Malcolm Hamer is a self-confessed sports addict who has worked extensively in the field of sports management. In 1971 he founded his own agency. He has represented many top sportsmen, among them golfers such as Johnny Miller, Sam Snead and the young Severiano Ballesteros. He is an enthusiastic golfer himself, although these days he no longer plays off a single-figure handicap. As a writer, his pieces have appeared in a wide variety of magazines and newspapers, including the *Daily Telegraph*, *The Sunday Times* and the *Observer*. His recent books include *The Ryder Cup – The Players* and *The Guinness Continental Europe Golf Course Guide*, as well as three previous Chris Ludlow novels, *Sudden Death*, *A Deadly Lie* and *Death Trap*. Together with his wife, Jill Foster, he has published a successful series of guide books, *The Family Welcome Guides*. They live in London with their daughter, Polly.

Also by Malcolm Hamer

FICTION
Sudden Death
A Deadly Lie
Death Trap

NON-FICTION
The Ryder Cup – The Players
The Guinness Continental Europe Golf Course Guide
The Family Welcome Guide
(with Jill Foster)

Shadows on the Green

Malcolm Hamer

HEADLINE

First published in 1994
by HEADLINE BOOK PUBLISHING

First published in paperback in 1995
by HEADLINE BOOK PUBLISHING

10 9 8 7 6 5 4 3 2 1

ISBN 0 7472 4686 6

Typeset by CBS, Felixstowe, Suffolk

Printed and bound in Great Britain by
Cox & Wyman Ltd, Reading, Berks

HEADLINE BOOK PUBLISHING
A division of Hodder Headline PLC
338 Euston Road
London NW1 3BH

To Jill

Prologue

Calvin Blair was a happy man as he drove home through the Sussex lanes. The meeting that afternoon had gone his way and tonight he could celebrate. It had been a tough few months.

To an outsider, designing golf courses for a living might seem like an easy option; to a professional like Blair, it was a difficult game, full of traps for the unwary, which provided few good opportunities to create something worthwhile. The afternoon's planning decision in his favour had just given him one of those opportunities. He intended to savour the moment.

The shadows of evening were lengthening as he eased the big BMW down his drive. He was later than expected but his wife and daughter wouldn't care about that. They knew how much this commission meant to him. Blair smiled. He could taste the champagne already.

As he approached the garage he activated the electronic door and watched it swing upwards. He edged the car forward.

He saw two bundles of clothing on the garage floor ahead of him and braked. How odd of Jane to leave washing in the garage, he thought.

Blair stopped the car and looked more closely at the bundles. Oh Christ, that wasn't washing! In his panic, he threw the heavy car door open so vigorously that it bounced back and trapped his arm for a moment. He tumbled out of the BMW and into the garage.

No, it wasn't washing. Lying on her side, her arms tightly bound to her body with brown tape, was his beloved Jane. Her dress was stained with congealed blood and her face was white; a dribble of saliva had dried at the corner of her mouth. Rebecca too lay on her side, her T-shirt patched with blood, her face as pale as her mother's and with the same terrible stillness.

Crying their names over and over, Blair scrabbled helplessly at the tapes that bound them. Then, with tears starting from his eyes, he stumbled out of the garage towards the house.

Chapter 1

The stony face of defeat confronted my partner and I as early as the eighth tee at Waterside Golf Club. We were three holes down, and lucky it wasn't more. By now, I was thoroughly convinced that I should never have got involved in this match in the first place. The day, dingy and overcast, was wrong, the opposition was unfriendly – and the stakes, at £500 per man, were decidedly uncomfortable. Above all, I disliked the course, a new one in the affluent suburbs of Surrey. The architect had no doubt been paid a small fortune to design and build a course which would have suited Florida very well, but not this gentle stretch of English countryside. With its vast tracts of water, eccentrically-shaped bunkers, profusion of mounds and hillocks and panoramic greens, it showed gross insensitivity on the part of the architect and stupidity on the part of the owners. The classic courses that lay nearby made Waterside look like Disneyland. How I would have loved a chance to do the design.

I was there at the urgent request of Barney Mustoe, a friend from the days when I worked in the City. An ebullient character who was an enthusiastic presence in the wine bars and restaurants of the Square Mile, Barney worked for a firm of stockbrokers which was now owned by a French bank. He was one of the top analysts in the property sector, a fervent supporter of Tottenham

3

Hotspur, and he played golf at a north London club off a highly
questionable handicap of 14. On the only other occasion I'd
played with him he'd looked more like a 24.

Although I was between jobs at the moment and welcomed
any diversion, I'd reacted cautiously to Barney's phone call on
the previous Monday morning.

'Chris, how's your golf?' he asked in his rapid tones.
'Fancy a hit on Friday? At Waterside.'

'Love to, but why Waterside? Swimming isn't my strong
point.'

Barney ignored my comment. 'Look, Chris, help me out, old
son, will you? I'm in bother. Shot my mouth off the other day
about golf at a lunch. Ended up with a heavy bet, a monkey a
nob.'

'Five hundred quid?' I asked in disbelief.

'Well yeah. You know how it is – I was a bit pissed at the
time.'

'A bit?'

'Anyway, Chris, my partner's dropped me in it. He's
buggered off to New York. Will you fill in? I'll cover your end
of the bet.'

'Who's the opposition?'

'A bloke called Simon Hanley. He's a lawyer, does a lot in
the property game. He's not really my cup of tea but I have to
keep in with him – you know how it is. Hanley's connected with
Shere Forest; his father-in-law owns it or something. Anyway,
this guy Hanley's bringing somebody called Giles Cockburn –
a merchant wanker, apparently. Cockburn's the reason we're
going to Waterside; he's just bought a debenture there, flash git.
At thirty grand a pop I suppose he wants to play there as often
as possible.'

'Where does he usually play? What handicap?' It was wise to gauge the other side's strength.

'He's off five at Royal St George's, I think.'

'Five at St George's! He'll be big trouble in that case – a proper golfer.'

'Yeah, yeah, Chris, but not as big trouble as you, eh?' Barney said winningly. 'Are you on?'

'OK,' I said reluctantly. 'But you really will have to cover my stake. Remember, I'm one of the army of unemployed. I really am skint.'

'Great.' Barney sounded enthusiastic. 'I want to beat that slob Hanley. On the tee at nine thirty? See you for coffee at nine.'

Nobody would have guessed Barney Mustoe's true opinion of Simon Hanley amid the easy banter with which he greeted him. Hanley was overweight for a man in his middle thirties and had a soft and petulant look to his face. More interesting was his partner, Giles Cockburn, who came straight from the practice ground to the first tee. He was rather stooped, with flat and inexpressive features under a white cap. Shades of Ben Hogan. I hoped he didn't play like Hogan . . .

Barney and I won the toss for the honour of playing first – and that was the only thing we did win over the next seven holes. Since I was playing off a handicap of 2, I was giving shots to the other players; nine to Barney and Hanley who both played off 14, and two to Cockburn with his handicap of 5.

Despite his lunging, flat-footed swing Simon Hanley kept his ball reasonably straight and, at the second hole, showed that he had an adept short game. A nicely controlled pitch over a deep bunker and a firm putt gave him a win.

5

He and Cockburn went two up at the fourth hole, the hardest on the course and acknowledged as such with an index of 1 on the scorecard. At 465 yards and with an array of ponds on the left-hand side and meandering outcrops of scrub and sand on the other, it was the toughest of propositions. The way Cockburn was playing I guessed I would need a birdie to hold him, and I was right. A three-wood from the tee and a one-iron put him ten yards from the front edge of the green. He chipped beautifully to within six inches of the hole and my putt from twenty feet shaved the left lip of the hole and stayed out. Two down.

Two down became three down at the seventh hole, which Cockburn birdied. I knew that if we went any further behind, the game would probably be beyond retrieval. Barney had not yet managed to use any of his shots; the tension of the occasion, despite his apparent good spirits, had affected his game. He wanted to win so much that he was trying too hard. A keen club cricketer, he had a good eye and hit the ball hard with an abbreviated swing; but today his timing had deserted him.

While we surveyed the eighth hole I spoke quietly to him. As a sometime caddy on the professional golf circuit I didn't have any qualms about offering advice to an amateur player.

'You're trying to steer the ball, Barney. Stand up and give it a good smack. Don't worry about anything else.'

'Feeling the heat a bit, are we, Barney?' interrupted Hanley. 'I hope you've brought your chequebook with you.'

The eighth was a short hole of just under 200 yards, and both Hanley and Barney received a shot. Although Hanley hit a poor shot into a bunker, Cockburn hit a long iron to within a few feet of the flag. It was vital that Barney got his ball somewhere on the green to give himself a reasonable chance of a net birdie.

I grinned encouragingly at him as he pulled his five-wood

from his bag. 'Right down the line,' I said quietly, 'as if you're hitting a straight six.'

As Barney took his club back, I heard the jangle of Hanley's clubs as he shifted his bag slightly. My partner had no chance to abort his shot but hit his ball head high and left. Fortunately he hit it hard enough to clear the water in front of the tee and the spin brought it drifting back, from left to right, towards the green. It was going much too hard to hold the putting surface and I had visions of Barney having to chip back from the edge of the lake behind the green.

Barney's ball bounded across the green, and the beginning of Hanley's apology was choked at its source as the ball hit the flagstick with a brisk *clang* and settled about four feet away. Barney grinned lavishly at me. With the pressure off, I flew my own ball onto the centre of the green.

Cockburn missed his putt for a birdie and conceded the hole. We were now only two down; it seemed that luck was finally smiling our way. As we walked to the next tee Barney muttered, 'That prick Hanley; that was deliberate.' I agreed and resolved to watch him carefully during the rest of the round.

Barney's irritation at the lawyer's gamesmanship had dissolved his inhibitions and he was hitting the ball with an authority befitting a man with a much lower handicap. He birdied the long twelfth hole and reduced our deficit to one.

There was precious little conversation between the two teams. An onlooker would have surmised that this was a very serious game – and with £500 at stake, it was. But the atmosphere, initially one of friendly banter between Barney and his two opponents, had become more highly charged. Some 'needle' had crept into the proceedings. Although this can be a treacherous emotion on the golf course, some people thrive on it, and I was glad to see that Barney was one of them.

The next four holes were halved and Barney and I came to the short seventeenth in the perilous position of needing to win one of the last two holes in order to save our money – or rather, Barney's money. One hundred and sixty yards of water lay between us and the plateau green; the lake ran along the right side of the green and extended around the back of it. The only 'bale-out' areas were at the front of the green and on the left, where three bunkers were positioned amid the scrub and heather.

Barney's ball ended up in the middle one of those bunkers, and so I elected to hit the safe shot – a high fade into the centre of the green. I nearly undercooked the fade and my ball just stayed on the left edge of the green . . . at least thirty feet from the hole.

'Very safe, Chris,' Cockburn drawled, 'but perhaps not *quite* the best shot in the circumstances. We are one up, aren't we, Simon?'

Then Cockburn hit his ball – too well. It hopped through the back of the green and into the water.

Barney did not bother to suppress his delight. With a grin he said, 'Better get your wellies on, Giles.'

To Hanley's great credit he hit an accurate iron shot to within about twenty feet of the pin and gave his partner a look of triumph, which implied that he had shut us out and made the match safe. That was a mistake. Barney had two hacks in the bunker and picked up his ball, as did Cockburn. Hanley and I were left to contest the hole.

Faced with a testing putt across a saucer-shaped depression in the green, I was keenly aware that the pace was the critical factor if I were to get the ball within a couple of feet of the hole. As I addressed the ball I was conscious of Hanley behind me and to my right. Nevertheless, I felt comfortable and decided not to ask him to move out of my peripheral vision. As soon as I started the putter back I was conscious that he was on the move. Steady, I thought. Take the putter smoothly and firmly through; don't let the bastard put you off.

The ball rolled across the green, gathered pace into the depression and made the climb up the other side. I'd misread the break slightly but I was less than a yard from the hole. I knew that the putt would not be conceded, rightly so in the circumstances. I decided not to mark the ball but to putt out and exert a little extra pressure on Hanley. With my head rigid I tapped the ball sharply into the back of the hole. Barney came across and gripped my arm in congratulation. 'Let's see what the slob can do now,' he whispered.

Cockburn nodded to me and said: 'Well putted, in the circumstances.' He held the flag for his partner who putted up to the same distance as I had but, whereas my second putt had been uphill and relatively simple, Hanley's was downhill and left to right across a slope. If I'd ever seen an arse-gripper putt, this was it. He looked hopefully at both of us to see if we would give him the putt. Some chance.

Hanley studied the line from several angles and conferred with Cockburn. He crouched over the putt and then straightened to take another nervous look at the line. I thought he had very little chance of holing out successfully but, to make quite sure, I dropped my putter on the green just as he settled into his stance.

'Terribly sorry, Simon,' I muttered. He went through the whole business of settling himself once again, only to miss the hole by several inches, at which he slammed his putter irritably into the turf.

Cockburn gave me a wry look and Barney said loudly, 'All square and all to play for.'

As we walked to the next tee, Cockburn remarked, 'I hear you're unemployed at the moment.' I nodded and he continued, 'You worked for Andrew Buccleuth, I'm told. Why don't you give me a call at Browne's?'

I thanked him, but never did get around to that call because another offer, one I couldn't refuse, materialised soon afterwards. Just as well – I couldn't see myself as a merchant banker.

On the eighteenth tee Barney's normally expressive face was tight. It wasn't a matter of money to him any more; he was playing against a cheat and wasn't going to let the bugger win. I felt the same but, in my present impecunious state, would find £500 very handy – and tax free.

As all eighteenth holes should, this one imposed a severe test of nerve on the players. The tee shot had to be carried over a stretch of water to a plateau fairway. There was more water on the right and a wasteland of sand, scrub and thick bushes on the left. The message from the architect was clear enough: hit it straight or I've got you.

He nearly got Barney, whose ball just stayed on the lip of the fairway next to the water. He rubbed his head and gave a quiet whistle of relief. It was a hole of over 400 yards, and I faded my drive onto the left side of the fairway. A medium iron to the green would give me a chance of a birdie – and a win.

'Nice and smooth,' Cockburn advised his partner, as Hanley prepared to drive. But the lawyer's action was far from that. His grip on the club was so tight that his knuckles showed white, and his swing was jerky and quick, sending the ball soaring to the right and splashing into the water.

'One down and one to go,' murmured Barney.

Cockburn chose to hit his one-iron and the ball hummed off the club head. It was a beautiful strike but his right hand was a shade too dominant and the ball hit the left centre of the fairway and kept on going left into the scrub.

'It should be OK,' Cockburn said pensively, 'but I'll play a provisional.'

He put his provisional ball into the centre of the fairway. If his first ball were lost, his next shot would be his fourth.

He watched Hanley play a second ball from where he calculated that his original had crossed the boundary of the water hazard. With his penalty shot, I reckoned that he could do no better than a six for the hole. I advised Barney to hit a quiet seven-iron towards the green and he did so; he was well-positioned to make his five.

It all depended on what sort of a lie Cockburn had in the rough. If he could hack his ball up the fairway so that he was within range of the hole with a short iron, he was capable of getting his par.

As we all searched the rough, Cockburn confirmed that he was using a Maxfli one.

'Balata, of course,' he said.

Professionals and good amateur players use golf balls with a balata cover. It is softer and therefore has more feel than the harder, two-piece balls which are used by the majority of club golfers.

Although I found a ball and Barney found two, none of them was a Maxfli one. When the five minutes allowed for a search were over, Cockburn shrugged, strode over to his provisional ball and rapped it casually onto the green. The best he could score was a five and he was a long way from the pin. I hit a five-iron to just over ten feet and Barney gave me a stage wink and a thumbs up. I doubt he'd have made a good poker player.

Hanley had isolated himself from the rest of us and walked disconsolately along the right-hand side of the fairway.

Our opponents both missed their putts and recorded sixes for the hole and I encouraged Barney, who had played a neat third shot to the centre of the putting surface, to hole out in five shots to win the match.

Hanley's handshake was perfunctory and, on the way to the clubhouse, he produced a chequebook from his golf bag and scribbled out a cheque for £500 in Barney's favour.

'Cash only, old son,' Barney said, deadpan. 'Never trust a lawyer, that's what my old dad used to say.'

Hanley snatched at the cheque but Barney skipped out of range. 'Only kidding,' he said. 'When I've cashed it, I'll frame it and hang it on the lavatory wall. Just to remind myself, every morning.'

With the briefest of farewells, Hanley headed for the car park and moments later we heard the screech of tyres as he left. It wasn't long before I met Simon Hanley again – and the experience proved to be just as unpleasant as this first encounter.

It was Cockburn's turn to delve in his golf bag; he produced a roll of notes held by a gold clasp and peeled off ten of them.

'Well played,' he said, handing them to me. 'I knew we were up against it when I saw your first shot.' He nodded at Barney. 'I don't wish to be churlish but I must get back to the office. I've a proposal to finish for Monday morning. Thanks for the game.'

Barney and I had a lively lunch and I knew that he would delight in the story of his victory, suitably embellished, for many months . . .

On the Monday morning, a courier arrived at my door and

handed me a heavy parcel. I tackled its thick packaging on the kitchen table and eventually brought forth a magnum of Krug champagne.

A small bubble-wrapped package was attached to the bottle. Inside I found a golf ball and a note 'from the desk of Barney Mustoe'. It read:

'A smashing game. Thanks. I thought you might like this ball because I know you use balata. Cheers, Barney.'

The ball was a Maxfli one.

Chapter 2

This is the life, I thought, popping the final juicy slice of nectarine into my mouth and filling my cup with coffee. It was an elegant cup, with a blue pattern and gold trim, which held plenty of coffee and sat on a deep saucer. One of a pair, it was a gift from my neighbour, Mrs Bradshaw, a widow in her mid-sixties. While she had been away on an extended holiday in South Africa, I had looked after her flat and redecorated her kitchen. The cups were her thank-you.

The decorating was a small favour for a good neighbour who, without any fuss, had taken over some of the domestic tasks that she'd decided I was incapable of performing. Mrs Bradshaw gave my flat a thorough clean every Wednesday and occasionally brought me some home-cooked food – usually with the excuse that she had made too much of some recipe or other and didn't want it to go to waste. In return, I kept a careful eye on her investments, did odd jobs in her flat and sometimes joined her in a visit to the cinema. My neighbour had a passion for Clint Eastwood and Jack Nicholson that was not entirely proper in a lady of her mature years.

Through the good offices of my old employer, Jack Mason, whose bag I had lugged around the fairways of Europe for three years or so, I had landed a job in the golf course design business.

The four days a week for which Blair Associates had hired me, had so far averaged five and my employer, Calvin Blair, had insisted I take today off.

Although I was less than halfway through my probationary period of six months, the job with Blair Associates seemed to have been made in heaven for me, and I was more than ever convinced that I had found my right niche. I had been closely involved with golf since I was a teenager – obsessed, said my father, who longed for me to join him in his highly prosperous computer software business. Dad pictured me carrying the flag into the next generation; like most fathers, he wanted to build his own little dynasty.

I knew I had disappointed him, especially when I became a caddie. How do you explain such a job at a smart dinner party in Esher or over a business lunch at Langan's Brasserie? In my youth I had aspired to be a professional golfer, but the essential talent was missing. Although I had played the amateur circuit for a year, I soon realised that I would never reach the uncompromising standards demanded by the professional game. My dreams of glory faded, but I was consoled by the fact that, as a caddie, I was involved at the highest level.

For a few years I happily combined my activities on the links with a job for a golf-mad stockbroker, but grim recessionary days brought the demise of many indulgences in the City, and a part-time employee like myself was at the top of the hit list.

A few weeks before, I had just returned from a lengthy jog around Richmond Park and was trying to decide between catching up on the ironing or poring over the Appointments pages of the *Telegraph*. Frankly, I was inclined to do neither, and I'd just decided to wander over to my golf club for a beer and a sandwich instead, when the telephone rang. The familiar voice of Jack Mason said: 'How do you fancy a job designing golf courses?'

Would an alcoholic turn down a glass of claret because it was a bad year? I paused and said, 'I hope no one has been stupid enough to ask you to build one, Jack.'

He had pronounced views on how courses should be built and never hesitated to express them, much to the annoyance of the Professional Golfers' Association, which had fined him on several occasions for his excoriating comments about some of their tournament venues.

'Not bloody likely,' he replied. 'But Calvin Blair needs help. You know he's remodelling Shere Forest?'

'Not before time.'

'Can you meet him at that Italian place over there, the Terrazza, on Wednesday?'

I certainly could.

I just about remembered Calvin Blair from his days on the circuit and, when we met, found him little changed, apart from thinner hair and a thicker waistline. His long face was characterised by a heavy jaw and bright humorous eyes. He had a slight and agreeable Lancashire accent and, as he greeted me, I recalled that Blair had always been a fluent talker, able to produce a quotable opinion on most aspects of golf. While still a tournament player he had capitalised on this ability by writing articles for golf magazines and by doing the occasional golf commentary on television. He had always been alive to the business opportunities within his sport.

Before we had finished our main course, he had offered me a job. The rewards were not what you'd call generous, but then, I reminded myself, Blair was from the north, and they were 'nobbut careful' with their brass up there. It didn't worry me

17

because I relished the idea of the work, and we could always negotiate again when my trial period was over. Or not, as the case might be.

I was optimistic because Blair had several golf courses in various stages of development, including one in Spain and one near Biarritz. Perhaps I could be his man in Europe. Delicious images of the sun-drenched coasts of the Mediterranean filled my mind's eye . . .

'Of course, this Shere Forest job is just a bit of superficial tarting up, for the sake of the sponsors.' Calvin Blair's voice brought me back to earth. 'Do you know Peter Gresham who owns Shere? The man's as tight as a fish's arse. He'll only do the minimum to keep the sponsors happy and to hang on to the British Classic. Meanwhile, I've got to screw an extra penn'orth out of every shilling to try and make it look good.'

'So what are the main changes?'

'We've been reshaping some of the fairways and a couple of greens, enlarging some tees, and we've built a few new tournament tees. We're also putting in extra bunkers, at the same time as taking several out because they're obsolete. Even from the members' tees they're superfluous and, as you know, they're expensive to maintain, so good riddance. The course was built in eighteen ninety and I sometimes wonder if it's been touched since then.'

'Didn't Harry Colt have a go at it in the twenties?'

'Aye, he did, Chris – and he really gave the course its wonderful quality. But modern equipment has distorted its shot values. We need to tighten it up, and a little extra length here and there would be helpful. That's not the be-all and end-all, but we've got to toughen its defences, maintain its challenge *and* its integrity. You know the old maxim, I'm sure, that golf is a battle of wits between the player and the course designer – but it must be a fair contest. I need to make it tougher for the pros but I mustn't make it too penal for the members. It's their course, first and foremost.'

'A hole should be a difficult par but an easy bogey.'

'That's right. We have to remember that a course should always be fun to play and the risks and rewards should be plain to see. You give the club hacker a fair chance, but you demand the utmost from a really skilful player if he's to get par or better.'

I was encouraged that Blair did not want to move into Shere Forest with a fleet of bulldozers and ruin a great course. He had put the emphasis on making enough subtle changes within the existing confines to keep the professionals at bay. It could certainly be done. Some architects seemed to think that only monstrously long courses would defeat the professional golfer, who had benefited from greatly improved equipment over the last couple of decades. Nowadays, the balls went further and the clubs were much more forgiving. America in particular is littered with those huge unrelenting courses, where poor hackers have to slug the ball over mammoth tracts of water and negotiate bunkers big enough to provide camps for tribes of nomads. No wonder these poor lost souls need motorised caddie carts and all day to play eighteen holes.

'Presumably Gresham's doing the clubhouse up as well?' I asked.

'Yes. He's hoping that a lick of paint on the outside will satisfy the sponsors but it won't, of course. They need to gut the place and start again. You should have seen old man Gresham's face last year when a deputation of players demanded a crêche. He went purple.' Blair chuckled at the memory.

'It sounds as if Mr Gresham lives in another world.'

'He does that – pre-World War Two,' Blair said drily. 'But Jack will tell you more than I can about him.'

'What would happen if the sponsors took the Classic elsewhere?'

'For a start the club would lose a thumping great facility fee from the PGA. Then there'd be the loss of prestige: "Shere Forest, the home of the British Classic" – all that palaver. It brings the societies in, as you know. Eighty or more blokes at well over a hundred quid a time. Think of all the Pimm's and claret and Kummels they sink, and the gear they buy from the pro's shop. They do about two societies a week – that's an awful lot of turnover and an awful lot of profit. In effect the societies subsidise the members because their subscriptions are ridiculously low. Eventually they'd lose a lot of that society income if the Classic went elsewhere.'

Blair drained his cup of coffee. 'I think the biggest blow of all would be to Peter Gresham himself,' he concluded. 'He loves to talk about "his" tournament although, in fact, he has bugger all to do with the British Classic. It's all done by the PGA and the TV boys these days.'

'But what about this new course that's supposed to be built?' I asked.

'Well, that's the really interesting bit. Everybody hopes that planning permission will be granted but there are problems.'

My antennae sprang into alert mode. His tone of voice and the look he gave me suggested that those 'problems' would be mine most of all. Maybe my new career in golf course design would be short-lived . . .

Blair went on to explain that he had little faith that Gresham ever intended to carry out the work. 'I hope he does because it would be a wonderful spot to build another eighteen,' he enthused. 'Heather, gorse, plenty of trees, natural undulations . . . it's all there, all the makings. I'd just have to make sure that I took the maximum advantage of what Mother Nature has already provided. Between you and me, Chris, I'm thrilled at the idea of doing it but I'm also a bit frightened. Daunted by the task. It's almost as if Van Gogh has handed me a canvas. He's drawn in the outlines, mixed the paints and numbered where the colours should go. It ought to be a masterpiece, and yet . . .'

'But you say the course may never happen?'

'I'm doubtful. I think Gresham is just using the idea of the new course as a smokescreen. He'll say to the sponsors that he's committed to radical change and a brand new championship course, but that it all takes time.'

'And money.'

'Yes – money which he hasn't got.'

'But he could raise the necessary amount,' I argued. 'It wouldn't be difficult to find investors for a club like Shere Forest, surely.'

'I'm not sure Gresham wants any investors. Remember, it's "his" course, and the silly old bugger still refers to it as the finest test of golf in the south of England. Well, it could be if he'd let me have another few hundred thousand pounds.'

'You said problems, plural,' I prompted Blair.

'Yes.' He hesitated. 'Have you ever heard of the Green Disciples?'

I hadn't and Blair explained that they were a militant, 'Friends of the Earth' style organisation. He was convinced that their veiled threats to him and his family, to lay off the development, were far from idle ones.

21

'Jack thought that you'd be able to help out, if . . .' Blair's voice trailed off.

'If things got rough?'

'Well, yes.'

'Fine. But I can't be at your side twenty-four hours a day.' Blair nodded patiently and I continued: 'I don't think you need worry. There are so many of these lunatic fringe pressure groups – single-issue fanatics who are invariably harmless. They usually don't go beyond anonymous letters and abusive phone calls.'

'Those animal rights people have done a bit of damage, haven't they?'

'There's always an exception. Anyway, let's discuss the question of my danger money.'

Blair looked startled, then realised I was joking and smiled with some relief.

22

Chapter 3

After this interview, I rattled happily back to London in my old Porsche. With well over 100,000 miles on the clock, the car had every right to rattle but I was reluctant even to consider replacing it. Anyway, I couldn't afford to.

The sensuous sounds of Fauré's *Requiem* were being sung to me by my brother's Cambridge college choir. The cassette was a present from Max, who liked to remind me that he was the clever one of the Ludlow brothers. A first in maths certainly made him so by quite a distance. In his irritatingly casual way he had augmented his academic accomplishments by turning out for various university teams: rugby, athletics and hockey. And chess, as well. It put my time at Sussex University in the shade – but at least I'd played golf for the English universities team.

Max was due back in England in a few weeks and I was looking forward to seeing him again. He had been up in the north of Canada helping with some environmental survey or other. Perhaps he could help with the project at Shere Forest. Max would be a good ally. Not only did he have a particularly incisive intelligence, but he possessed a ruthless physical self-confidence. This could be unnerving, even for me and I was used to him. From our early teenage years, and Max was only a shade under two years younger than me, we had gone to self-defence classes at the insistence of our father. Max absorbed the lessons enthusiastically and soon adapted them to form the basis of a comprehensive armoury of offensive tactics. After he left Cambridge he had spent three years in the Army, much of it in Northern Ireland, and I still didn't know what he'd been doing there. Whatever it was, I felt sorry for the opposition.

As I drove along the narrow confines of the A3 I speculated happily about a future in the golf design business. The portents, as long as I could strengthen my first flimsy grasp on the opportunity, were excellent. There existed a huge demand for golf facilities of all kinds in Britain, not just for the traditional members' clubs but for basic courses where anyone could turn up, pay a few pounds and play. Interest in the sport was zooming, even more so in Europe. The sun-and-fun spots of southern Spain and the Algarve had always been popular destinations for British golfers, and courses had been built to satisfy that demand, but the golf bug had now bitten deeply into the veins of the native European population. The French, Germans and Scandinavians had taken to the game in droves, and golf courses were being planned and laid out at an extraordinary rate.

I reached Putney and parked my car outside the solid Victorian mansion, now converted into flats, where I lived. I was in a good mood. For once the future looked rosy.

As I fumbled amongst the small change in my pocket for my front door key, Mrs Bradshaw came around the corner of the building. She had a pair of secateurs in one hand and a large clump of herbs in the other.

'Rosemary,' she said. 'For the lamb. Daisy's coming over for a meal.' Daisy Warburton was Mrs Bradshaw's friend and bridge partner, a more steely-eyed partnership it would be hard to imagine. My neighbour looked at me closely. 'You seem pretty pleased with yourself, Chris. Won the pools? New girlfriend? Handicap reduced?'

'A new job, I'm glad to say. I start on Monday.'

Mrs Bradshaw kissed me on the cheek and told me how delighted she was. As we parted in the hallway she issued instructions that I ring my mother with the news immediately. 'By the way,' she finished, 'the new Clint Eastwood is on at the Odeon. Shall we go on Sunday?'

I waved my agreement and went into my flat. On the ground floor, it had the advantage of those high ceilings and generous proportions that the Victorian middle classes demanded; the tall windows of two of the rooms looked out over the back garden.

I thought I should celebrate my new job by having a beer, or maybe several beers, but I was still suffering the effects of my unaccustomed heavy lunch. A session on the exercise machine in my spare bedroom was sorely needed before I downed more booze. It was dark and lonely work, as someone once said in a different context . . . but it helped to keep me fit.

Despite my words to Calvin Blair concerning the Green Disciples, I thought it wise to stay in good condition, just in case. For one thing, I wanted to be as sharp as possible for the challenge of my new job. As I pushed and pulled the weights, Beethoven, turned up loud, helped me through the tedium.

Blair's misgivings were understandable. The doings of extremist groups such as the animal rights activists were never far from the front pages of the newspapers; and demonstrations and disruptions, even the occasional explosion, were the common currency of our television screens. I wondered whether the persistent Irish problem, which had brought death and destruction into everyday life in Britain, had made it more difficult for other less lethal extremists to make their mark. When whole areas of the City of London could be devastated, how could the likes of the Green Disciples make a sufficient impact?

Presumably by stepping up their activities. Could personal violence, or even murder, be next on their agenda? No wonder Calvin Blair, with a family to protect, was worried.

After a shower and a mug of tea, I phoned Jack Mason to thank him for his introduction and tell him about its happy outcome.

'Any time, Chris. We'll share a bottle of fizz soon, I hope.'

'Look forward to it. Can you tell me anything useful about Calvin? I know he's an old mate of yours but . . .'

'Nothing that would worry you. Actually, he's very straight. If you do a good job for him, Chris, he'll reward you.'

'He seems to be worried about these Green Disciples.'

'Hmm. Considering our Calvin's built like a tank, he does act like an old tart sometimes. Mind you, nerves were always his problem; that's why he never quite made it on the circuit.'

'Tell me more.'

'Well, you know the scene. It's the final round of the tournament. You're two shots off the pace. I don't have to tell you how often I've left my breakfast in the clubhouse loo just before my tee-off time. You have to cope. Poor old Calvin couldn't, which is why he retired early. And I don't blame him.'

My second call that afternoon was to Toby Greenslade, Golf Correspondent of the *Daily News*. The *News* is the sort of newspaper that bills its sports writers as 'controversial' and 'fearless' – but Toby was only fearless when he had a wine list in his hands – he'd try any wine once. Toby was writing for the wrong newspaper. His editor's curiosity about sportsmen stopped at the bedroom, just as it did about show-biz personalities, politicians and the Royal Family.

In contrast, Toby had a genuine love of golf and wrote about it well, *when* he was given enough space. That was a rare occurrence, but he tolerated the *News* for the sake of the salary and generous expenses; in return they tolerated his sometimes erratic behaviour.

Toby was an invaluable source of information, rumour and gossip about golf and I hoped he'd be able to fill me in about the goings-on at Shere Forest. From what Blair had told me it sounded intriguing enough to have caught the attention of my journalist friend. It was as well for me to be forearmed.

As the direct line to Toby's desk at the *News* buzzed several times I wondered if he was engaged in a particularly lengthy lunchtime session. I usually tried to catch him in the late afternoon, that elusive period between lunch and his early evening 'liveners', but lunch would sometimes merge jovially into the cocktail hour.

At last, a far from jovial voice answered the phone. 'Greenslade, scribe, speaking.'

'Ludlow, formerly unemployed, calling,' I replied.

'Unemploy*able*, surely, dear boy? What foolish or desperate individual has offered you a position? It's not some love-struck female, is it?'

'That's rich, coming from you, Toby,' I said nastily. So far, Toby had been divorced by two wives, both charming, both attractive, and neither able to contend with his mercurial behaviour. The second wife once told me that it was not unusual for Toby to turn up twenty-four hours late for a dinner party.

'Less of this banter. You may not realise it, young Chris, but journalists have deadlines to meet. I must pen five hundred words of diamond-sharp prose about the latest golfing prodigy from Spain by teatime. We'll celebrate your good news tomorrow. Lunch. On me this time, your shout as soon as your first salary cheque is banked. See you at the San Remo at twelve.'

Chapter 4

The restaurant, a favourite of Toby's, faced the river, not far from Tower Bridge. Housed on the ground floor of a former warehouse, it was very much a haunt of media people. Consequently the prices were high, the wine list eclectic, the food forgettable and every other waiter had a novel with a publisher or a script with a producer. The San Remo was noisy and cheerful, humming with gossip and intrigue. When I examined the menu and its prices, I was glad the *Daily News* was footing the bill.

From his first gulp of an Australian sparkler, Toby was more than willing to tell me all he knew about Shere Forest and the people there. He was encouraging about Calvin Blair and described him as an excellent course designer.

'He's very prudent, a traditionalist, and he'll always deliver a good course within the budget. Straight as can be, although a bit tight with the money. He'd be a very good match in that department for Peter Gresham. Calvin will treat you well. He's a great family man, of course. I've never heard a hint of his having anything on the side. Talking of which, Chris, what are you doing on the horizontal-jogging front?'

'Nothing, unfortunately.'

My eyes followed the shapely form of a young woman as she

29

swayed past our table. A skintight, very short dress emphasised contours that some men might kill for. She had spiky blonde hair and, when she returned a few minutes later, I saw a face whose wide-eyed innocence was denied by lips that were lush and inviting. Catching my eye, she winked at me as she sashayed past. Half embarrassed, I grinned back.

Toby smacked his lips lasciviously. 'A beauty, isn't she? Publicity girl at Highlight Publishing. Very, very expensive.'

'Not my style, Toby. I mean, would I be able to take her home to Mother?'

'She's not a girl anyone would take home to Mother, thank God,' he stated with relish. 'Which leads me, since we are discussing the two most entertaining pastimes in life, golf and sex – in that order of course – to the gallant Captain Nigel Burnside of Shere Forest.'

'The Secretary?'

'Yes. He's what they used to call "a ladies' man". Now, as you're between partners and, judging by the glances you swapped with that pretty girl a moment ago, looking for some action, I think I should warn you to be careful while on Burnside's patch. He regards the ladies' section as his own private harem, and I'm told that his strike rate is impressively high. Anyway, Burnside's birds would be a bit on the matronly side for you.'

'Doesn't Peter Gresham mind Burnside making hay among the lady members?'

'If he knows he probably doesn't care. He and Burnside went to war together. Well, that's a gross exaggeration, they were in Germany together in the early sixties. Same regiment. Their only manoeuvres were probably in the German bars and brothels. They are buddies, comrades in arms. It's odd, isn't it, how men cling to these sentimental ties,' he mused. 'The old school, the regiment, this or that club.'

Toby refilled our glasses and leaned forward confidentially. 'The comrade in arms expression is particularly apposite. It reminds me of a bit of gossip.' The gruff boom of his voice only carried across half a dozen tables. 'Burnside is a bit younger than Gresham – let's say middle fifties as opposed to early sixties. You probably won't believe me when you meet Hermione Gresham, but she used to be a bit of a racer – and one of her riders was Captain Burnside . . .'

'I assume Gresham wasn't in the know. He isn't a complaisant husband, is he?' I asked.

'No, no, I'm sure not, but it'll make you laugh when you see her. She's Mrs Colonel to a tee, lady of all she surveys. A crashing snob, of course. If you're not Eton and Keble and the Guards, you're simply not worthy of serious attention. She rules the ladies' section with a rod of iron . . .'

'I thought you said Burnside did that.'

'Smutty. Anyway, I wouldn't imagine that old Gresham was much concerned about sex, once he'd done his duty and banged a couple of kids out. He was more interested in his golf. However, the gallant Nigel went at it like a good 'un, as a junior officer should. By the way, our Nigel's other considerable talent is the booze. Don't *ever* get into a session with him. He's lethal.'

I blinked at the thought of someone who could out-drink Toby. As I did so he waved at a waiter and a bottle of Australian red was quickly placed on the table. I asked him to tell me more about Peter Gresham.

'Born with the proverbial silver spoon. Marlborough. Scraped into Oxford, God knows how, it must've been his golf. Played in the Walker Cup once, while he was in the Army, I think. He inherited a bloody great estate in Wiltshire and is a director of the family building firm. The Greshams have always had money and his father passed on his interests in Shere Forest to lucky Peter.'

'How come?'

'The family own the land and nearly all the shares. Peter has most of them. His son, Nick, owns a few and so does Simon Hanley.'

'Simon Hanley, eh?'

'Yes, he's a solicitor – works in the City. Married to Francesca Gresham. She, now, is delightful, a real cracker.'

'I've played golf with Hanley.'

'He's a typical City boy, isn't he? You've met them by the cartload. Money is his real passion but he struck me as being reasonably shrewd and rather nasty.'

'And Nick, the son? Do you know him?'

'Only slightly. He usually plays in the British Classic pro-am. He's a charmer, a lightweight, the complete opposite of his father. He's in the City, too, and needs every bonus he can get. It's the horses and the casinos with him.'

'So money isn't his passion. Throwing it away is.'

'Yes, Chris, but you can cut the look of prim disapproval. You worked for a stockbroker. That's gambling too. Gambling with other people's money.'

'Maybe, but backed up with theory, research and experience.'

'Contrarian investing, the efficient market hypothesis, the random-walk theory . . . all mumbo-jumbo. I'd have as much faith in a man with the *Sporting Life* in his lap and a Woodbine stuck on his lower lip.'

Toby and I had played many variations on this particular theme over the years. It was verbal ping-pong: my argument for expert City knowledge would be countered by his accusation of illegal insider-dealing. But my usual defence of City expertise had not been helped by a picture which had recently appeared in several newspapers. It showed a chimpanzee which had selected a share portfolio in Norway by throwing darts at the listings. He had comfortably beaten all the other experts on one of the financial magazines. The humans, that is.

As we toyed with some slivers of cheese and Toby sailed into a large glass of vintage port, he told me that he had saved his best piece of gossip for last. With the reflex action of a journalist, he leaned towards me and spoke directly into my ear – an unnecessary precaution, since the noise level in the San Remo had now reached its peak. Toby's voice cut through it with ease.

'It's the usual problem at Shere Forest. Money, although there's enough in the kitty to upgrade the original course and tart up the clubhouse a bit. The sponsors of the British Classic insist upon it and Gresham will do just enough to placate them. He'll try to get away with the bare minimum though, because he's mean. Whatever he spends will hurt him, particularly when it's at the dictate of a multinational whose headquarters are in America.'

'He's anti-American, is he?'

'Completely anti-foreign. Wogs, messed-up food and nasty diseases start at Dover.'

Toby paused and looked appreciatively at the Highlight publicity girl as, once again, she weaved her way between the tables.

'The poor girl must have a weak bladder,' he muttered spitefully.

I looked at her table and saw several empty bottles of

champagne which had been shared between three. I wondered where she would be sleeping it off.

'Pay attention,' Toby said sharply. 'This is the interesting bit. My sources were adamant that there is not the slightest chance of Gresham stumping up one and a half to two million quid for a second course – especially when he thinks that he already has the finest course in the south of England. He simply hasn't got the money. His building firm is just about surviving the recession and he certainly wouldn't sell his estate in Wiltshire, even if anyone had the money to buy it.'

'So Calvin Blair can forget his dream of building a showpiece championship course?' I tried not to sound too disappointed.

'Not necessarily. There is a property company waiting in the wings, ready to buy Gresham out and acquire Shere Forest. He wants to keep the club under his control, but his son Nick and the son-in-law Hanley are both trying very hard to persuade him to sell.'

'Why are they so keen?'

'Because they need the money from the sale. They've lost bundles of cash at Lloyds and Nick also has his gambling habit to feed. They would both cop a very tidy sum when the sale went through, not just from their shares in Shere Forest but, I would guess, in fees from the purchaser. Hanley represents the property company and Nick is bound to be in on the deal, too.'

'It sounds sensible to me to take the money and run,' I said.

'Well, you're pragmatic and unsentimental, Chris. But Shere Forest is Gresham's baby and he wants to hang on to it. He'd probably have liked to stop the world in the fifties, when professional golfers were forelock-tugging servants of the club who only spoke to the members when spoken to, and when the course could be maintained by two men and a dog.'

'From what I remember of Shere Forest, it *is* still stuck in the fifties. There's a tiny changing room and only a couple of showers that dribble rusty water. How on earth do the pros put up with it?'

'Rentacabin move in with all mod cons for the week.'

'Brown Windsor soup, steak and kidney pie and treacle tart for lunch.'

'Nothing wrong with Brown Windsor soup. Anyway, you were lucky to have a changing room. The ladies didn't have one, not until the doughty Hermione got interested in the game, that is.'

'Encouraged by Captain Burnside?'

'No doubt. Special lessons, I expect. Anyway, she made sure the ladies were catered for in no uncertain terms. A changing room and a ladies' lounge appeared almost overnight.'

'If this property company gets its hands on the club, they'll run it as a business. It'll be viewed as an asset . . .'

'A grossly under-used asset at that,' Toby agreed. 'They've only got about three hundred members though the club could easily cope with four hundred, and most of the old buffers hardly play. The average age must be way over sixty. Of course, it's as hard to join Shere Forest as to enter the kingdom of Heaven.'

'Harder, by the sound of it.'

'It was like a morgue when my elegant swing last had an outing at Shere Forest.'

Toby had a swing that creaked like a rusty gate.

'There was one member in the bar – one member! And he was only having a cup of tea and a scone. It probably cost him just over a pound, and yet it took several people to prepare and serve. If Bertie Wooster had strolled in, complete with plus fours and monocle, I wouldn't have been surprised. I think we saw four other players on the course.'

'And down the road at the municipal course they were probably queuing from first light to get a game.'

'Yes, Chris. It's crazy. We need more courses.'

'And we need to use existing golfing resources better . . .'

'. . . and I'm not sure that a property company is the answer.'

'They'd more than double the number of members. They'd jack up the subscriptions and make sure that the bar and the dining room made money. And the members would revolt,' I said.

I asked Toby who else I should look out for at Shere Forest.

'There's Jake Petersen, the pro. His gear is always twenty per cent dearer than anyone else's. He rips off the societies and all the other visitors, especially the Americans and the Japanese.'

'And no doubt the steward and the catering manager are both on the fiddle?'

'No doubt at all, because Captain Nigel Burnside, the Secretary, prefers to be in the bar with a glass of Scotch in his hand to doing his job.'

'Shere Forest seems to have all the constituents of a bad situation comedy.'

'Absolutely, Chris. I wish you joy of it.'

As Toby paid the considerable bill, I reflected on my newly gained knowledge of Shere Forest and its various personalities.

Chapter 5

My initial brief as a new employee of Blair Associates was to stick closely with Calvin and assist him whenever possible. He began by explaining two of the cardinal rules of golf course design: never start with a short hole because it delays play much more than a straightforward par four, and ensure that the first and the last holes do not play into the sun. These were obvious things but I'd never had them pointed out to me before.

Blair was more than happy to use me as a sounding board for his views on how the course at Shere Forest should be reshaped. The main changes had already been approved by the club's committee and put in train by the architect. Peter Gresham chaired the committee and, in effect, his was the only opinion which mattered. But there were many details which had to be resolved, and anyone could see the tension in Blair whenever he had to deal with Gresham. Their meetings usually took place in the clubhouse, in the privacy of the Secretary's office and, as a humble assistant, my presence was not required. Gresham clearly preferred to carry out his manoeuvres on his home ground, but he did appear in the site office one day as Calvin was busy explaining to me the way he intended to alter the shape of the twelfth hole.

It was a fairly straightforward par four of just over 400 yards.

The only bit of devilry was a small pond on the right-hand side a little less than 200 yards from the tee. It acted as a magnet for most of the club members' balls, even though there were acres of space to the left. Water seems to have a stupefying effect on the ordinary golfer – however innocuously it is positioned. With contorted body and lunging swing he will manage somehow to propel his ball straight into the drink. So it was at Shere Forest's twelfth hole, and Blair had decided to increase the psychological pressure by extending the pond towards the fairway by a few yards, at the same time narrowing the fairway by bringing it in towards the pond from the other side.

'It'll make it a tough hole for everybody,' he said, practically smacking his lips. 'From the back of the tee, the members will have to make their minds up whether to try and hit that narrow strip of fairway, or carry their ball beyond the water, or play short.'

'And from the tournament tee, the pros will have the same choices?'

'Exactly,' Blair said with a smile.

As Blair was expounding these ideas, there was a brief tap on our office door and the formidable person of Peter Gresham appeared. It was the first time I had seen him at close range and I beheld a man of well over six feet in height, rather stooped, with broad fleshy features interrupted by a thin white moustache. He obviously trimmed his moustache and should have given his eyebrows the same treatment; they were bushy and tangled and their fecund growth was echoed by the hairy forest which emerged from his ears. He glanced at me momentarily when Blair introduced me as his new assistant and I noticed that his eyes were unusually dark, almost black. He was dressed in Home Counties mufti – cord trousers, brown brogues, tweed jacket and a striped tie which could have been military, club or old school. It certainly wasn't the tie of Sussex University. He carried an ash walking-stick and his golden retriever trotted at his heels.

'Now, look here, Blair,' he said, without any niceties. 'Your design for the twelfth will never do. It'll make the damned hole much too difficult for my members. The landing area for their drives is going to be too narrow for most of 'em and it's a tough enough hole as it is.'

'That's the whole idea, Peter,' my boss said patiently. 'It's the right time to have a tough hole. The tenth is a shortish par four and the next is a medium-length par five. We've got to hit them with something difficult and make them fight for par. The average player still has a safe route; he can lay up short of the pond and settle for a bogey or an outside chance of a par with a good chip and single putt. But the good player can risk the carry and have a chance of a birdie.'

'Well, they won't like it and nor do I. There's too much emphasis on water hazards these days. All those damned American designers, that's all they think about. We'll end up playing golf in water wings. Why don't you just put a couple of bunkers in, instead of extending the pond?'

'There are several reasons why not. Bunkers don't have the same psychological effect. You remember how Bobby Jones compared the two?'

Clearly Peter Gresham didn't; neither did I.

'Landing in a water hazard is like being in a plane crash – it's final, but landing in a bunker is like a car crash – there's a chance of recovery. Of course, bunkers are more expensive to maintain,' Blair added, getting Gresham where he knew it counted, 'and there are important environmental considerations.'

'We do enough for the damned environment as it is,' Gresham grumbled. 'Look at all the wildlife on the course – foxes, squirrels, all the birds. They wouldn't be here if this was a council estate, would they, eh?'

'Of course not, and we can get some more Brownie points with the environmentalists by extending the pond. Parts of it need to be dredged anyway, and at very little added cost, we can enlarge it. We'll look after it properly. You'll see the plants proliferate – bulrushes, marsh orchids, meadowsweet and watermint. A whole host of plant life.'

I was impressed by Blair's knowledge, Gresham was silenced by it, and Blair continued: 'All that'll encourage insects and the amphibians that have them for dinner – the frogs and toads and newts. And the birds, too – they live off the insects. Your members will probably enjoy seeing wagtails, curlews, redshanks and maybe even wildfowl and waders. The conservationists will certainly be impressed.'

'I hope those Green whatevers will damned well take note,' Gresham muttered irritably.

'The Green Disciples?'

'Yes. Bloody stupid name. Have they been bothering you at all, Blair?'

'Just a few minor irritations.'

'Hmm, we've had a call or two and some silly letters.' Then Gresham cheered up. 'They got the rough edge of Hermione's tongue the other day. She told them to go and do something useful if they cared about the environment, like demonstrate against that nuclear waste reprocessing plant.'

To get the conversation back on its original track, I said: 'The golfers will have to use their intelligence. They can play short with a three-wood if they don't fancy a big shot with a driver. The pros will be forty or fifty yards back on the new tee and they'll have the same decisions to make.'

Gresham looked at me as if he had noticed me for the first time. 'Do you actually play the game, young man?' he asked.

'Chris is off two and used to be a caddie.'

'A caddie? Whatever next.' But Gresham seemed to regret this remark since he added quickly. 'Well, I'll play a few holes with you some time.' Then he paused, hands behind his back, and grunted to himself a few times.

'It's what the sponsor wants,' Blair said quietly. I looked innocently out of the window.

'Damned sponsor,' Gresham sighed, then, more loudly: 'Very well, Blair, I'll see what I can do. I take your point.'

Blair smiled at me as Gresham went out of the door. 'That means yes, go ahead. By the way, did you smell anything?'

'Yes, I did. It wasn't Gresham, was it?'

'No, it's that bloody dog Hannibal. He's got a very bad case of canine BO but the old boy doesn't seem to notice it any more.'

I laughed, then asked Blair what all the fuss had been about. 'Haven't all these changes already been discussed and approved?'

'They have, in principle. But Gresham likes to have his pound of flesh. You see, he thinks he knows more about golf and golf courses than anyone. Just because he's on the R&A committee and once played in the Walker Cup.'

'Now then,' I said, 'let's not have any inverted snobbery.'

Professional golfers were sometimes irritated by the fact that the ultimate authority in their game was the Royal and Ancient Golf Club – what they called 'a bunch of bloody amateurs'. Along with the United States Golf Association it was the final arbiter of the rules and regulations, but even the most diehard professional would probably have admitted that golf was by far the best administered of all the international sports. The many scandals which regularly afflicted other sports were rarely heard of in golf.

'Oh well, he was quite a tidy player,' Blair conceded. 'Come on – let's walk down to the twelfth and stake out where the pond will go.'

By the time we'd finished, it had been reshaped into a wickedly tight hole from the tee. 'I hope the members are all proficient with a one-iron,' Blair said with a smirk.

'Even God can't hit a one-iron,' I said automatically, and recalled the story of an American professional who, while retreating towards the clubhouse during a violent thunderstorm, held his one-iron in the air to ward off the lightning.

We checked on how the work was progressing elsewhere and then Blair took me on a quick tour of the 200 acres where the new course would be laid out – should it ever go ahead. As we bumped across the gorse and heather in Blair's four-wheel drive truck he gave me an enthusiastic summary of his ideas. With the help of topographical maps and aerial photos and some rough measurements, he had already done an outline of the course. It was to be the classic configuration of four par five holes, four short holes and ten par fours of varying lengths. There was ample room to make a series of very large tees, so that both the handicap golfers and the professionals would face similar challenges. Whereas the club members would play a course of around 6500 yards, it could be stretched to over 7000 yards for a professional tournament.

'Just look at this land.' It was clear that Blair could hardly wait to get started. 'It was put here to make a great golf course.'

We had stopped on the edge of a heavily wooded knoll and he gestured expansively at the ground which rolled and swooped in every direction.

'We won't even need to move much earth; the natural rises and falls are already there.'

'Except for the tees and the greens.'

'Oh yes, they always take up a lot of the budget, especially the greens. You need a top-class shaper, that's the first priority.'

'And have we got one?'

'Yes, indeed – Barry Miller. He's a rough bugger but a real artist behind the wheel of a scraper. I just hand him the designs and leave him to it.'

'Let's hope it goes through without any hitches.'

'There are always hitches, Chris. Getting planning permission is a ruddy minefield. I've tried to clear the decks with some of the conservationist bodies well in advance but you've seen what Gresham's like – he prefers to pretend they don't exist. And he certainly won't spend any money.'

'What have you done so far?'

'Talked to the Nature Conservancy people. They're helpful but that old sod Gresham wouldn't let me go beyond doing a pilot ecological survey. Too expensive, he said.' Blair shook his head sadly. 'If they come across some rare butterflies like the ones they found on a site in California, the Bay Checkerspot I think it was called, we'll really be in the mire. When they discovered some blind spiders at a projected golf course in Hawaii – the smallest daddy-longlegs in the world, apparently – the developer was forced to abandon the project.'

'For the sake of a piddling arachnid,' I said. 'I think I might have been tempted to apply a size ten Footjoy to said spider and hope for the best.'

43

Blair grinned. 'All the same,' he said, 'the conservationists have their part to play and I'd be a fool if I didn't want to work within their code. If they want to look after some SSSIs, so be it. I can handle that.'

'SSSIs?'

'Sites of Special Scientific Interest. I can incorporate them into the course. It's Gresham with his old-time patrician outlook who's the difficulty. He doesn't understand that we must show how we encourage wildlife, not destroy it, especially when golf course developments are under attack.'

'The property spivs do us a great disservice, don't they?' I mused. 'They just want a golf course as a lever to put up a hotel and a conference centre. Then there's a leisure centre, and before you know where you are they've built several dozen executive lodges along the fairways.'

'Right. Golf can do without them. The wide boys with their mobile phones . . .'

'. . . and rented Mercs . . .'

'. . . and blonde assistants with legs up to their shoulders.'

Our chorus ended and we grinned in mutual sympathy.

'How *do* you become a property spiv?' Blair asked with a laugh, then, more seriously, 'We really do need more golf courses, don't we?'

'The right kind of courses, yes – and in the right places. Like your municipal one up in the north-east.'

'And the second Shere Forest course.'

'Let's hope so.'

'As far as the environment is concerned, when I've built the second course, or rather *if*, you'll hardly know it's there. There'll be no huge bunkers scarring the landscape, and it'll be as natural as I can make it, I promise you.'

Although he had often suffered in the past with the cumbersome and frustrating process of gaining planning permission, it was apparent that Blair had a cautious approach to building a golf course. His instinct was to preserve, rather than move in with a battery of giant earth-movers and pound the terrain into submission.

He was particularly protective of trees, many of which he planned to transplant. The abundant clumps of wild flowers were to be left wherever possible and classified as 'ground under repair'. A golfer would not be allowed to play his ball out of such areas; he would drop his ball in an adjacent spot and play from there without penalty. It seemed to me that Calvin Blair was very much on the side of the environmental angels.

We stopped again on some higher ground and Blair pointed into the distance. 'We can have a wonderful par four here – a short one. Straight down this shallow valley for about two hundred and thirty yards, and then sharp right around that grove of trees to a plateau green. Some of the big hitters will be tempted to take the heroic route, across the corner and over the trees. It's a big risk but, although the green will be bunkered on the left and the right, I'll leave a clear way in at the front. So the reward for a long and accurate shot will be there.'

'That'll give them something to think about.'

'Should do. But I'm going to clear the undergrowth and thin the trees out a bit. It'd be sadistic to have both trees *and* rough – too penal. One or the other but not both; we don't want to break their hearts.'

'Then what?' I asked.

'Then a short hole downhill into another grove of trees, with a smallish green and plenty of bunkers. Then a long par five. A proper three-shot hole, almost six hundred yards. Remember that this is the second half of the course and we want to give them a really fierce finish.'

As we jolted down the hill and Blair turned the vehicle towards the clubhouse, I saw a flash of colour as two small birds with dark red bellies disappeared into a thick patch of gorse. Robins, I presumed.

Blair put his foot down. 'Hold on to your hat, I want my lunch.'

Chapter 6

Over the next couple of weeks the work on the existing course was pushed onward at a good pace, while Blair continued to refine his ideas for the new one. The British Classic Tournament was only a couple of months away and a collection of builders, carpenters and decorators arrived to give some cosmetic attention to the poor old clubhouse, which was badly in need of a full face-lift.

The process of trying to revive its jaded looks found no favour with Calvin Blair. 'A total waste of money,' he pronounced firmly. 'It needs half a million quid spending on it. A paint job won't hide the crap underneath for long, I can tell you.'

But at least the news about the planning permission that filtered down from Peter Gresham was encouraging. On one of his rare visits to Blair's office he seemed as benign as I'd ever seen him.

'Good news, you chaps. My sources tell me that permission for the new course is only a formality now and should be through in less than a month. Thank God the local council is staunch Conservative.'

Blair winked at me. 'Are you a staunch Conservative, Chris?'

'No, Monster Raving Looney Party. How about you?'

'I can't bring myself to vote for any of the buggers. They're all raving loonies in my opinion.'

Gresham couldn't quite decide how to cope with this. 'Be that as it may,' he responded gruffly, 'we're damned lucky to have a Conservative council. They're friends of the businessman, mark my words.'

'So the new course will go ahead?' Blair said.

Gresham quickly changed the subject. 'I'm playing a few holes after lunch. Would anyone care to join me?'

I looked questioningly at Calvin Blair. 'Not for me, Peter,' he said, 'but young Chris here will give you a game.'

'Three o'clock, then,' said Gresham. 'We'll play nine.' And he stumped out of the office, his retriever at his heels. A powerful smell of ancient damp wool hung unpleasantly in their wake.

Peter Gresham's golf swing was simplicity itself, his method anchored in an unhurried and rounded action. He had obviously been a golfer of the highest class and still played to a handicap of five. If his years prevented his hitting the ball very far, he more than made up for that with his accuracy. I had to play some stern golf to stay level with him. Gresham took advantage of the one shot I had to give him over the nine holes and went ahead at the sixth, but I won the seventh with a birdie to square the match.

Like many players of his generation Gresham was a very quick player who rarely lingered over a shot and we walked briskly down the fairways. Hannibal lagged behind us which, in view of his personal hygiene problem, was just as well. As we played, Gresham went through the familiar inquisition. Which school? Which university? Did my father play?

He was non-committal over most of my replies and only

showed real interest when I mentioned my time in the City with Norton Buccleuth.

'So you worked for Andrew, eh? First-rate chap. He sold out to some damned Swiss outfit, didn't he?'

I nodded and Gresham said, 'I hope he got plenty from them. Too many of our assets have been sold on the cheap.'

The harsh economic climate of recent years had taken its toll of many City firms and the truth was that Andrew Buccleuth had been forced to bring in some foreign investment to keep his company afloat.

It was a good opportunity to sound Gresham out about the new course, although I knew I had to tread softly with him. 'Assuming that the new course gets the green light,' I began carefully, 'I'm sure that Andrew could introduce some investors if extra money were needed.'

I watched as he plucked a five-iron from his small bag of clubs and ran his ball onto the green. Thirty yards further on I hit a soaring shot with my eight-iron and saw it settle close to the pin. If only I could do that every time . . .

'Nice shot,' my opponent said, but money interested him even more than golf. 'What sort of money could Buccleuth come up with?'

'I know he's got a few Japanese clients looking for opportunities in golf.'

'They would not be of any interest to me.' Gresham's face lost its temporary animation and he reverted to his normal gruff self. 'I'll bear your other comments about Andrew in mind.'

That seemed to be the end of *that* topic and we walked down the seventh, whose green lay on the very edge of the course. Over the fence lay the land earmarked for the new course.

As we approached the green I noticed someone standing very

still by a group of tall silver-birch trees which pointed proudly skywards on the far side of the perimeter fence. After we had holed out on the green, Gresham walked towards the fence with a muttered, 'Who the hell's that?'

The figure turned as Gresham reached the fence, revealing a young man in his late twenties, dressed in an olive green waxed coat and dark cord trousers. He had a thin pale face with an earnest expression. Around his neck he carried a pair of binoculars and, as I approached in Gresham's wake, he was jotting something down in a small spiral-bound notebook.

'Can I help you?' Gresham barked.

'No, I don't think so,' the man replied in a gentle and accentless voice. 'Thank you,' he said as an afterthought.

'Well, you're on private land. I'll direct you back to the road.' Gresham had adopted a parade-ground voice which seemed to have little effect on the trespasser.

'No need,' he replied politely. 'This seems to be a footpath and this was all common land for several centuries.'

'Not any longer, it isn't. It's been in my family for nearly a hundred and fifty years, I'll have you know.'

'More's the pity.' The man remained apparently unmoved by Gresham's aggression.

The older man's face darkened with anger. 'If it wasn't for my family this place would probably be a damned housing estate or industrial site by now.'

'Instead of which it's a rich man's playground.'

The intruder seemed to be losing his calm and I intervened to dissipate the rising hostility between the two men. 'Bird-watching?' I asked.

'Sort of.'

'Anything interesting?'

A smug smile briefly visited his face. 'Plenty, thanks. But I won't keep you from your game. I'm off anyway.' And he strode away towards the distant main road.

Gresham looked after him, a scowl on his face. The faithful Hannibal stood close and I moved upwind of him.

'Didn't like the look of the fellow,' Gresham stated. That was pretty obvious.

'He was some sort of naturalist, I suppose.'

'Naturalist, poppycock! What was he up to? One of those damned environmental johnnies, I expect. A bloody nuisance, all of 'em.'

Gresham was still chuntering away as he propelled his ball down the middle of the eighth fairway. We halved the hole and the match and with a brief, 'Thank you for the game, young man,' he marched off into the clubhouse, his retriever trotting at his heels.

It was about a week later that the relatively smooth progress towards the acceptance of the second Shere Forest course was interrupted. The telephone rang in our office and, after a short conversation, Blair said, 'I've been summoned to a meeting. You'd better come with me. That was Gresham in a right old state. There's an objection to any new golf course developments on environmental grounds because of some bird. That's all we need.'

Blair turned away and crashed his brawny fist down on one of the tables. Several pencils jumped in the air and one rolled gently over the edge and onto the floor.

'I begged the silly bugger to get smart, to play the ecological game and take some basic precautions but no, he still thinks he can steamroller everything through. He hasn't a clue just how important these pressure groups are.'

'But he should know. He's in the building business, isn't he? He must deal with planning problems all the time.'

'No, he's just a figurehead. The other directors do all the hard work. He's hardly ever seen except for the monthly board meeting and he grumbles enough about that. The head office is in Slough, which is not his favourite habitat.'

'What should he have done?'

'First off, he should have commissioned a full ecological survey,' Blair said, thumping the desk emphatically, 'to provide an analysis of all the flora, fauna and wildlife on the land in question. There are plenty of people who'll do it and one of the best is not far away. He's the bloke who runs the Department of Ecology at Surrey University. He's the top man. Naturally, that idiot Gresham balked at the cost. I managed to persuade him to let the guy do a preliminary survey . . .'

'How much for the full report?'

'Oh, about ten grand – which is peanuts in the context of the whole project.'

'And it would show that we're on the side of the angels?'

'Exactly, instead of coming on like some turn-of-the-century lord of the manor. Those days are over.'

'What else?'

'Get the local Wildlife Trust on our side. Ask them over to have a good look around. Give them a nice lunch and listen to their advice. Confrontation is just what we don't need. These issues about the environment are too sensitive for that.'

'In other words, Gresham is playing right into the hands of groups like these Green Disciples?'

'Unfortunately, they're as bloody-minded as he is. So, let's go and see how big the problem really is.'

Chapter 7

The Club Secretary's office looked like most Club Secretaries' offices – untidy. The files and papers scattered over Nigel Burnside's desk had overflowed onto another wooden table and were also stacked up on top of the filing cabinets. A bag of clubs leant in one corner and there were boxes of golf balls, walking sticks and hats amongst an array of objects strewn haphazardly around the room. A corner cabinet contained a good selection of bottles and I noticed that both Gresham, who was sitting behind the Secretary's desk, and Burnside, who was leaning nonchalantly against a filing cabinet, had glasses in their hands. Smoke drifted from a cigarette held in the Secretary's other hand.

Calvin Blair introduced me to Burnside, who gave me a barely perceptible nod and buried his nose in his tumbler. He was tall and slim, with fair wavy hair that beat a hasty retreat from his forehead. A pair of pale blue eyes looked out over a small nose and a narrow rosebud mouth. Not bad-looking, I supposed, in a damp sort of way. But then, I've never understood what turns women on.

Gresham wasted no time and certainly did not offer us a drink. 'We have a problem. An objection has been lodged to the new course. Apparently some bird has been spotted on the site. A very rare one, a protected species.' He addressed Blair as if the problem were entirely of his making, and in a manner that suggested he would shortly receive just punishment.

Blair stood up well to being addressed like one of the other ranks. 'What sort of bird?'

'Dartford Warbler,' replied Burnside.

His voice suited his looks; he spoke in a light drawl. I watched as he put down his glass and lit a fresh cigarette from the end of the old one. The smell of the smoke failed to mask the stench of Gresham's dog, which was curled up under its master's feet.

'They nearly died out in the sixties,' the Secretary continued. 'Down to ten pairs or less. Doing OK now, but still an endangered species in Britain.' He smiled slightly in Gresham's direction and I realised that he was actually enjoying the situation.

I remembered the birds I had seen when Calvin and I had been looking at the site of the new course. 'Is it quite small?' I asked. 'With a long tail and wine-coloured belly?'

'That's the birdie,' Burnside answered cheerfully. 'They live in the gorse. Heathland is their habitat.' He gestured at the window. 'Shere Forest is just right for them. They don't migrate, so not many of them survive the winter, alas. Unlike our members, eh, Peter? We could do with a cull amongst the oldies, that's for sure.'

He laughed loudly and I guessed that, although it was only just eleven o'clock, the whisky which he had just finished was joining several others. He wandered over to the cabinet and topped up his glass.

Gresham's agitation was clear as he fidgeted in Burnside's chair. With his forefinger he explored his ear and then sent the same finger poking tentatively into a nostril. With an apprehensive glance around the room, he quickly replaced his hand on the top of the desk. I assumed that his wife had tried hard to break him of that particular habit and, after thirty-odd years, still hadn't succeeded. Gresham shifted in his seat and accidentally kicked Hannibal, who snorted in his sleep.

'I'll bet it was that damned rude bugger I found lurking about by the seventh the other day. I knew he was up to no good,' Gresham said. He nodded at me. 'You remember him, young fella?'

'It's Chris,' I said. 'He seemed harmless enough, but he did have binoculars and a notebook, so . . .'

'I'd like to get out there with my shotgun,' interrupted Gresham. 'That would solve the problem. Damned Warblers, blasted environmentalists.'

'Which would you shoot first?' Burnside inquired smoothly.

'It's no laughing matter,' Gresham snapped. 'I suppose it's those Green Disciple people.'

'Why don't you buy them off?' Burnside said with a quick grin.

'Because they're damned fanatics. They wouldn't listen to reason.' Gresham turned to Blair. 'Well? Where do we go from here?'

'If you'd listened to me six months ago we wouldn't have to go anywhere. The battle would have been won. A bloody walkover.' I noticed that Blair's Lancastrian accent had become more pronounced as he emphatically made his point. 'If we had commissioned that ecological survey, we'd have been in the clear.'

'Twenty thousand pounds for some long-haired academic to tell us things we either know already or don't want to know,' Gresham said bitterly.

'Ten thousand – and worth every penny, as we're about to discover!' Blair's voice rose. 'I suggest we get him in now, tomorrow if possible, with as many of his students as he can muster to do the best he can in the time available. Whatever the cost.'

'It's easy for you to say "whatever the cost" when it's someone else's money,' Gresham declared. 'It's my money. God Almighty, it's *my* property! Surely I can do what I want with it?'

Blair sighed and spoke as if to a child. 'You know well enough that you can't. You wouldn't expect to put up a factory or a housing estate without permission, would you? And a golf course is just the same, we all know that.'

There was silence for quite a time, punctuated only by the sound of sharp intakes of cigarette smoke into Nigel Burnside's abused lungs and a snuffle or two from the dreaming retriever.

Finally, Gresham spoke. 'I suppose you're right, Blair. Talk to those ecology fellows, then – but keep the cost down. This project will put me in Carey Street if I'm not careful. Do whatever's necessary, within reason.'

'What else *is* necessary?' I asked.

Calvin looked at me gratefully for providing him with an opening. 'First of all, we mustn't antagonise anybody. We must emphasise how much we care about the environment, which I do. We will get the course approved, provided we co-operate with various bodies and do exactly what we must to protect not only these Dartford Warblers but the rest of the wildlife here.'

With great firmness he went through his plan of action, which was to keep in close contact with the local planning officer and to consult the various interested bodies: the Nature

Conservancy Council, the Countryside Commission, the County Wildlife Trust and the Council for the Protection of Rural England.

'And don't forget Prince Charles,' Burnside sneered.

'He's not a golfer – unfortunately.' Blair's good humour was back. He rubbed his hands together purposefully. 'We'll show that planning committee that we will do everything in our power not just to protect the environment but to enhance it.'

As Calvin spoke I remembered reading something about the local Wildlife Trust and a name jumped into my head: Charley James. She was a wildlife and ecology expert who, in recent years, had made a name for herself through several television series. The popularity of such programmes never seemed to falter; no doubt it was the enduring appeal of all that sex and violence. And Charley James, an extrovert even by television standards, had shouted and waved her enthusiastic way into millions of British homes.

'We need that Wildlife Trust on our side,' I said. 'Charley James is involved.'

'Who's he?' Burnside asked.

'She,' Blair replied. 'Ecology's answer to Patrick Moore. It's very important, as Chris has said, to get her and the Trust on our side.'

'How?'

'Chris and I will deal with that. We'll ask her over, get her to talk to Dr Michaels and his merry band from the University. They're bound to find some sensitive areas in addition to the places where the Dartford Warblers nest and feed. There are some wetland sites to consider and they'll probably spot some sand lizards or a smooth snake or two and rare butterflies and plants. Then we can ask the Trust to manage those areas. They'll be as happy as larks.'

There was a spluttering sound from the direction of the desk. I thought for a moment that Gresham's dog had finally lost its battle against incipient incontinence, but it was Hannibal's owner who seemed about to explode.

'I cannot believe all this!' Gresham spat. 'We're going to allow those damned weirdos to crawl all over Shere Forest, sniffing around every stone in their search for rare species, and now you want to give them some of my bloody land!'

'Not give, let them manage some of it as a nature reserve. You've got over three hundred acres out there and we only need half that for the new course. It makes sense, I promise you.'

'None of it makes sense to me, old boy,' Burnside said unhelpfully, topping up his glass and reaching for another cigarette.

'What is more,' continued Blair, ignoring him, 'we must form an ecological committee to manage both courses for the next decade or so. Someone from the Trust, a director of the golf club, either myself or Chris, and one or two others. We did this up at the Solway Firth club and it worked a treat.'

'This is all very clever,' Burnside drawled, 'but do we actually need another golf course? Do the members want it?'

'That's irrelevant, Nigel,' snapped Gresham. 'We must get the planning permission, whatever happens.'

The Secretary had a good point; this was often one of the environmentalists' strongest challenges. Blair and Gresham agreed that they had all the facts and figures about the availability of golf courses in the area and the number of golfers who wanted to use them. Nowhere in the world was the need for new courses more apparent than in the south-east of England.

'Nevertheless,' I said tentatively, 'perhaps we ought to put the facts down on paper. We could produce a little leaflet summarising all the statistics and the argument for more courses, plus all the ecological stuff.'

'Good idea.' Blair was enthusiastic. 'And we can try to get Charley James involved.'

'Dave Swanton might agree to write the golf bits,' I added. Dave was a television commentator who had made himself more prominent in golf than the players themselves.

'More money,' Gresham said gloomily.

'No,' I said. 'Charley James would probably work for nothing and Swanton's fee would be modest. But you'll need someone to put it all together in a hurry so that it can be distributed before the planning meeting. What about Toby Greenslade?'

'Yes,' Blair agreed. 'Would he want a fee?'

'A case of Krug would suffice.'

'I don't have an unlimited budget, you know.' Gresham was horrified. 'Krug indeed, for a journalist!' He subsided into his seat and his dog stretched and wheezed at his feet in sympathy.

Blair now spoke directly to Gresham. 'Peter, you know many of the councillors. Do some more lobbying. Bring them up here and show them what we're doing. Give them a good lunch . . .'

'Show them a good time, old boy, fine wine and naughty girls and perhaps a present in their back pockets to send them on their way,' interrupted Burnside. 'That's how you do it in the building trade, isn't it?'

Both Blair and Gresham ignored him and the architect continued: 'You know what to do, Peter. Emphasise the importance of the Classic to the whole area. Talk economics to them. Remind them of all those jobs that are provided during the Tournament, and all the visitors who fill the local hotels and restaurants. And not just during that week but all the year round. Shere Forest is important to the area and the new course will secure its long-term future.'

'And the long-term future of the Gresham family, too,' Burnside smirked.

'Shere Forest *is* the Gresham family,' Peter Gresham said sharply. 'You will do well to remember that, Nigel.'

At that moment the office door opened and the tall figure of Hermione Gresham appeared, dressed in a green tweed skirt and a moss-coloured cashmere sweater. Her round face was distinguished by a large and determined chin and she looked formidable. However, the overall effect was tempered by her widely spaced eyes and the soft curls of her grey hair.

'What would Nigel do well to remember?' she asked in a voice which, though unmistakably used to issuing commands, was gentler than I'd anticipated.

'Nothing, Hermione,' Gresham replied evasively. 'We're just discussing the new course, that's all.'

'Well, your discussions must be concluded, Peter, or you'll be late for lunch with the ladies' committee. You know how important it is to show the flag. We have many questions for you about the new course.'

'Yes, yes.' Gresham sighed irritably.

'And you, Nigel,' Hermione continued with a thin smile, 'you are joining us, I take it?'

'Wouldn't miss it for the world, Hermione, my dear,' he replied, as he drained his glass of whisky.

No, I bet you wouldn't, I thought to myself.

* * *

As we walked back to the site office I congratulated Calvin on his handling of Gresham.

He smiled and held up two crossed fingers. 'All I want him to do is chat up some of his councillor chums. I don't want him near the planning officer or anyone like that. Gresham's such an arrogant old bastard. As for Burnside, I wonder whose side he's on. What did he mean by "the future of the Gresham family"? It sounded pretty snide to me.'

I shook my head at Blair to indicate that I too was in the dark, although I was pretty sure that I knew what the Secretary's remark meant. To change tack, I suggested that we chase up Charley James as quickly as possible since she was important to our overall strategy.

After several phone calls, I heard Blair thanking someone for their help and I looked inquiringly across at him.

'Her agent. Nice guy – plays at Royal Wimbledon. He's going to ask her to call me. Fortunately she's around at the moment. She's just finished recording a series so we might be in luck.'

By the end of the day Calvin had contacted Dr Michaels at Surrey University and Charley James had rung him and agreed to visit Shere Forest two days later. Things were on the move.

Chapter 8

The initial planning committee meeting was scheduled to take place in less than three weeks, and Calvin Blair had gone into action without delay. On the following afternoon Dr Michaels, a bustling man with a rotund figure and a cheerful smile, appeared with several assistants and promised to deliver an ecological survey within ten days.

'That's about a thousand quid a day,' Blair commented ruefully.

In addition, Blair chased the various environmental groups for general counsel and also particular advice about protecting the Dartford Warblers.

Blair had been through these procedures before, most notably in securing approval for his course on the Solway Firth. Coastal areas are notoriously sensitive in environmental terms and, as well as ensuring that public access to those areas would not be affected, the architect had to work to a closely defined ecological plan. Calvin had been smart enough to improve the access to the coastal paths, and he had also devised a wildlife trail which took in some of the outlying parts of the golf course itself. Visitors to the area were encouraged to pick up leaflets which described the wildlife and other natural features of the locality. As the finishing touch, the owners of the new club had agreed to make annual donations to several conservation groups in the area.

It was fortunate that Calvin Blair knew how to tiptoe through the environmental minefield, and his natural tact and sense of humour strengthened his cause. Left to his own devices, Peter Gresham would simply have tried to bomb the opposition out of existence. In World War One, British troops were known as 'lions led by donkeys'. There were no prizes for correctly categorising Gresham.

Calvin's charm was well to the fore when he greeted Charley James, after she had bumped and jolted to a stop in our car park. Her little yellow 2CV looked incongruous tucked between Calvin's powerful BMW and my ancient Porsche. I watched as she hopped out of the Citroën and saw a small neat woman, her oval face framed by cropped red hair. She was dressed in jeans, a dark sweater and trainers, and carried a dictaphone in her right hand.

She bounced up to the office door, exuding energy and a bright awareness.

After the introductions, she said, 'So you'd like some help in getting approval for your new golf course? I'm happy to take a look and make some recommendations on behalf of the Wildlife Trust.'

She smiled at both of us and I asked her if she played golf. 'No, but that doesn't mean I'm against others playing it. I'm for the environment. So, let's get on with it. Come on, Calvin, you show me around.'

She spoke to him as naturally as she would to an old friend, and I guessed that her easy manner had been an important factor in her success in the media. As well as appearing on television, she wrote regularly for a national newspaper and I'd read that her books sold in their hundreds of thousands.

They drove off in Calvin's truck and when they returned about two hours later, I saw that my boss's reserve, apparent when he had first met Charley James, had been swept away. They were chatting and laughing as if they'd known each other for years.

As they entered the office I asked how they'd got on.

'Like a house on fire,' Charley said. 'I've been preaching to the converted – Calvin is one of us. Or if he's not, he's putting on a very good act.'

She confirmed that she would drop in the following day to talk to Dr Michaels. As she headed for the door, she said, 'Oh, one last thing, Calvin. You ought to come to the Trust's AGM. It's in about a month's time.'

'Where?' asked Blair.

'In the local school hall – a pretty cheerless venue, I'm afraid.'

'Why not use the club's dining room?' Blair said quickly. 'There's loads of space – and no charge.'

'Are you trying to bribe me?' she asked in mock horror.

'Certainly I am. It would be an opportunity to demonstrate our goodwill and show that we want to work closely with you and the Trust.'

Charley James waved her thanks and walked purposefully to her car.

'You two seem to have hit it off,' I said.

'She's a smashing woman and I think I've sold her the package.'

'The package?'

'Nature reserves for the Trust to manage and access for the public, a conservation committee and so on.'

'Will she speak on our behalf at the planning meeting?'

'Depends on her conversations with Michaels, but if they go well, yes.'

'And do you think Gresham will actually allow the Trust to use the clubhouse? I reckon some of the older members will need their smelling salts when they get to hear about it.'

'The old bastard will have to agree,' Blair said grimly, '*and* lay on some wine and cheese. She could swing it our way on her own, no trouble.'

'The power of the telly, eh?'

'Let's have it on our side.'

The telephone calls to the office had started almost immediately. If you picked up the receiver you were either greeted with silence or an earful of obscenities, some so colourful that Blair and I learned some choice new phrases. For most of that week the calls were almost continuous; someone was spending an awful lot of time and money on us. Changing the number only gave us a couple of hours' respite, so we used mobile phones instead.

Next, the calls were made to Calvin's home number. Even though the first one was answered by the clearly youthful voice of Rebecca, Calvin's twelve-year-old daughter, the Green Disciple wasn't deterred, and gave her a mouthful of violent abuse. Calvin's wife, Jane, took the next one. She gave as good as she got, but she and Calvin were distressed for Rebecca and arranged for all subsequent calls to be intercepted.

The same tactics were used against the club itself and Nigel Burnside confirmed that he had received a series of abusive calls, as had Peter Gresham.

Then the Green Disciples decided to widen their activities. I'm not much of a letter writer myself; I tend to take the lazier route and seize the telephone when I want to communicate with other people. In consequence my daily post usually amounts to no more than a few circulars plus, of course, the odd bill.

That morning I had been on a short run around the fringes of Wimbledon Common and had my nose in a final mug of tea before leaving for Shere Forest, when I heard the clump of the morning's mail on the hall floor. There was no need to open my bank statement; I knew what it said and didn't see why it should blight the day so I left that envelope on the kitchen table with some other junk mail.

The only item of interest was a package about the size of a paperback blockbuster. I wasn't expecting a parcel, so I turned it over and looked for the sender's address but found nothing.

It was a sign of the times that I felt a twinge of suspicion. With a pair of kitchen scissors I levered the flap open. There was a muffled crack as I got halfway along the edge. Throwing the envelope away from me, I jumped back and instinctively put my hands over my eyes for protection. I could hear my heart thudding hard and felt adrenalin rush through my system. An acrid smell filled the air.

The initial shock waned but I didn't know if the envelope had more pyrotechnics in store. Gingerly I peered through my fingers and saw that the flap had peeled back of its own accord to expose a piece of white card.

Instead of calling the police or fire brigade, which common sense told me I should, I edged towards the envelope and got close enough to read a typed message

WE MESS UP PEOPLE WHO MESS UP THE ENVIRONMENT. OPEN THE ENVELOPE. WATCH THE ENCLOSED VIDEO.

With some trepidation and my head averted, I pulled out the video-cassette. With it came a sheet of paper with another printed message —

YOU BASTARDS AT SHERE FOREST ARE ALSO THE
GUILTY ONES. REST ASSURED THAT YOU WON'T
BUILD ONE SINGLE EXTRA HOLE.

It was signed —

THE GREEN DISCIPLES

The video lasted less than ten minutes. It opened with idyllic shots of the countryside; as a choir was singing 'Jerusalem' on the soundtrack, I thought it a reasonable supposition that this was the British countryside. Suddenly the scene shifted to nauseating pictures of battery chickens, featherless and crammed together in tiny cages; then it was back to England's green and pleasant land. Contrasting images then flashed onto the screen. Factories spewed out acres of black smoke and a happy family opened their Christmas presents; close-ups of skeletal children in Africa, their faces covered in flies, were followed by those of a smiling South African rugby team arriving at Heathrow; lovers strolled hand in hand through a sunny field, then the screen dissolved into images of Chernobyl after the reactor meltdown. I saw pigs being slit open in a slaughterhouse, foaming detergent on a poisoned river, a fox being torn apart by hounds, an injured cow forced into a truck with an electric prod. It was crude and effective, an unnerving catalogue of man's inhumanity to man and to the creatures around him.

The final sequence showed the sea covered in dead fish,

fields reduced to dust, a blighted landscape – a world without life.

The screen went black and a voice said: 'Man's headlong destruction of his fellow creatures and his own environment must stop. The Green Disciples are dedicated to ensuring that it will.'

I pressed the rewind button and was reflecting on the brutal shock tactics of the production, when the telephone rang.

'Have you opened your mail yet?' Toby's voice asked sharply.

'Yes, and I've received a present from the Green Disciples.'

'A present? I nearly had a heart attack. And I wasn't alone – most of the golf writers seem to have been targeted. Who are these jokers?'

'They're obsessed idealists, absolutely convinced that they're right. That's why they're so dangerous.'

Toby perked up as the newspaper man in him came to the fore. 'They're certainly putting the screws on you lot at Shere Forest. What happens next?'

'You don't think we're going to wring our hands and give up the project, do you?' I said impatiently.

'Of course I don't. But Calvin is more vulnerable than you. You'll have to look out for him, I imagine.'

'That's the main reason he employed me, Toby. Look – I must get over to the club.'

'Give me a call if the Green Disciples have burned the clubhouse down, won't you?' Toby sounded positively cheerful now. 'Or hanged Peter Gresham from the flagpole. I need a good story for tomorrow's edition. In the meantime I'll see what the *News* has on file about them. Nothing much, I'm sure. My editor isn't too bothered about political extremists unless they cause a major riot with blood flowing in the gutters.'

To my surprise Calvin hadn't received the video. With the thought that it might arrive with the second post he rang his wife and warned her not to touch anything from an unknown source.

I tried to play down the sinister aspects of the video and told Calvin it was just a highly professional piece of propaganda. I should have saved my breath. He was unconvinced and I had to agree with him that the Green Disciples might have devised something nastier for the architect, whom they probably regarded as their prime target.

They might also have put Peter Gresham in the same category, but we discovered that both he and the Secretary had received a copy of the video. Shortly after my arrival at the office, Gresham came storming through the office door. He waved the video at us both and said: 'Bloody anarchists. I've called the police about this. It might have blinded us. Poor Hermione nearly had a seizure – knocked a jug of milk all over Hannibal. Had to give him a bath.' Calvin and I exchanged looks which said plainly, 'Every cloud . . .'

Gresham continued: 'These people have gone too far. I damn well won't be intimidated by them. I'll get that course approved even if I have to appeal to the Department of the Environment. Not that it will be necessary, between you and me.' He treated us to a conspiratorial smile. 'I've got most of the councillors in my pocket. They'll wave it through when it comes to the crunch. We've given all of them VIP treatment at the Classic over the years – champagne, a good lunch, a chance to meet the players . . . Their wives love it. And now it's time to collect on our little investment.' He was giving a good impression of a Home Counties Godfather.

'I assume there are some Masons among them?' Blair observed drily.

'A few, certainly, but that's of no significance. The primary concerns of the Freemasons' movement are charitable. We help the needy,' Gresham stated pompously.

'And the greedy,' muttered Blair.

'What was that?' Gresham snapped.

'Yes, indeed,' Blair said quickly.

Gresham glared at him, told us that he had work to do, as though we'd been detaining him, and barged out again.

On the following day we learned from Nigel Burnside that every member of Shere Forest golf club had received a registered letter in which the Green Disciples affirmed their unrelenting opposition to any attempt to build a second golf course. The sting was in the letter's tail, with its threat that they would hold every member individually responsible for any disturbance to the environment.

'The members won't like that,' Burnside said sardonically. 'Much too near the bone. Their worst fears will be confirmed – Socialism, violence on the streets, revolution. Damn near as earth-shattering as putting up their fees.'

My attempt to calculate the cost of sending 300-odd registered letters to the members was rudely interrupted by the noise of a motorbike skidding to a halt outside in the car park. A motorbike is *not* the favoured mode of transport among Shere Forest members, and I felt the hair prickle on the back of my neck as I prepared to earn my money as Calvin's protector.

The driver was hidden under a helmet and a visor and his passenger's long hair straggled from beneath the sort of round helmet which is affected by members of the Hell's Angels. The skull and crossbones on his black leather bomber jacket confirmed his allegiances and I couldn't try to kid myself that he was a prospective Shere Forest member or the man from the Pru.

These guys meant trouble – and they weren't going to waste time. Before I was even out of the door I saw the passenger produce a large and businesslike hammer from inside his bomber jacket.

He ran at Calvin's pristine BMW with the hammer raised and the first blow smashed the rear lights. I started after him, praying that the noise of his destruction would mask my approach, and that his experience of head-to-head violence was limited to Saturday-night posturings down at his local. I wasn't keen on the fact that his hammer and crash helmet gave him a distinct advantage over me.

I nearly made it but, at the last moment, the driver, who had remained astride his machine, saw me and shouted a warning. The hammer whistled past my ear as I ducked low and took Skull and Crossbones in the ribs with my shoulder. He was already off-balance with the violence of the attempted blow and as I thudded into him as hard as I could, he lost his footing and fell onto one knee.

Fortunately he lost his grip on the hammer at the same time. As he scrabbled for it, I kicked out and caught him solidly in the crotch, regretting only that I wasn't wearing something more substantial than my trainers. The man's scream of pain told me that I had hit the target. The Marquis of Queensberry would not have approved.

My ambition to break a few of his ribs was thwarted when I heard the roar of the motorbike and saw it hurtling towards me.

I jumped for my life across the bonnet of the BMW and saw the bike circle round on the other side. The driver yelled, 'Get on, you stupid bastard.' He had the indeterminate South London accent of a Radio 1 DJ. The motorbike was a powerful Honda, its numberplates illegible under a layer of mud.

As the stupid bastard started to crouch-run towards the Honda with his hands between his legs, I fancied my chances of having another go at him and tried a rugby tackle, but received a hefty kick in the shoulder for my pains. This loosened my grip sufficiently for the man to haul himself onto the back of the bike. But I wasn't done for yet. As it revved up to a numbing crescendo, I clawed at my adversary's neck, grabbing what I could. Strands of lank hair slipped between my fingers and, in a last despairing move, I caught his right ear. For a moment I had my forefinger stuck in his ear and my thumb at the back of his earlobe – not an orthodox method of dealing with the enemy, I grant you. Then the bike moved off with a jerk and a shower of dirt from the spinning back wheel. As I hit the ground I heard another scream of pain and wondered why.

By now, Calvin was at my side, breathing hard, and I realised that the whole incident had taken only the time it took him to run from the office.

'I'm sorry, Chris. I wasn't much use to you, was I?' he said. He was all for following the pair in his car, but, thank God, allowed himself to be dissuaded.

He pointed at my right hand which was sticky with blood. It didn't hurt, though, and when I flexed my fingers, they seemed to be in full working order. As we examined my hand for the source of the bleeding, Calvin noticed something caught on my sleeve. It was an earring, speckled with blood.

He held it up for my inspection. 'No wonder he screamed

like a stuck pig – you must have ripped this out of his ear. First blood to Blair Associates.'

'Yes – and his wedding tackle will never be the same again, either.'

We wished our leather-jacketed visitor a journey of potholes and bumps. It was a consoling thought.

'That's why I didn't rate a video,' Blair said thoughtfully. 'That was intended as my own special message from those delightful Green Disciples.'

I wasn't so sure, and my doubts were confirmed when Blair received a call from his wife late in the afternoon. She did most of the talking and all I could hear at my end were his exclamations of annoyance.

I looked up as he put the phone down and saw that his solid and fleshy face was tinged pink with anger.

'Those bastards. Do you know what they did?' he asked rhetorically. 'They sent that wretched video to Rebecca's school – to the headmistress. No exploding envelope, thank God, but with a letter saying that Rebecca Blair's father was one of the people who were trying to destroy an environmentally valuable part of southern England. That we were intent on ruining the wildlife, including endangered species like the Dartford Warblers.'

'What did she do? The headmistress?'

'Rang Jane. Didn't say anything to Rebecca. Destroyed the letter and the video.'

'Good for her.'

'She's a sensible lady. But it's worrying, isn't it? They've had no difficulty tracing their targets' homes and the school. They're way over the top. They seem to have lots of money and endless resources.'

'Try not to worry too much. We've seen them off this time and it'll all blow over as soon as that planning permission comes through.'

It wasn't long before my easy words, intended to lend comfort, came back to haunt me.

Chapter 9

The next couple of weeks encompassed a period of intense activity as Blair marshalled his evidence and his witnesses to demonstrate that Shere Forest would be a model of ecological correctness.

Dr Michaels' survey did not uncover any unforeseen difficulties. Calvin knew the Dartford Warblers habitat and the positions of various areas of wetlands, and he had already altered his outline plan of the new course to take account of them. He did not know, however, about the pipistrelle bats which inhabited an abandoned barn on the edge of the Shere Forest land, nor about the barn owls which had been seen in one of the woods. But they did not pose any problems to him and would be an added attraction for members and visitors with an interest in wildlife.

The campaign gathered strength on all fronts. On a couple of occasions I glimpsed Peter Gresham and Nigel Burnside in earnest conversation with middle-aged and besuited gentlemen who could only be local councillors. They were being shown the site of the new course and how carefully it had been planned to accommodate the designated conservation areas. The boring bit concluded, Gresham and Burnside then plied their visitors with the club claret and made a serious pitch for their support over the vintage port.

The personable Charley James had been won over to our cause, especially when she saw the first draft of the ecological survey. It was then that we sent the fearless Greenslade into action. Within a couple of days, and despite his complaints about the deadline, he produced a nicely argued piece, supposedly from the pen of golf commentator Dave Swanton, about the urgent need for more golf courses, particularly in the south-east of England. It was balanced by comments from Charley James about the ecological implications of golf courses, the duties of designers and golf club administrators towards the environment, and how those duties would be properly discharged at Shere Forest.

It was my task to get our vital piece of propaganda produced. Fortunately I found a local printer who ran off a thousand copies within twenty-four hours. These were distributed as widely as possible but especially to the councillors, people who lived in the vicinity of Shere Forest and to the local media, which amounted to a radio station and a couple of newspapers, one of which was a freesheet. All three dutifully ran items about the project and I was surprised when Toby managed to insert a short item into the *News*.

The headline read: TV NATURE GURU WELCOMES NEW GOLF COURSE and the report went on: 'Charley James, TV's irrepressible nature girl, has put her stamp of approval on the proposed new course at Shere Forest, home of the British Classic Golf Tournament. Cuddly Charley said yesterday, "It's a triumph of ecological common sense. I wish the club well and I'll be serving on the conservation management committee."'

A picture of 'Cuddly Charley' alongside the article showed her holding a tiger cub in her arms.

I could not resist a call to Toby, ostensibly to thank him for his publicity. Since it was only ten o'clock in the morning I rang him at home and was greeted with a rather terse 'Hello, Greenslade.'

'You sound a bit rough, Toby. Out on the town last night?'

'A book launch, dear boy. Another turgid golfing tome by a semi-literate which will be here today and mercifully gone tomorrow. Why do these publishers bother? The wine was supermarket plonk, probably from a screw-top bottle and the food – ugh, sorry, *canapés* – not much better.'

'You enjoyed yourself, then?'

'Oh yes, I usually manage to do that,' Toby said wearily.

'Thanks for the plug about Shere Forest. I'm sure Cuddly Charley liked it too. So, you got that close, eh?'

Toby groaned. 'My God, the standard of the sub-editing at that rag gets worse. Any woman under the age of fifty, especially if she appears on the telly, is sexy, or toothsome, or statuesque – or bloody cuddly. It's English on autopilot. Tabloid tripe. No, I did *not* get that close. Anyway, your boss Calvin was positively dancing attendance on her. I think he's got more than a cuddle in mind.'

'Toby, they may have taken to each other but Calvin isn't smitten. He's not a womaniser.'

'Oh no? It took me back to my teenage days.'

'Come off it, Toby, you were never a teenager. The day after you were born, you turned up at the offices of the *News* with a hangover.'

'Hmmm. Very droll.'

'Maybe Calvin's playing a deeper game than you think. He's attentive for the sake of his project. Her support is crucial, after all.'

'You're a very cynical young man, as I've had cause to remark to you before. I just hope his delightful wife doesn't hear anything untoward.'

'Toby, you've been working on a tabloid for too long. I'm sure that Calvin treads the straight and narrow. Charley is very sparky mind you, very attractive.'

'Talking of the straight and narrow, and in the hope that no officers of Her Majesty's Inland Revenue service is listening in, what about my fizz? It was a hard-earned fee, I can assure you.'

'What would you like?'

'Krug rosé, please.'

'Rosé?' I queried. 'You've always said that rosé is neither one thing nor the other, a tart's tipple.'

'And I was right. But Krug rosé is very special and, above all, it's very expensive and the cost will annoy that bladder of meanness, Peter Gresham.'

'OK,' I agreed. 'It's a deal.'

On the morning of the planning committee meeting, Calvin and I walked down to a local pub for lunch. It was a relief to get away from Shere Forest for an hour or so. That morning we had checked that we had done everything that was required not once but many times. Over our pints of Tetley's we checked again and then Calvin said, 'I think that's it – we've done our stuff. Famous last words, I know, but I can't see that we'll have any problems.'

He went to the bar and returned with two more pints and a plate of sandwiches. 'Chris, you've done more than your fair share. I hate to think what I owe you in overtime, so why don't you have the rest of the day and tomorrow off? I'll call you at home as soon as I know the decision.'

I didn't need any persuasion and half an hour later was pointing the nose of my Porsche towards Putney.

In order to wind down, I played a few holes of golf at my own club. Recently, I'd noticed that I was looking at the course with new eyes; not only at the wildlife which proliferated there but also at the plants. When my opponent got into the rough, my identification of horseshoe vetch and clustered bellflower spoiled his concentration and he dropped a shot. Wildlife helped him to get his own back at the next hole, though, when my concentration was spoiled in turn by a fox sitting fearlessly near the edge of the green watching my approach putt with an apparently critical eye. As well as the foxes, we had a family of badgers – a protected species which I think the greenkeepers would have preferred to have taken up residence elsewhere.

I got back to my flat shortly before six o'clock and the telephone rang about half an hour later. I snatched it off its stand in my eagerness. The normally calm Calvin Blair almost shouted: 'We've done it! It sailed through!'

'No problems?'

'Some dissenters and a bit of a demo outside. Green Disciples with placards. I didn't recognise your friend – the one you duffed up. I was looking for someone with a limp and a squeaky voice,' he said with a laugh.

'Great news. Well done.'

'I think we'd have got there anyway but Charley really knocked 'em in the aisles,' Blair said enthusiastically. 'We knew the Conservatives would swing it our way, but by the time she'd finished, the Lib Dems voted for us as well.'

'She's become a real friend, hasn't she?'

'Oh yes. Great girl. Anyway, we'll finish the alterations to the old course and crack on with the new eighteen. There's just one hurdle . . .'

'What's that?'

'Will Gresham come up with the money? One thing at a time, though. I'm going home now to have a bottle of champagne with Jane and I hope you'll lift a glass to celebrate as well.'

Ten minutes later I was doing just that, along with my neighbour, Mrs Bradshaw. She'd only take one drink, since it was her bridge night and she didn't want to let her partner down. Aware as I was of her razor-sharp mind, I didn't think there was much danger of that. On the contrary, I felt sorry for the opposition.

When she'd gone off to do battle, I put the remains of a chicken casserole in the oven; it could heat slowly while I finished the champagne.

In an effort to educate myself in the principles of golf course design, I'd read several books on the subject. The latest was *The Golf Courses of Robert Trent Jones* and I was making very slow progress with it.

I opened the book and settled down, champagne at my elbow, to read a chapter before dinner. It seemed only seconds before the insistent ring of the telephone made me jerk upright from a deep sleep. The book fell on the floor but thank goodness the champagne stayed put. I headed for my desk.

In reply to my 'Hello,' there was no sound for a moment.

'Hello,' I repeated sharply and heard a sort of snuffle from the other end, a truncated sob. A heavy breather? I didn't attract many of those.

Suddenly a voice at the other end said my name: 'Chris, I need help.' Hoarse and cracked as it was, I recognised it as Calvin's. What the hell was wrong?

'What's the matter? What's happened?' I asked urgently. There was silence then I heard the sounds of a man trying to get control of himself.

'Jane, Rebecca. They're dead.' His voice tailed off again and I had to shout above his sobbing and retching, trying to find out where he was ringing from and whether he'd called an ambulance or the police.

'Calvin, can you hear me? Come on, man, where are you?'

His only reply was a small 'Home,' followed by a smaller 'Help me,' and I shouted, 'I'm on my way!' and headed for the door, just remembering to turn off the casserole.

Thank God I'd only had two glasses of champagne. The deep ennui induced by Mr Trent Jones's golf courses had probably kept me legally sober, and I'd certainly never felt so sober in my life. As I burst out of the front door to the flats I nearly knocked over my upstairs neighbour who was cradling two bags of shopping in her arms, about to insert her key in the lock. 'Sorry,' I called back, adding superfluously, 'in a hurry.'

Although I had only visited Calvin Blair's house a couple of times, I remembered the way there pretty well. At just after eight o'clock in the evening, the rush hour was over and, as I did all Porsche drivers an enormous disfavour by slicing and bullying my way past the traffic, I prayed that there were no police cars lurking on my route. Although my heart was pumping and my whole body trembled in the effort to get to Calvin, a part of me enjoyed the challenge as I hurtled the car into Sussex.

I couldn't understand what had happened to Calvin's family and at this moment didn't even want to speculate. I concentrated instead on the road flying beneath my wheels and tried to blot out everything else.

The journey seemed to take for ever, but in fact I'd probably broken all records as I swept into Calvin's drive, missing the ambulance that was coming the other way by the thinnest coat of car polish. Arc lights were glaring upon the house and two police cars sat by the front door. Thank God he'd called the police. I hadn't known how I could possibly cope with a couple of bodies. I leaped out of the car and almost into the arms of a young uniformed policeman.

'Can I help you, sir?' he asked.

'I'm a friend of Mr Blair. He rang me about his wife and daughter. What's happened?'

I tried to walk past him towards the front door but he blocked my way and said, 'Just a moment, sir. Come with me, please. I'll check with the guv'nor.'

He made me wait at the front door until, after a couple of minutes that felt like hours, a man came out and introduced himself as Inspector Gilder. I was startled for a moment by his sheer size; he looked just like the Michelin Man. Rolls of flesh were trying to escape from his rumpled, dark blue suit. Above his florid face his hair stuck out in patches of grey abandon. I guessed his weight to be considerably over twenty stones.

'You must be Mr Ludlow,' he said, in an unexpectedly quiet and well-modulated voice. 'Calvin has been asking for you.'

'Where is he? What's happened to Jane and Rebecca?'

'He's in the house. He's had a terrible shock but he'll be all right.'

'Yes, but Jane and Rebecca?' Impatience sharpened my voice. 'They're not all right, are they? They're dead.'

'Not so, thank goodness.'

Not dead? The shock and relief paralysed me for a moment.

'Look, Inspector,' I said, losing control, 'I've broken virtually every traffic law in the book to get here. Tell me, please, what has happened to Calvin's wife and daughter?' I was shouting at the man by now.

As I finished, Calvin himself appeared in the doorway. He was stooped, his arms hanging loosely in front of his body and the normal healthy colour of his face had been replaced by a waxy pallor.

'It's very good of you to come, Chris,' Blair said, as if I'd turned up for cocktails, but as I walked towards him I saw that his eyes were overflowing with tears. The weeping of an outwardly strong man is always disturbing and, as he collapsed into my arms, I found it difficult not to cry along with him.

'They're all right,' he whispered. 'I thought they were dead, I thought I'd lost them for ever. They've taken them to hospital but they're all right.'

The bulky Inspector Gilder rustled alongside me and said quietly, 'Whoever it was tied them up, daubed them with ketchup and gave them some sort of drug which slowed their pulses right down. Mr Blair assumed the worst, as anyone would in a situation like that, and as it was intended he should.'

'Come on, let's sit down,' I said and guided Calvin into the sitting room.

For some time he talked through what had happened, interrupted by the occasional question from one of several coppers who were busy working in and around the house and garage. Gradually he became calmer and his voice stronger. Finally, he announced, 'It was those bastards, the Green Disciples.'

'How do you know?'

'Because they left a note. You must see it. That Inspector took it.' He left the room in search of the policeman and for the first time I looked at my surroundings.

The room was very large, with a number of unmatched sofas and easy chairs scattered about. A solid oak refectory table was pushed up against one wall, an array of magazines distributed on its top. One wall was covered with a wide variety of books and the others with prints and paintings of golfers and cricketers, interspersed with landscape watercolours and architectural drawings of golf holes, presumably designed by Blair. A six-sided conservatory had been built onto the end of the room and through its windows I could see a wide, lawned garden. It was a room at once comfortable and attractive; a family room. My examination of some of the book titles was rudely interrupted by a noise from the hall.

'For Christ's sake, I only want him to have a quick look at it.' Yes, Calvin's voice was getting stronger by the minute.

'But it's been tagged for evidence, sir,' Gilder replied.

'I don't give a shit,' came the forceful reply. 'I want Chris to see it. He's here to help.'

I walked into the hall to see Inspector Gilder open his mouth, close it again and motion to a uniformed colleague. A few moments later the officer returned with a piece of white card which had been placed in a plastic bag. It read: 'This is just the beginning. Next time it's for real. Save the planet. *The Green Disciples.*'

Chapter 10

'And who are these Green Disciples when they're at home?' Gilder asked. 'I've never heard of them.'

As briefly as I could, I explained the background to the Shere Forest project, Calvin Blair's role in it, and what had happened so far in the way of reprisals by the Green Disciples.

One of the easy chairs creaked as Inspector Gilder shifted his weight and observed, 'So it's another anarchic pressure group, a bunch of loonies who think animals are more important than people?'

'Not just animals, Inspector,' I told him, 'the whole environment – the flowers, the trees, the shape of the land itself.'

'We'd still be living in caves if we carried on like that,' Gilder said.

'Maybe, but a smattering of their philosophy might have saved us from industrial deserts, tower blocks and cities gridlocked by cars,' I said.

'And Slough and Milton Keynes,' muttered Blair.

'I'll look forward to discussing their philosophy with them when I've got these people banged up in a cell,' Gilder said grimly. 'I'll ask Special Branch for a hand. They'll have a file on them along with all the other nutters, like the animal rights boys . . .'

'When can I see my family?' Blair interrupted.

Gilder looked at me, a warning in his eyes and replied, 'Not tonight, Mr Blair. Very unwise, I would have thought. You should get some rest, take one of those pills the doc gave you and get some zeds in. I'll ring the hospital and see how they are.'

Gilder paused in the doorway and beckoned to me to follow. I joined him in the hall and he asked if I'd stay with Calvin for the night.

'He's still in shock you see, sir, and he shouldn't do anything for a while. He should be OK tomorrow and so should his wife and the little girl. The doc didn't know what they'd been drugged with – let's hope it was harmless.'

He lumbered towards the telephone and I rejoined Calvin. He seemed relieved when I offered to stay at the house with him and asked me to pour him a Scotch. I found a bottle of Glenmorangie and offered the Inspector a glass when he rejoined us.

'Thank you, I will have a splash. It's been a longish day.' He took a hearty swallow and smacked his lips appreciatively. 'I've rung the hospital and Mrs Blair and Rebecca are in no danger, sir. They're still out for the count, though, and the doctor reckons they were given some sort of tranquilliser-cum-beta-blocker and that's why their pulses had slowed right down.'

'Beta-blocker?' queried Blair.

'Yes, as used by some sportsmen,' Gilder said.

'To calm their nerves,' I butted in. 'Snooker players have tried them and so have musicians. And didn't they have a problem in the rifle-shooting at the Olympics a few years back?'

'Who'd notice another drug at the Olympics?' Gilder asked cheerfully. 'There are enough drugs in an Olympic village to keep the whole of London stoned for a week.'

'I wish I'd known about beta-blockers when I was on the pro tour,' Blair said wistfully. 'I might've holed a few more putts.'

I was relieved to see that some of his normal ebullience was returning and asked Gilder if there were any more precautions Blair should take, in addition to his burglar alarm system, to protect his family and himself.

Gilder was pretty sure that the Green Disciples wouldn't have another go at the Blair family, and expressed himself well satisfied with the existing alarm system and window and door locks. However, he recommended getting a dog. 'I have two Labradors myself. Lovely deep barks. Frighten people off, you know, although they'd only lick any burglar to death.'

Calvin declared his strong preference for the independent and arrogant cat over the helpless and stupid dog and, as though on cue, a brown Burmese appeared round the door and made a beeline for Gilder's lap.

Inspector Gilder quickly downed the rest of his malt whisky and told Blair that he would call round on the morrow to take a full statement. I walked him to the front door.

'Look after him, Mr Ludlow. These Green Disciples are clearly not short of money, personnel or commitment. I'm going to see what we know about them.'

As I opened the door a man in an anorak and corduroy trousers appeared in the porch. 'Hello, Don,' he said to Gilder. 'What've you got for me?'

'Sod all, Sid,' the Inspector replied. 'A small domestic accident, nobody seriously hurt.' Gilder gestured at the thin, middle-aged man who cupped his hand around a cigarette as he drew on it deeply. 'This is Sid Lacock. Chief ambulance-chaser for the local rag.'

'And the local stringer for the *News* and the *Chronicle*,' Lacock said with a grin. 'Who's this?' he asked with a nod in my direction.

'A friend of Mr Blair's,' Gilder replied. 'Now leave them in peace, Sid. If you want to know more, I'll make a brief statement in the morning.'

Inspector Gilder put a massive hand on the journalist's shoulder and urged him away from the front door towards a small car parked near the gate. 'Off you go, my lad. I'll see you tomorrow.' No doubt aware that he needed to remain in the formidable Gilder's good books, Lacock did as he was told.

A constable held open the back door of the police Rover, and it tilted heavily as Gilder settled in his seat. He gave me a wave and was driven away.

I suddenly realised that I was ravenously hungry and asked Calvin to point me at the kitchen. Like the other rooms, it was large and seemed to contain every gadget and utensil any cook would ever need. I rooted around in the freezer, found some salmon steaks, and shoved them in the microwave to defrost. A few minutes later I had thrown together a salad, cooked the salmon and opened a bottle of Beaujolais.

I called Calvin to the kitchen table but, despite my encouraging him like a Jewish Momma, he only ate a couple of mouthfuls. After some cajoling, he agreed to take a sleeping pill, which he downed with some of the wine.

It was ironic that I was the one who slept badly. If only I'd brought the Trent Jones book with me, I'd have gone out like a light. At about six o'clock, I gave up the struggle, splashed cold water over my face and into my eyes that seemed full of grit, and padded downstairs.

An hour later I was on my third cup of tea and well into a

collection of Henry Longhurst's golf writing, when Calvin wandered into the kitchen. He looked a lot less haggard than on the previous day, although his eyelids were heavy with the after-effects of a drug-induced sleep.

'Chris,' he said, as though surprised to find me there. 'Erm, yes, it was good of you to stay.'

'Did you sleep OK?'

'Not badly, but I had some terrible dreams. Well, only terrible in that I dreamed I kept getting holes in one when I should have been dreaming about Jane and Rebecca. That is terrible, isn't it? I must ring the hospital.'

'Not until you've had a cup of tea and then I'll drive you down there.' The Jewish Momma act was becoming a habit.

Blair nodded in agreement, wandered over to the radio and switched it on. It was tuned to Radio 4 and we listened to a mildly interesting interview with the Foreign Secretary, a very tedious one about the latest crisis in the marital affairs of a minor member of the Royal Family, and then came the sports round-up.

The summary of the news consisted of the usual catalogue of death and disaster but the fourth item was of real interest to both of us.

The newsreader stated: 'Parts of London's Westminster were still cordoned off this morning near the Department of the Environment where a bomb went off during the night. No one was injured but extensive damage was caused. An obscure group of environmental activists calling themselves the Green Disciples have claimed responsibility.'

Chapter 11

At the hospital, all seemed reasonably well with Jane and Rebecca. I lingered only long enough to establish that both had regained consciousness and seemed no worse physically for their ordeal, before heading back to Putney. Calvin and I agreed that we would meet at the Shere Forest office on the following day to begin putting the finishing touches to the course in anticipation of the start of the British Classic Championship.

My first call was at my flat for a shave and a change of clothing. Warily, I gathered up my mail and hoped it contained no more inflammatory communications from the Green Disciples. An over-large electricity bill apart, it was harmless enough and I turned my attention to my answering machine, whose red light was winking at me self-importantly.

Toby Greenslade asked me to give him a call 'as soon as convenient, but immediately' and the second caller was my brother, Max. He was arriving in London that day and could I offer him a bed for a couple of nights? I was pleased at the thought of seeing Max again and hoped that he might have some knowledge of the Green Disciples.

Of course Toby knew about the incident at Calvin Blair's house and berated me for not giving him a call.

'I had my work cut out just looking after Calvin,' I protested.

'You should have called me with an on-the-spot report,' he grumbled. 'That bloody stringer for the *News* is useless.'

'Sid Lacock?'

'Yes. How the hell did you know?'

'Because he was hanging about on Calvin's doorstep last night.'

'You could've helped me with an exclusive from old Calvin! What are friends for, for God's sake?'

'Not for providing you with scoops,' I said sharply. 'Calvin was in no state to talk to anyone – and especially not a journalist.'

Toby grunted at the other end of the line and said: 'Well, I've been busy researching on your behalf. I've been checking up on your Green Disciples – with very little success, I'm afraid. I drew a blank in the *News'* library, so I tried the Press Association . . .' There was a pause and I heard Toby swallow something. Coffee, probably stiffened with brandy.

'All I found was an article from a year or so back which just said that they were radical and believed in direct action.'

'That much we know.'

'Oh yes – and they've got money. Apparently the movement started in Germany and spread quickly into Holland and Belgium and parts of Scandinavia.'

'Let's hope they haven't embraced the ideals of the Baader-Meinhof bunch,' I said.

'Not so far. Anyway, I thought these green groups were meant to be non-violent.'

'Non-violent to all animals except the human one.'

'Right, Chris. I know it's not much but that's all I have to tell you so far. Now, can you do me a favour? Ask Calvin if he and his wife will give me an interview. My editor is, as always, on my back like the proverbial camel's hump.'

'Not a chance.'

'Please, won't you give it a try? You'd rather your dear old friend from the *News* got the story than some slimy dyslexic from one of the other tabloids, wouldn't you? You know I'll treat them gently.'

Yes, I knew he would. I promised to do my best with Calvin.

Shortly after six o'clock that evening, Max turned up on my doorstep. He carried a small bag and a briefcase in one hand and two bottles of wine in the other. My baby brother looked as fit as ever but his sun-tanned skin didn't quite conceal the grey rings around his eyes.

Over a cold bottle of champagne I asked him where he'd been. Although I'd received the occasional postcard during the previous months, they were uninformative, just greetings.

'Where haven't I been?' Max said and then gave me a quick-fire summary of his activities. He had been helping with some research for an environmental group which was based in Geneva.

'They've got pots of money,' Max said. 'A girlfriend recommended me. I had special responsibility for sport and leisure – its effect on the environment, et cetera. It sounded a doddle but I've never worked so hard.'

'What about the girl? She supplied the leisure activities, I presume.'

'For a while but we, erm, parted company in Thailand.'

'I see.' It was a familiar story; my brother had unfailing charm and an unflagging appetite for women who were beautiful and bright. His relationships always teetered on the edge of melodrama and rarely lasted for more than a few weeks.

I told Max about my job in the golf design business and our difficulties with environmental pressure groups.

'If I'd known you were interested, I'd have got you involved, Chris. But I thought you'd be back in the City by now.'

Then he told me more about his work, particularly of the problems caused by people's leisure activities.

'Take skiing,' Max said. 'There are too many skiers and too many ski runs. The landscape is being eroded in Switzerland and Austria, just like the so-called beauty spots here in Britain. Too many feet, too much damage. Enjoy the peace and tranquillity of the Lake District? Some chance when there are hordes of others trying to do the same thing.'

He paused while he took a sip of champagne. 'In Thailand, you should see what they're doing in the name of our favourite game, Chris. They're opening new golf courses at the rate of one a week and they're destroying virgin forest to do it. Deforestation is one of the world's biggest environmental problems, as I'm sure you know. The trees are the main devourers of carbon dioxide and yet the forests are diminishing by the minute. What a bloody awful race we are.'

Max shook his head sadly and went on: 'Canada and America have been the worst offenders and about half the earth's rainforest has gone in the last twenty years – the Philippines, Indonesia, Malaysia, Brazil. And all for the profit of businessmen who can see no further than the end-of-year accounts and their own fat wallets.'

Such was Max's despair that I changed the subject back to Thailand and asked him about the new golf courses.

'They want foreign visitors,' he replied, 'especially the Japanese and so they're obsessed with those artificial, over-engineered courses that the Americans love and the Japanese imitate.'

'Emerald green grass, vast stretches of water, acres of sand, heavily watered greens . . .'

'Spot on. And they're heavily dependent on chemicals to keep the courses that way. The more they destroy the natural processes, the more they have to rely on chemicals. It's self-defeating and they don't give a damn.'

'I suppose they put blue dye in the lakes to make them look more attractive?'

'Yeah, they do, and the dye kills off the fish, the plant life and the insects. Then the birds and the small mammals desert that habitat and the whole natural balance is destroyed. And they throw up large hotels and condominiums to house the tourists. It's environmental bedlam.'

'But golf courses don't have to be built that way,' I protested. 'Why doesn't the government regulate the process?'

'No chance. The local businessmen know exactly who to bribe and how much. The place is rotten with corruption. Anyway, this is a depressing conversation. Tell me more about what you're up to, Chris. Talking of corruption, I'm glad to hear that you're no longer in the City.'

I grinned at him. This was more like the Max I knew. 'That particular gravy train is temporarily in the sidings,' I conceded. 'My work with the golf course designer is my only employment, but it's close to full-time and I'm learning the craft. And we're working *with* nature, not against her.'

I poured him another drink and explained about Calvin Blair and the Shere Forest project. When I reached the part about the Green Disciples, Max interrupted.

'When I first heard of them a few years back, I thought they

97

were just what the Green Movement needed. They were well-organised, radical, and prepared to focus on big issues but at a local level.'

'Like Greenpeace, you mean?'

'With a different emphasis. Greenpeace beat a very loud international drum. They hit the headlines on a world-wide scale on major environmental issues – and good luck to 'em. That's what we need. The Green Disciples, as I see it, aim to tackle the same problems but at a lower level. For instance – a road that the local inhabitants don't want, a beauty spot that's threatened by a new factory – they'll mobilise the locals, rally support among all the other environmental groups and go to it. Like Greenpeace they don't shirk direct action. They chain themselves to bulldozers and lie down in front of lorries. If the Green Disciples are in there taking notice of your project, you'd better know exactly what you're dealing with, Chris. However, I lust for a good Indian meal – you buy me one and I'll tell you everything I know.'

As we walked to my local Indian restaurant, Max described to me how the Green Disciples organised themselves. They operated in a series of local cells, each one unknown to any other but all controlled by a small number of regional commanders – a set-up which gave them great security inside as well as outside the organisation.

Max studied the menu and chose for both of us. As we tucked in, it was a relief to let off steam about all the difficulties we'd had with the Green Disciples, from their overreaction to the presence of Dartford Warblers at Shere Forest to the attack on Blair's family.

'That's exactly their style,' Max nodded. 'A perfect illustration of their methods.'

'But I thought these Greens were non-violent. That attack on Jane and Rebecca is difficult to reconcile with the normal Green philosophy.'

'Normal Green philosophy, maybe, but the Disciples are not normal.'

'Well, we feel more relaxed about them now that the Shere Forest planning permission has gone through – with the support of the local wildlife and conservation people. We're hoping it was the Green Disciples' last spiteful throw of the dice, a final act of revenge.'

'I wouldn't count on it, Chris. During the last couple of years they've moved a long way from their original position as an environmental protest group. They're now an extremist, highly motivated political organisation which is using environmental issues as an excuse to disrupt society.'

'Come off it, Max, you sound like a delegate to the Conservative Party conference.'

My brother's information about the group quickly destroyed my complacency and his stories of some of their activities made my blood run cold. Nearly all of their attacks were aimed at middle-class targets – golf being one of their prime concerns, together with fox-hunting and all the other field sports. I wished Max had been around when they first came on the scene and wondered how he knew about them in such detail.

'During one of my research trips I discovered that someone is pumping a lot of money into the cause. And I managed to get to know one of them quite well in Brazil.'

'Female?'

'Yeah.' He gave me what I think is called an old-fashioned look. 'No, Chris, no hanky panky. She's Jodie Hesse. A very interesting woman, tough as they come – mentally and physically.

I'm sure that she was involved in some trouble at one of the logging factories out there.'

'I wouldn't fancy taking part in a demo in Brazil. You could end up dead.'

'Two of Jodie's chums did, beaten to death by security guards. She got away. One of the security guards was shot dead and I wonder . . .' He left the sentence unfinished while he wiped some nan bread round his plate.

'Oh come, Max, you're not suggesting she killed him?'

He shrugged his shoulders. 'She's in London. You should meet her. In fact, I'll arrange it.'

He went off to telephone but didn't succeed in speaking to Jodie. 'God knows who that was,' he said. 'He sounded very suspicious but agreed to take your number and ask her to call. Perhaps it's a husband she forgot to mention.'

'That's never held you back.'

'Now, big brother, I've told you – Jodie would have none of that.'

Max expressed a desire for several pints of bitter and, after paying the bill, we set off to fulfil his need.

When we returned home, there was a message on my answering machine from Jodie, who asked Max to ring her again on the following morning.

While I prepared breakfast Max shut himself in the living room with the telephone.

After a few minutes I glanced up and saw him leaning in the doorway. 'I spoke to Jodie. She seems to know some of the Shere Forest background. She reckons that the new course is just a ploy to push planning permission through for a hotel with a leisure centre and conference facilities, followed by several dozen cottages and apartments, after which the place will be marketed as a superior sports and holiday centre.'

I motioned Max to sit down at the kitchen table and poured our tea. 'That's rubbish,' I said. 'I've been working at Shere Forest for several weeks and there hasn't been a whisper of any such scheme.'

'Of course there hasn't. Why should you, or Calvin for that matter, know anything about it? You're only the hired help and you, Chris, are being bloody naive. This new course is a Trojan Horse to enable Gresham and his pals to develop Green Belt land. That trick is as old as the hills and as insidious as hell.' My brother was speaking with real heat. I thought he was talking tripe, but tried to damp down his rising anger by pointing out that Gresham hadn't even got the money to build the new course, let alone spend millions on hotels and apartments.

He remained unconvinced. 'Gresham and his chums will soon find the money, don't you worry, and then they'll ride off into the sunset with their fat profits.'

'You're wrong, Max – and anyway, what's wrong with profit? You're beginning to sound like a trade union leader.'

'There's nothing wrong with profit, in the right context – but not if it's at the expense of the environment. Places like Shere Forest are unique, their survival is vital. All over the world there are thousands and thousands of similar situations. And people like Jodie are fronting up to them and so should we all if this planet's to have a future.' He gulped down some tea. 'Sorry, sermon over.'

Max toyed moodily with his food while I tried again to reassure him that what we were planning at Shere Forest was another golf course and nothing more; that our design would not disrupt nature but encourage it.

'I'll show you, shall I?' I urged. 'Come with me this morning.'

'OK. I've told Jodie to meet us at the club. We'll go for lunch.'

'And I'll introduce you to the Club Secretary, Nigel Burnside. He should know the truth about any planning applications for new buildings.'

'Ah – but would he tell you?'

I was left pondering the question.

Chapter 12

As soon as we arrived at Shere Forest I took Max over to Burnside's office. Inside, the Secretary had been making his usual valiant tobacco-based contribution to air pollution. He was toying with a cup of coffee and casting some baleful looks at a large pile of correspondence on his desk.

I introduced my brother and Burnside raised a weary eyebrow when I asked if Max could play a few holes before lunch.

'Why not?' he said. 'There's a group of visitors out there already. Surveyors, accountants or something. Probably can't break a hundred, any of them. You'd better play the back nine. You have a handicap, I take it?'

'Last time I checked it was eight,' Max declared with his most charming smile. I knew that his true handicap lay nearer to half that figure and I never gave him more than two shots a round.

'I'm researching golf course development,' Max continued, 'for an institute in Geneva.' He produced an engraved visiting card from his wallet and handed it to Burnside. 'Are there any plans to develop Shere Forest beyond building a second golf course?'

The Secretary frowned and said, 'None whatsoever.' He gestured at the papers stacked on his desk. 'Look, I don't want to be rude, but the Classic starts in a couple of weeks. The admin and the demands from the sponsors and those arrogant bastards at the TV company get worse every year. So, if you'll forgive me . . .'

'Of course,' Max said, but instead of making for the door, he pulled a chair up to Burnside's desk, sat down and made himself comfortable. 'I won't keep you a moment, Captain Burnside, but I might be of some help. I have a contact with the Green Disciples and they think you're going to ride roughshod over the planning constraints around Shere Forest. Is that true? What planning permissions are you after?'

'Your brother doesn't waste time with small talk, does he, Ludlow? You could go down to the offices of the local council and look it all up.'

'Quite true,' Max replied. 'But since I'm here, sitting in front of you, you can save me the time and trouble.'

Burnside lit another cigarette, drew heavily on it and said, 'OK. There are some outline planning permissions. For example, to convert a barn to a dwelling for a member of staff. Maybe for me. We also have the same outline consent to build a leisure centre and some outdoor tennis courts. That's it. For myself, I hope to God nothing comes of the leisure side. Sweaty tennis players and keep-fit enthusiasts everywhere! Heaven forbid. This is a golf club first and last and I don't want to see it transformed into some ghastly country club. I've got enough on my plate as it is.'

Burnside looked pointedly at his correspondence, Max thanked him for his help and we left his office. As we passed the Secretary's window I glanced in just as he picked up the pile of letters and shovelled the whole lot into his wastepaper basket. It was probably his favoured way of dealing with such time-consuming matters and I guessed that Burnside was about to make his first foray to the club bar. He would undoubtedly make a worthy drinking companion for Toby Greenslade.

I saw Max on his way off the tenth tee and, although his swing was a little rusty, he still got his club head through the ball very firmly. If he ever bothered to apply himself to the game, I knew that Max could probably get very close to a scratch handicap. What an infuriating person to have as a brother. Mr Perfect . . .

When I entered the office, Calvin was trying to prise a progress report on the state of the course from the head greenkeeper, a monosyllabic man from Dorset named Martin. He had worked at Shere Forest for over twenty years and made it clear that he resented the presence of a golf architect on his patch.

'OK, thank you, Martin,' Calvin said resignedly. 'I'll take a look at everything later.'

As the recalcitrant Martin left the office, I asked Blair how his wife and daughter were faring.

'Pretty good in the circumstances. They'll be home tomorrow. Rebecca is chatting away like mad. At first she was a bag of nerves but now regards it as a high old adventure. The story gets better every time she recites it and she can't wait to get back to school and thrill her chums with it all.'

'And Jane?'

'More of a problem. She thought they were going to kill her and Rebecca. She's become withdrawn, doesn't want to talk about it. She'll need some counselling. It's worrying.'

'I'm sorry, Calvin. If there's anything I can do . . .'

'Well, next time you get hold of a Green Disciple, knock seven bells out of him, would you – and then give me a free hit.'

Calvin's tone was bitter and his hands clenched into fists. He gave me an embarrassed smile and I asked him how the intruders had got into the house.

'From what I can gather it was very easy. Two ordinary-looking blokes knocked on the door. They had a large bag and were selling something or other. You know the form, Chris, there's lots of unemployed lads trying to make a living selling dusters, tea towels, kids' toys . . . Jane usually buys something though she reckons she's got enough dusters to last her well into the next century. Sometimes she offers them a cup of tea and a biscuit, although I've told her to be wary if I'm not around. Anyway, these men simply stepped into the hall, slammed the front door behind them and grabbed her. Rebecca heard the rumpus and came running and that was that.'

'Thank God they weren't real villains.'

'They were bad enough, but I know what you mean. I don't even want to think about it.'

'What was the drug that was used? And how?'

'Beta-blockers of some kind – injected. And there were traces of something called Digoxin, which slows the heart right down. These people are dangerous, they know what they're about.' Blair paused and shuffled some papers. 'Jane's pretty level-headed. She just needs a little time.'

He stood up and said vigorously, 'In the meantime, we have a course to prepare. God help me if it's not perfect for those pampered professionals who'll arrive in their courtesy cars and cashmere in a couple of weeks.'

'It wasn't like that in your day, was it, Calvin?'

'No, it bloody wasn't—' He stopped himself. 'Are you winding me up?'

I smiled. 'Jack Mason will wind us both up if anything is

less than perfect. Let's go and take a look.'

Despite his unco-operative manner, Martin and his band of greenkeepers had already trimmed and pampered the course to near its best. On the opening day of the Classic it would look perfect. Its fairways would be manicured in sharp outline against the darker green of the semi-rough, which in turn would contrast strongly with the wilderness of heather and gorse, long grass, and clumps of variegated trees which awaited any ball which was hit badly off line. The turf on the banks of the streams which criss-crossed several of the holes had been cut neatly back and, such was Calvin's attention to detail, he had given two of the greenkeepers the task of brushing the loose sand which accumulated around the edges of the bunkers back into them.

The major changes to the course, such as new tees and bunkers and the reshaping of several greens, had been carried out during the previous autumn and the new turf and the reseeded areas had all been successfully established.

'Now, if God will just organise showers alternating with sun for the next week or so, it'll be perfect,' Calvin said.

'You sound just like a farmer. Never happy, always asking for meteorological miracles.'

Calvin grunted and suggested we take a look at the sixteenth green. 'It's the only one that worries me. It gets too much water running off the bank on the left. I'd like to dig it up and start again some time. I've got a stimpmeter in the truck – let's see what it tells us.'

A stimpmeter is a simple device to measure the speed of a green. A ball is rolled down a thirty-inch funnel, set at an angle of twenty degrees, onto a flat part of the green, and the distance it travels is measured. Nine feet means a stimpmeter speed of nine. That's quite quick, but I knew that Calvin wanted to get the greens just above the speeds recommended for tournament play by the Professional Golfers' Association. He was aiming for eleven on the stimpmeter. The greens at Augusta, where the renowned US Masters Tournament is played each year, are often quicker than that and induce nervous paralysis in even the best golfers; a precise and courageous touch is required on those roller-coaster greens. Anyone with whisky fingers might as well stay in the clubhouse; it's safer there. As a disenchanted American golfer once said of Augusta: 'Those greens are faster than a fart in a hot skillet.'

Calvin Blair measured the roll of the ball on the sixteenth. 'Eight,' he muttered. 'Not bad. I'll get it more or less up to speed on the big day.'

I looked over at the seventeenth tee and gave Max a wave as he teed up his ball. His swing looked slower now as he flew the ball way down the right side of the fairway.

'Who the hell's that?' asked Calvin. 'I wouldn't play him for money. Great swing.'

'My brother.'

'Jack Mason told me about him.'

'Did he? Well he's taking me to lunch to meet a member of the Green Disciples.'

'He's *what*?' Calvin didn't believe me and I repeated my remark. 'For God's sake, Chris . . .'

'Before you say anything more,' I interrupted, 'she's had nothing to do with Shere Forest or the attacks on your family. Max can vouch for her and she might help us.'

'Well, you might ask her what her attitude is to attacking women and children and planting bombs in the middle of London,' Calvin said fiercely as we got back into his truck. That was his last word to me on the subject. He confined himself to brief comments on the course as we took a circuitous route back to the office, where Max was waiting for me.

'You must be Calvin Blair,' Max said cheerfully. 'What a super back nine.' Calvin's bleak expression softened a little, especially when my brother continued, 'I played some of the holes off the back tees. The twelfth is brilliant, a great golf hole.'

'I only tinkered with it,' Calvin said. 'It had all the makings. Anyway, enjoy your lunch. See you later.' He went into the office.

Max nodded in his direction. 'Problems?'

'Only that I told him we were meeting a member of the Green Disciples. They're not his favourite people, as you can guess. I told him she might help.'

'I wouldn't bet your next salary cheque on that,' Max replied.

Chapter 13

As we walked the few hundred yards towards the clubhouse verandah and our rendezvous with Jodie Hesse, Max told me a little about her background. She was in her late twenties and her mother was part of an aristocratic German family.

'They were anti-Hitler . . .'

'Weren't they all?' I remarked.

'Her grandfather was murdered in forty-four. He was one of the army officers who tried to assassinate mad Adolf – Claus von Stauffenberg and so on. Jodie's mother married a British Army officer named Reynolds whom she met in the early sixties – and here's the rub; old man Reynolds used his Army contacts to set up in the arms business. He made a fortune during the seventies and eighties.'

'Not difficult,' I said. 'What with the Middle East, Africa, South America, maybe even Ireland.'

'I don't think he stooped that low, but it was far too low for Jodie. She was a high-flyer, graduated in philosophy at Tübingen.'

'What's that?'

'Only one of the best universities in Germany.'

'On a par with Cambridge?'

'Don't be silly, Chris. But it's very good, nevertheless.

Naturally, Jodie was a pacifist and a passionate Socialist.'

'Feminist too?'

'That goes without saying. She reverted to her mother's name when she was sixteen and went on to study sociology in Amsterdam. I think that's when she got involved with the Green Disciples.'

At that moment we rounded the corner of the verandah and I set eyes on our guest. I knew it was her because lady members didn't normally wear skintight purple jeans, baggy 'Save the Planet' T-shirts and green berets perched jauntily on their heads.

Max had done nothing to prepare me for such a magnetically beautiful woman. The clinging jeans did full justice to her perfect bottom and long slender legs and, even though the T-shirt was loose, her every movement hinted tantalisingly of the charms that lay beneath. No wonder Max was keen to get to grips with her. Her face was tanned, with sharp cheekbones and large but distant eyes. Very superior, I thought, but a second glance revealed that she wore contact lenses. Thank God she wasn't flawless after all.

My brother pecked her on the cheek, waved in my direction as an introduction and said how wonderful it was to see her.

Jodie gazed out across the Shere Forest fairways for a moment and said, 'It's beautiful here, isn't it? What a pity it's only for the benefit of golfing élitists.'

Her voice was clear and high-pitched but her English was unaccented. It hadn't taken her long to leap aboard her environmental soapbox and I wasn't going to let her get away with it.

'Golf has been a traditional sport in Britain for several hundred years,' I said tonelessly, 'and to play it you need plenty of space. It may be "élitist" in this part of England but it's far from that in Scotland, for instance, and even down here it's much less élitist than it is in Germany or Italy. You will also notice that there is plenty of common land in use all over Britain, including the cities. London, for instance, is ringed with parks which everyone can use.'

'Is your brother always this touchy, Max?' she said with a thin smile in my direction.

'Chris is in the golf business,' Max replied. 'And he's prepared to defend his calling. But before we start any wide-ranging discussions let's get some food and drink in front of us.' He grasped Jodie firmly by the arm and led her towards my car. I hung back for a moment or two to observe her elegant walk from behind. It was quite a view and I saw Hermione Gresham register it from the other side of the verandah doors. Her look seemed to mingle outrage and admiration in equal measure.

I waved a greeting in her direction but she ignored it, turning back to resume her conversation with the noble Captain Burnside.

I caught up with Max and Jodie and hoped we would not run into Calvin Blair on the way. We were in luck and, with my brother sprawled in the uncomfortable space in the back of the Porsche, we made the short trip to the local pub.

The White Horse was relatively unspoiled. No attempt had been made to transform it into some interior designer's hazy version of Merrie England or the British Raj or the inside of a Chinese junk. It offered the patron an unadorned wooden floor, plain wooden tables, photographs of bygone village cricket and football teams on the walls, and a pretty garden. The pub was owned by two men who looked to be well-preserved forty-somethings. One did the cooking while the other served the customers, and as both were very particular about what came out of their kitchen the result was imaginative and plentiful.

Edgar, the one who did the waiting, made a great fuss of seating Jodie Hesse at a garden table. He took a little of the wind out of her sails when she asked him about vegetarian dishes.

'It's a very short menu, dear, because it's all freshly cooked. No microwave in our kitchen. There are two veggie dishes today. Veg casserole – all the ingredients organic – and lentil bolognese with wholewheat pasta.'

Jodie chose the casserole and Edgar produced a wine list with a flourish, pointing out his selection of organic wines. She gave him an appreciative smile but ordered a glass of water. I opted for the pasta and Max the jugged hare.

'Very free range,' he said to Jodie with a grin.

'Let's hope it hasn't been at the pesticides,' she replied.

Christ, doesn't she ever let up? I thought, but when I looked at her she gave me a glowing smile which took the pomposity out of her remark. I realised for the first time that she might be teasing me a little.

When the drinks arrived Max asked Jodie why she was in England. Her reply was vague enough to arouse my suspicions and I pressed her. 'Some research? Who for?'

'Oh, just general research on Green issues,' she replied.

'For the Green Disciples?'

'Partly. Max has obviously told you that I help that organisation.'

'At Shere Forest perhaps?' I asked.

'No. I don't get involved at grass-roots level. As I said, I organise research, analyse strategy. It's a big subject.'

'So presumably you report to someone at the centre, a director of operations here in England?'

'I didn't say that, Chris, and I don't know anyone in the hierarchy. I'm asked to do reports and make recommendations and that's what I do, as best I can. As it happens, the Disciples do want me to assume a higher public profile in Britain and I'm here to try and put their case. I'm hoping to be the acceptable face of Green radicalism.'

'Make sure you don't get arrested,' Max said. 'Extremist groups are not very popular here.'

'If you think that our wish to stop man destroying himself and his planet is extremist, Max, then, yes, I'm an extremist.'

'Do you agree with the use of violent means, such as attacking women and children and planting bombs, to attain your ends?' I asked.

'Sometimes there has to be suffering for the greater good of mankind,' Jodie said. It was bizarre to hear such a heartless philosophy from someone so beautiful.

It also apparently jarred Max's sensibilities, for he said, 'I'm a hundred per cent with you on many of the environmental issues, Jodie – but surely you cannot condone violence?'

'I don't accept that the Green Disciples were behind the attack on Calvin Blair's family or the bomb at the Department of the Environment. Any lunatic fringe group could be using us as a scapegoat. And it isn't unknown for the boys at MI5 to do some damage and then put the blame on a pressure group they don't like.'

I could see that this line of inquiry was going nowhere and I asked Jodie what the Green Disciples stood for.

'How long have you got, Chris?' she asked, eyebrows raised. 'It's quite difficult to encapsulate all the horrors of colonial and industrial society into a couple of sentences. For centuries the Western world has plundered the resources of the rest of the planet. Nature and its inter-relationships have been turned topsy-turvy and the full horrors are just beginning to become apparent.'

'Like what?'

'The energy crisis, starvation in half the world while the other half is overweight, deforestation, soil erosion, diminishing water resources, the poisons that are now inherent in the whole of nature because of indiscriminate use of pesticides and fertilisers. The whole food chain is riddled with poisons.'

'That's a horribly apocalyptic view,' I said.

'Do not borrow off the earth for the earth will require its own back with interest,' said Jodie.

'That must be a quote from *Silent Spring*,' Max stated.

'No, but it could have been. I learned that book at my mother's knee. It was a sacred text in the Hesse household.'

'So what do we do?' Max asked gently. 'Stop the world and get off?'

'At least try to get back to a simpler way of life. The industrial society and big business have blown it. We need decentralisation, small local communities which can be self-sufficient. We've got to learn that we're part of nature and that it's not something we can exploit for ever and a day.'

'How romantic,' I sneered. 'Let's get back to some innocent Golden Age, a village society with kindly adults working in harmony and caring for their rosy-cheeked offspring. I've read the history books. I know that life a few centuries ago was nasty, brutish and short, that most people died before they were thirty after a life of abject poverty and that babies had a less than fifty per cent chance of survival. Where was this happy land, Jodie?'

'I suppose I deserved that, but even if we can't stop the world, we could slow it down and return it to some vestige of sanity. For all your cynicism about the past, is there anything much you like about the present?'

'Central heating, Australian Cabernet, Seve's golf swing, liberated women,' interrupted Max brightly. He ordered another couple of beers for us and Jodie asked for a herb tea.

'Let's get away from the general,' he continued, 'and look at specifics. Why can't the Green Disciples lay off Shere Forest? As my brother will tell you, the people there have bent over backwards to do all the right things to protect the environment of the new course. They'll preserve the wetlands, they're setting up some SSSIs which will be managed by the local Wildlife Trust, fertiliser usage will be kept to an absolute minimum and so will watering. What's the problem here?'

'The problem is golf's record in general. It's an obscene devourer of land especially in emerging countries like Thailand, Indonesia and Malaysia. Huge hotels and tourist villages are thrown up around the courses. Golf is symbolic of many of the things we hate, like the exploitation of the land and its ordinary people for the sake of an élite.'

'So we're back to class warfare, are we?' I said.

'That's a part of it, sure, though you should be used to that in Britain. And the courses are an environmental nightmare. Everything that's living there – the trees, and the flowers, the plants and insects, the birds and the animals, must perish in the name of golf.'

The heat of her argument had brought a flush to Jodie's face but it slowly subsided as the attentive Edgar bustled over to our table and stated firmly, 'You beautiful people should do more eating and less squabbling. What about a pud? They're lovely. All made by Howard's own fair hands.'

We couldn't resist. My brother and I indulged ourselves in

117

crème brûlée and Apple Charlotte, while Jodie ate a superb-looking fresh fruit salad. Max and I finished with a pot of coffee.

Max spoke severely to his cup: 'I hope your beans were politically correct – hand-picked by liberated Colombian peasants who are happy in the knowledge that they have private health insurance and safe pensions.' Jodie relaxed enough to acknowledge his teasing with a mock scowl.

I attempted to use the moment of good humour to press our cause further. 'Let's get back to golf for a moment and especially Shere Forest. We're working with nature there, not against it, just like many of the other better British courses. Look at St George's: it's just as much a nature reserve as a golf course. So are Birkdale and Gleneagles, and even a humbler course like Church Stretton is kept in harmony with its natural surroundings.'

'That's a good sell for golf at Shere Forest, but the Green Disciples think and act on a global scale – and golf is one of the many sports that we totally oppose.' Jodie was folding and unfolding her napkin as she spoke. 'All this destruction for the sake of a game. Men and their games – why don't you all grow up, for God's sake?'

'Everybody has different forms of relaxation,' Max said briskly. 'Golf happens to be one of ours. I don't really know what Jodie does in her spare time,' he continued, with a sly wink in my direction, 'though I do know that she writes Latin verse . . .'

'Perhaps you are aware that Plato wrote about the dangers of deforestation,' Jodie said, 'and we've had warnings aplenty in every generation.'

Max ploughed on. 'What I can't understand, Jodie, is your inflexibility. Do you really mean that you'll keep up the pressure on Shere Forest despite all their efforts to appease the conservationists? After all, the Dartford Warblers and the other species will be protected. Even Charley James is satisfied with that.'

'Charley James?' Jodie echoed, her voice fierce with contempt. 'She's just a telly personality. I'll bet she goes gooey-eyed over red squirrels and wets her knickers over pandas and dolphins. She's probably on committees with Prince Philip and Lord This and That. What use is she?'

'And you're a dyed-in-the-wool radical, are you?' I said sourly. 'You're going to change the world?'

'Or disrupt it?' asked Max. 'The way your movement is run is not a million miles from a hardcore revolutionary movement. Is that your real aim, to cause social chaos? Is there some lunatic skulking in the background planning to seize power when our decadence results in terminal social breakdown?'

'What utter nonsense, Max. You're much too intelligent to believe in conspiracy theories. We want to change society and we may have to apply a few shocks to the system in order to put our message over, that's all.'

'My blood runs cold when someone like you starts using euphemisms,' Max said. 'Shocks to the system, the Final Solution...'

Max paid the bill and we dropped Jodie at the nearest railway station. Our two pairs of eyes followed her elegant figure as she strolled towards the ticket office.

'What is she, Max?' I asked. 'A starry-eyed idealist? An avenging angel of the environment? Or just a hard-edged anarchist who's daft enough to cause havoc in society?'

'Maybe she doesn't even know herself,' he said. 'There's a messianic gleam in her eye that spells trouble, whatever her objectives. But hey – check out that body! I'd love to get her into a locked room for an hour or two.'

I groaned melodramatically and pointed the Porsche towards Shere Forest.

Chapter 14

With just over a week left to ensure that the course was in pristine condition for the British Classic, intense pressure was exerted on the greenkeeping staff. The studied indifference of Martin, the head greenkeeper, continued; he could not conquer his resentment at the presence of Calvin Blair. But Calvin's breezy good humour and breadth of knowledge enabled him to motivate his staff to greater exertions than ever before.

The course was groomed to perfection and the vigorous growth of late spring added the final touches to its beauty, as the flowers bloomed and the trees assumed their new leaves. Even a brief look at such a scene made me dismiss the prophecies of Jodie Hesse. Surely nature would always have the strength to renew herself, whatever the vile assaults of man. It was a time for optimism.

As we all beavered away on the golf course, so the circus which attends any major professional golf tournament gradually took shape around us. A tented village was established, rigged with a myriad of exhibition stands, all of which sold something to inflame the desires of the club golfer: a new driver to put twenty yards on his tee shot, irons which would automatically correct a hook or a slice, golf balls which would go further and straighter, putters which never missed the hole, holidays of a lifetime, instructional books and videos which would make him into a scratch golfer, devices to keep his knee or elbow straight or flexed and which would cut his handicap in days . . . dreams, dreams. At every tournament I visited I was amazed anew at the ingenuity of the golf equipment manufacturers.

The television technicians were out in force, trailing miles of cable rather than clouds of glory, plotting the positions of their camera towers and asking each other plaintively how much overtime they could expect. But among the variety of T-shirts which strained to cover their substantial bellies, I saw not a single one which urged me to 'Save the Planet'.

Grandstands mushroomed around the greens, but the huge hospitality area took pride of position by the eighteenth. From there the sponsor, AMC, one of the major car manufacturers, would wine and dine its clients to the brink of cardiac arrest. That, after all, was the whole point of the exercise. The soft sell was in attaching the AMC name to a prestigious golf tournament, and the hard sell took place in the hospitality suites where the fleet buyers and their wives and girlfriends were entertained and where decision-makers in business and politics were flattered and cosseted.

At this stage of the event, PGA officials were much in evidence. Apart from checking the general condition of the course, they were also preoccupied with inspecting its boundaries. It was particularly important to mark clearly the out-of-bounds areas, water hazards and ground under repair. A large number of red, white and yellow stakes were required and gallons of white paint. Given the volatile nature of many of the golfers and the vast prize money for which they were playing, it was inadvisable to allow any ambiguity. I could vividly remember in my early days as a caddie for Jack Mason how a dispute over an out-of-bounds line had escalated. Jack had been convinced that his ball was still in bounds and the tournament referee was equally sure that it was not. To the amazement of the spectators, Jack had plucked several of the posts out of the ground and hurled them away into deep rough. I had restrained him from doing the same to the hapless referee and thereby kept his fine down to a manageable sum.

I had heard nothing more from Max, who had gone to Edinburgh in connection with his environmental survey but, on the Monday before the Classic began, a package arrived for me at our office at Shere Forest. I didn't recognise the handwriting and, remembering the shock of opening the video from the Green Disciples, I turned it over warily.

Calvin looked up as I opened the package and took out two books, one of which was a copy of Rachel Carson's *Silent Spring*. A white card contained the message, written in green ink: 'I know that you're not a complete environmental illiterate despite your addiction to golf, so I thought you might like to read these. *Silent Spring* is the classic Green book and the other one has some interesting ideas. Love, Jodie.'

I glanced at the other book, a slim tome published by an American university. It's portentous title, *New Dimensions for Green Political Thought*, did not exactly whet the appetite and I flicked quickly through its early pages. The phrase 'the historical situatedness of the Green Movement' caught my eye and I resolved to give it to one of the charity shops.

'Books in a plain brown wrapper, eh? What are you up to, laddie?'

'I think someone's trying to convert me to environmental correctness,' I said warily. 'It's from that girl Max introduced me to, Jodie Hesse.'

Calvin grunted. His attitude to the Green Disciples was even more antagonistic since his wife had returned home. He had told me that Jane was listless and would not leave the house on her own. Her counsellor could not predict when she would return to normal; she might spontaneously recover or it could take months. In Calvin's eyes the attack by the Green Disciples had temporarily deprived him of the woman he loved.

He stood up. 'Come on, Chris, it's a lovely day,' he said. 'Let's have a stroll around. I want to have another look at that practice green.'

I knew he was concerned that its condition should mirror, as closely as possible, the greens on the course itself. Nothing irritates a professional golfer more than a significant difference between the practice green and the real thing, and professional golfers are easily irritated.

The sun was flooding across the course and the benign conditions had encouraged a number of golfers to get in some early practice. The majority of them had doubtless missed the cut at the previous week's tournament, and had been eliminated after two of the four rounds. The real stars would make their entrance tomorrow, play in the pro-am tournament on the Wednesday and be ready for the real battle on Thursday.

Calvin and I chatted to some of the players on the practice green and they seemed satisfied enough with its speed. It read nine on the stimpmeter and Calvin reckoned that, with a double cut that evening and another on the following morning, the surface would be well up to standard.

We watched the line of golfers working on their swings. Each one was hoping that it would all fall beautifully into place, that this would be their week, a time of glory and profit.

'Poor buggers,' muttered Calvin. 'Not many of them will ever get above the breadline.'

'Maybe not,' I replied, 'but they're holding on to their dream. You must have been the same, surely?'

'Of course I was, Chris, and it's still great to be a part of it all, even if it's only from the sidelines.'

Like Blair, I was content to be a part of a big golf tournament once again. I had been away from it for a while and had forgotten what a jolt of adrenalin it gave me. Although I wouldn't be striding the fairways with a golfer and his bag in my care, I felt that my present role gave me an equally strong interest.

As we walked back to the office, I asked Calvin if Jane was fit enough to visit the tournament.

'Yes, she's promised to come on Sunday with Rebecca.'

Chapter 15

At five o'clock on Wednesday morning my alarm clock hauled me out of a bad dream. I was all alone in a gaunt landscape, where the ground was bare and pitted with mud, and the few trees were skeletons of rotten wood. Everything was the colour of the starved earth and the green of natural vegetation had departed. As I stood there with a five iron grasped uselessly in my hand, only silence surrounded me. I groped my way out of bed and blamed it all on Rachel Carson and her vision of hell on earth.

Still, at least it had got me up nice and early. I had promised to be at the club by 6.30 at the latest since it was the day of the pro-am.

The PGA officials were responsible for such matters as positioning the holes on the greens, and today these would be in friendly places near the centre for the sake of the amateurs. But Calvin knew that we should both be there to solve any problems when they arose. He was also anxious about the reception which his course changes would receive.

The first match in the pro-am teed off at 7.30. It was going to be a long day because each group contained five players – a professional and four amateurs. This unwieldy format, copied from America, enabled the sponsor to issue more invitations to his clients. Even though it was decreed that only the two best scores on each hole would count, it was inevitable that the rounds would last for five hours or more. I felt sorry for the professionals, most of whom loathed pro-ams, but the rules of the PGA were absolute: the top thirty or more pros had to turn out to support the sponsor. This, after all, was the day when he pushed the good ship *Hospitality* down the slipway.

After a couple of hours in the office I wandered out to find myself some breakfast and a cup of coffee. I ate a bacon sandwich and strolled over to the first tee. The sponsor's products were much in evidence on the course and their top-of-the-range model, an 'executive sports saloon', was stationed in all its dashing glory by the first tee. Every conceivable refinement was included in the price. No wonder AMC's products had rocked the confidence of the German manufacturers who had in the past dominated the executive car market.

Although there was only a scattering of spectators as yet, the tension of the occasion unnerved the already shaky swings of many of the amateurs. Their rigid and contorted bodies propelled the ball in curious directions. I noticed that many of the pros chose to look into the far distance in their efforts to ignore the bizarre consequences of their partners' actions. The professionals had to cope in their different ways with a lengthy round in the company of, mostly, very poor golfers. Some tried to block the whole occasion out and ghost through it as if heavily sedated; others tried to take a leaf out of Lee Trevino's book and be the life and soul of the party. My old boss, Jack Mason, was unpredictable and his mood often depended on his intake of beer the previous evening.

I watched an American player, imported by the sponsors at great expense, crash his ball high and long into the rough on the left of the fairway. Since he didn't seem too concerned, I wondered whether he was planning to take the sponsor's shilling, miss the cut and go shopping with his wife for the remainder of his visit.

As I pondered that cynical thought, I felt a tap on my arm and turned to face Captain Nigel Burnside. He wore his usual dark blue blazer with regimental buttons and tie, and the ever-present cigarette drifted smoke into the still air. Hermione Gresham was at his side; she seemed to spend more time with him than with her husband.

'The course looks in fine fettle,' Burnside said. 'Full marks to Blair Associates.'

'Thank you,' I said.

'Will it be enough to satisfy the sponsors, do you think?' he asked.

'I'm sure they'll take a sensible view of Peter's efforts,' interrupted Mrs Gresham. 'Shere Forest is the traditional home of the Classic and that's where it will remain.'

'Especially with the new course about to get under way,' I added helpfully.

Burnside dropped his cigarette on the grass, stamped on it and said grimly, 'If it's ever built, it'll be the end of Shere Forest as a proper golf club. We'll be awash with debenture holders, Flash Harry types from the City and foreigners. It won't be the club that your husband inherited, my dear,' he said to his companion.

'What nonsense, Nigel,' she replied. 'The Gresham family will always maintain control.'

'That's exactly what they won't be able to do,' Burnside

said. 'However, it's time for a coffee and a brandy. Are you going to join me, Hermione?' They turned and walked back towards the clubhouse.

I watched a few more groups drive off from the first tee and mulled over what Burnside had said. It was clear that he shared Toby's view that the new course would only be built at the cost of Gresham selling his controlling interest to an outside investor. No doubt he was concerned about his own future at Shere Forest. New owners would require the Secretary to concentrate on his duties and do a proper job.

I smiled at the thought of Burnside applying himself to running a busy golf club with several hundred extra members who would probably be infinitely more demanding than the current ones. The new regime, if there were to be one, would want its pound of administrative flesh.

Back in the office I was just settling down to look through some of Calvin's plans for the new course when Jack Mason's substantial frame filled the doorway. He strode in, Calvin at his heels.

'Hard at it, Chris? Good to see,' he said cheerfully. 'However, Calvin says I can borrow you. Come on. Spikes on. You're on the tee in twenty minutes.'

'Hang on,' I said, my innards turning slightly watery. 'I've hardly played in the last few weeks.'

'Look, if you played on one leg, you'd be better than most of those jokers out there. Someone's pulled out of our team this morning and you're the replacement. We're playing with Gresham, the top man from AMC and one of his main distributors. A bloody five-ball – they must be mad. But at least I'll have one good golfer on the team.'

'Gresham can still play a bit,' said Calvin.

'I dare say,' Jack replied, 'but he's a boring old fart. Chris, get moving. I'll see you on the tee.' With that final command, he left the office while I found my golf shoes and checked that my bag contained everything I needed.

On my way to the tee, I wondered why the Managing Director of AMC, the sponsors of the event, had been partnered with Jack Mason, who could be too outspoken for anybody's comfort. It seemed a risky pairing, but when I was introduced to Dick Fairbairn, the quietly spoken and soberly dressed Canadian who ran the manufacturer's European operation, he told me that he had requested Jack as his professional.

'He's no bullshitter,' he said, 'and I want his views on the changes that've been made here. I'll be able to bounce them off Peter Gresham.'

It promised to be an entertaining round.

The final member of our group was Paul Sturgis, the main distributor of AMC cars in the south-east. Tall and strongly built, with dark features and black hair which was just beginning to tinge with grey, Paul had one of those crushing handshakes which professional salesmen often affect, and he accompanied it with a wide smile which showed perfectly even teeth. He spoke with a slight Scottish accent and told us that his handicap was four shots.

'Well, gentlemen,' Jack said, 'we've got a powerful team here. Three low-handicappers and Mr Fairbairn off sixteen – and no doubt a very competitive sixteen. Remember, it's only the two best net scores on each hole which count. I don't suppose I'll be needed much. Let's enjoy our day.'

Jack led the way with a long drive down the middle of the first hole, a par five, and a long iron onto the green. Two solid putts gave him a birdie and, by dint of a slightly shaky pitch-

and-run shot that ended up closer to the hole than it deserved, I also made a birdie.

With a clap on my shoulder, Jack told me how nice it was to be back in business with me. We all hit the green at the next short hole. Dick Fairbairn took advantage of his shot to record a net birdie and our team was three under par after two holes.

As a comparative veteran of pro-am events (I had been much in demand when I worked in the City) it was diverting to watch the different approaches of the players. Peter Gresham, despite his long experience as a leading amateur, seemed ill at ease. I put it down to a certain amount of nervousness in the presence of the sponsor of the tournament; Fairbairn was obviously there to assess the changes to the course. I could also see that Gresham was irritated by the funereal pace of the round. Nevertheless, his golf was accurate and consistent.

So was that of Fairbairn, who possessed an awkward-looking swing that had clearly been manufactured for him by a teaching professional. But he was steady enough and played competently within his limits. The same could not be said for his distributor, Paul Sturgis, who was under the illusion that this was his opportunity to impress the rest of us, and especially Jack Mason, with his golfing skills. Such people are present in force at every pro-am; their motivation is to be able to tell their cronies at the weekend that they 'outdrove the pro on the ninth' or that they 'got inside Jack Mason's ball on the short fourteenth with a seven-iron.'

The average professional golfer is not concerned. He is out there to do a job for the sponsor and he will take a polite interest in his amateur partners. If it seems possible that some prize money can be won, he will even help them with their club selections and the line of their putts.

Paul Sturgis, however, was hovering at Jack's elbow throughout the first half of the round and I could tell that my old boss's patience was wearing thin. So was that of Dick Fairbairn who wanted to get Jack's reactions to the state of the course. Not that Sturgis was a bad golfer; it was just that, like many Scottish golfers in my experience, he thought he was a lot better than he really was. Perhaps it's the happy accident that there are so many great courses in their country that deludes the Scots into thinking they have a special relationship with the game.

After seven holes our team were eight under par, which was excellent scoring. As always when I played with Jack, his smooth and controlled swing rubbed off on me and I was going along very well at one under par. On the eighth tee, in response to Sturgis's inquiry about whether to use a one-iron for safety, Jack had replied gruffly: 'Just bash a driver down there, Paul, and leave the tactical play to me and Chris.'

The Scot had glared momentarily at me and then hit a colossal hook into the heavy rough on the left. He dropped his driver on the grass, lifted his eyes to heaven as if it were the first bad shot he'd ever hit, and then, in order to demonstrate his innate good humour, grinned at us.

'Should've hit a one-iron, eh, Jack,' he said. As he looked at us from under his eyebrows, bared his fine white teeth in a smile and shook his head in self-admonition, I was certain that he reminded me of someone. I watched Gresham hit a lovely shot into the centre of the fairway and realised that Sturgis bore a faint resemblance to Sean Connery. Some misguided person had obviously told him so and he worked hard to assume the actor's mannerisms. That explained a lot.

As we walked down the fairway I looked back and saw Jack still on the tee with Fairbairn. Jack was gesturing and I guessed that he was making some points about the eighth and the ninth holes – fairly straightforward designs which Calvin Blair had been keen to reshape. Gresham had refused on the grounds of cost.

A long putt gave me a birdie at the eighth and we scored two more at the next hole. Eleven under par at the halfway mark was very good shooting by anyone's standards. Jack insisted that we all had a glass of champagne and a smoked salmon sandwich at the hut by the tenth tee.

It had taken over two and a half hours to reach this point in the round and none of us needed any encouragement to take advantage of AMC's beneficence.

With his finger probing the luxuriant undergrowth of his right ear, Gresham asked Dick Fairbairn what he thought of the course so far.

'I'm reserving judgement, Peter, until I've seen it all. But Jack's made the point that those last two holes were rather dull – and could be improved quite easily.'

Jack finished his glass of champagne and smiled at one of the lissom AMC girls who refilled it for him. 'Yes, Peter. A little rerouting of the eighth and ninth would make them more attractive and more interesting to play. If you took the eighth tee thirty yards left and thirty yards back into the trees you'd have a different angle into the fairway and that would bring those left-hand bunkers more into play. Then dig up the green, which is bloody rubbish anyway, move it to the left and you've got a dog-leg hole. Much more fun. And do the reverse with the ninth. Same principles. Surprised Calvin Blair didn't think of it.'

'What do you think, Peter?' asked Fairbairn. 'Blair fell down on that one, eh?'

Calvin had wanted to do almost exactly what Jack had

suggested. Gresham looked at me and knew he wouldn't get away with any unjust criticism. He muttered something to the effect that it had been discussed. 'But there were other priorities.'

'Well, Peter, it'll have to be done, whatever happens,' Jack insisted. 'That green's been over-watered and there's thatch underneath. You might as well do it now rather than later.'

During the second half of the round Jack and the AMC boss spent a lot of time apart from the rest of us and in close conversation. It benefited Paul Sturgis, who played better golf once he had cast aside his urge to try to out-hit Jack Mason, and we finished the round at twenty under par. I was delighted that I had hung on over the difficult second half to finish my round at two under par.

'Well done, chaps,' said Jack in genial fashion. 'A shower and a change, a couple of pints and a late lunch is in order, I think. With luck, we should pick up a prize.'

There were smiles all round at this and Dick Fairbairn suggested that we gather in the bar in twenty minutes.

The usual buffet meal of poached salmon, prawns, roast beef, cooked ham and salads was augmented by a sushi bar and we all, with the exception of Peter Gresham, ate a variety of raw fish. Even Jack Mason, who was conservative in his tastes, declared it all delicious. When the coffee was on the table, Dick Fairbairn spoke up.

'I know you won't mind me speaking my mind about the course, Peter. You saw me nattering away to Jack, and I find his views, as a very experienced professional, simply invaluable. It isn't a question of going behind Calvin's back because Jack is a friend of his and I told Calvin what I was up to. I'm glad that Chris, his assistant, is here, too.'

He nodded politely to me and continued: 'I think that the

work done on the course is really excellent. The new tees and the reshaping of several fairways have transformed some of the holes. Jack and I agree that the twelfth is now a brilliant hole.'

Gresham was smiling and nodding his agreement. 'Oh absolutely,' he said. 'Blair and I worked very hard to get the twelfth right.'

The old hypocrite, I thought, but had to let it pass. Fairbairn replied, 'But you've only done half the job, in my opinion.' The smile disappeared from Gresham's face. 'Jack's point about holes eight and nine is correct. They're ordinary and you could enhance them dramatically with the changes he suggested.'

'Calvin's ideas originally,' Jack said. Thank you, Jack.

Gresham was gloomily excavating his left ear and he took the chance to say, 'This is a members' course, Dick, and we don't have unlimited funds. If you're talking about new greens, that's very expensive . . .'

'I'm glad you raised the subject because Jack thinks that at least half a dozen greens need to be lifted and rebuilt.'

'That's preposterous!' Gresham looked horrified. 'That would cost a small fortune.'

'Money well spent,' Jack said firmly. 'Whatever happens, you've got to take some of them out of play to treat them. So you might as well take the chance to extend them and to rebuild them in some instances.'

'The greens are one of the best features of Shere Forest,' Gresham said dogmatically.

'Were,' Jack replied sharply. 'They've diminished in size over the years, the edges have grown in. You only have to look at the old photographs to see. Also the undulations on some of them are too severe. It was OK back in the thirties when the greens were much slower, but the pace that's decreed for competitive play these days makes some of the slopes impossible to gauge.'

'You pros always moan about the greens,' Gresham said dismissively. 'Too slow, too fast, they're never right.'

'I'm not the one with whisky fingers,' Jack said unkindly. He had noticed Gresham's uncertainty over putts in the three to four feet range.

Fairbairn spoke, his eyes cold behind his spectacles. 'Right, Peter, we've covered the state of the course and it seems there's still a lot to be done. Would you agree with us, Chris? You've been at the sharp end.'

I nodded and the Chief Executive of AMC Europe continued, 'An even bigger problem for you though, Peter, is the state of the clubhouse. I've had a chance to take a good look round and I know you won't be offended if I say it has a certain antique charm.'

Gresham smiled mournfully in agreement and Fairbairn went on, 'Its facilities, however, are totally inadequate to host a major golf tournament. A few licks of paint just aren't enough. It needs complete refurbishment and expansion.'

'We plan to have it done in time for the opening of the new course.' Gresham was getting huffy.

'Not good enough,' Fairbairn said firmly. 'That's two or three years away. Wise up, Peter. This is AMC's tournament, it's a prestigious event which is part of our marketing mix, and it's extremely important that we put over our message of quality. Our cars are quality and everything we put our name to must be quality. Am I making myself clear?'

It was certainly clear and uncompromising enough to all of us at the table and I felt slightly sorry for Peter Gresham as he fiddled uncomfortably with his coffee cup for a few moments. But he wasn't giving in.

'I realise that you put up the money, Dick, but the Classic has been played here since before the war. Shere Forest is its home, and we helped to create its great traditions. You've only got to look at our champions – Henry Cotton, Dai Rees, Peter Thomson, Gary Player, Lee Trevino . . .'

'I was second a few years back,' interrupted Jack.

'There's quality,' Gresham blustered at Fairbairn. 'A great course produces great champions.'

Jack caught my eye and gave me a small smile of sympathy as he acknowledged my discomfort. I had no particular love for Peter Gresham, and in any event his problems had been brought about by his past meanness, but I wished this conversation was taking place in my absence.

Fairbairn leaned forward in his seat in order to emphasise his next words. 'I grant you all that, but I'm in business and your course – and above all your facilities – must be in tiptop order, in keeping with the company image.' He sat back in his chair again, took off his spectacles, rubbed his eyes carefully and issued his ultimatum. 'If I'm to continue at Shere Forest you must get your act together. We can always take the tournament elsewhere. I've no wish to do that but changes have to be made.'

'If we can finance them,' Gresham finally capitulated.

'I wouldn't be averse to putting up some of the investment in return for some equity,' Fairbairn said quickly, as he replaced his glasses. 'Let's discuss it after the tournament.'

He stood up, apologised for taking up our time with business and said he would see us all at the prize-giving.

As Jack and I wandered out towards the practice ground, he said, 'Fairbairn's what they call brutally honest, isn't he? "Do it or else." I wouldn't like to work for him, would you?'

'Well, he's honest – and he's right. But old Gresham's looking at a lot of expense.'

'The thick end of three-quarters of a million, I'd say. Two hundred plus on the course and at least half a million on the clubhouse.'

'He won't like that.'

'No, but he should never have let the course and clubhouse get into their present state. Whatever happens, he won't want to lose the Classic, will he? If he's going to build another course, why doesn't he raise three or four million quid and do the whole thing properly? It makes sense, surely.'

'To you and me, maybe,' I said, 'but people like Gresham don't think that way. "What was good enough for me . . ."'

We paused by the practice ground and watched the players who were slogging it out on 'Misery Hill' in preparation for the stiff test of their technique which was yet to come. Particularly impressive was a player who was practising on the edge of the range. His swing looked slow, almost lazy, compared to the others on view but he was generating great power with little apparent effort. I asked Jack who he was.

'Richie Riley – a young American. Their Amateur Champion a couple of years back. Hasn't done anything as a pro yet. Great swing, eh? Let's go and say hello.'

Riley was notable not only for his smooth swing but also for a shock of blond hair which he wore unfashionably long. With his broad shoulders and tanned face he looked like a throwback to the surfin' sixties. It seemed to my ears that he had the accent for it, too, and he later confirmed that he was a Californian.

'Hey, Jack, I've been looking for you. I need a caddie. The guy I had has disappeared with two of my cashmere sweaters, my watch and most of my golf balls. Any ideas?'

'The caddie master will find you someone for tomorrow.'

With what looked like enviable ease, Riley hit another towering iron shot up the practice ground. 'Well, OK, but I don't want some chicken-shit guy with holes in his trousers. Thought you might know somebody good.'

Jack looked at me, I looked at him – and shook my head. After all, I did have a more or less full-time job now. Jack took not the slightest bit of notice.

'You're looking at one of the best in the business, Richie.' Jack nodded towards me. 'Chris Ludlow. He looked after me very well for nearly three years. Doesn't steal, doesn't drink to excess and only speaks when he's spoken to.' That was a lie.

'Sounds great. What're you doing tomorrow, Chris?'

'Working for Calvin Blair, the golf designer.'

'Come on,' Jack said authoritatively, 'we'll go and fix it with Calvin. It'll do you good.' Jack never did listen to what he didn't want to hear and in fact the idea of caddying for this interesting player appealed to me immensely. I knew that Jack would smooth the way with Calvin.

Blair grumbled, but Jack teased him into agreeing to let me off for half a day on the Thursday and Friday. Richie Riley offered me a generous wage plus six per cent of his prize money. As it turned out, our team finished second in the pro-am, and I collected a set of cut-glass whisky tumblers for my efforts. Yet another collection to add to all those at home. Mind you, they came in handy when that famously thirsty golfing journalist Toby Greenslade, came to call . . .

Chapter 16

It was Sod's law that, after several days of limpid sunshine, we were greeted by a persistent drizzle on the opening morning of the British Classic Championship. On the previous evening I had spent some time checking the measurements of the course so that I could give Riley the exact distances for his shots. Since I had access to the scale drawings prepared for Blair Associates, I was confident that I would be better prepared than anyone. When I met my new, albeit temporary, master by the practice ground, he was half-hidden under a waterproof jacket with a turned-up collar, and a woollen cap pulled down over his ears.

'Good God,' I said, 'this isn't St Andrews in November, you know. It'll brighten up later.'

'So you say.' Richie smiled suspiciously and reminded me that Californians are thin-blooded.

Despite his bulky rainwear, his swing was as fluid as before and I thought that he would probably do well, as long as he didn't allow himself to be psyched out by the weather. All golfers have a comprehensive range of reasons for not playing well and the weather accounts for a high proportion of them. It's either too hot, too cold, too windy or too wet. The local food and drink comes next on the list of excuses and then the accommodation. As for the local people ... The list is endless

141

and when in doubt the golfer can also blame his caddie.

In bad weather the caddie's job is to ensure that his golfer is as dry and comfortable as humanly possible. Above all, that the grips of his clubs are wiped before every shot and that he is provided with a new glove whenever necessary. I rooted through Riley's bag and found everything we needed, including bananas and chocolate, but no bottles of beer. Jack Mason sometimes carried a few liveners with him, much to the delight of the spectators – but then they didn't have to shoulder the extra weight.

Riley's game was well under control for the first few holes and he was one under par when we reached the seventh tee. The other two players in our group, a Spaniard with a bright smile and very little English and a quiet young Englishman who was in his first year on the tour, were also playing neat and competent golf. The rain had stopped, as I had predicted, and a watery sun had appeared. There were smiles all round as waterproofs were removed and stowed away in golf bags.

'That's better,' Richie said, as he swung a club on the tee. 'Freedom at last.'

'What have you got in your hand?' I asked him. The seventh was a dangerous short hole of 240 yards and the pin was tucked away on the right side of the plateau green and guarded by a bunker.

'Two-iron,' Richie replied.

'Take one more and be sure,' I advised.

'It's enough, Chris. I'll make it easy enough,' he said impatiently.

I shrugged. He nearly made it but golf is littered with 'nearlys' and they usually add up to dropped shots. Riley's ball pitched on the green beyond the bunker, gripped on the second bounce and rolled inexorably back down the slope and past the bunker.

'Well, I'll be—' He left the rest unsaid and, although I couldn't help feeling a touch of the I-told-you-sos, I kept my mouth firmly closed.

Riley's ball was lying on a bare patch of ground with the edge of the bunker protruding into his line to the flag, which was less than twenty feet from the fringe of the green. It was a very tough pin position which invited a safe shot to the heart of the green rather than a heroic one straight at the hole. I looked quizzically at Riley when he asked me for his sand wedge and offered him my opinion: to try to play a delicate shot off a bare lie with a broad-soled club was too great a risk. 'Run the ball past the edge of the bunker with a seven-iron. You can get within three or four feet, it's the percentage shot.'

Riley glared at me. 'Chris, the sand wedge is my club. I can get the ball up and stop it.'

He didn't. His sand wedge bounced on the hard surface and drove the ball over the bunker and off the back edge of the green. He was lucky it didn't lodge in the front face of the bunker and cost him several shots. Although he played a reasonable shot back to the hole, Riley missed the putt and took five to go back to one over par.

As he came off the green, he threw his putter towards me. It whirled end over end as he strode angrily to the next tee. The young English player smiled sympathetically at me and tapped his head to indicate his opinion of Riley. I waited for a moment, picked the club up and followed him slowly. Riley was standing at the back of the tee and I waited until the Spanish golfer had flown his shot down the middle of the next fairway.

'Gimme the driver,' he snapped at me.

'You're going to hit a three-wood,' I said quietly, as I removed the metal club from his bag, 'and you're going to hit it right of centre on the line of the tallest silver birch.'

As he made to turn away, I grabbed him and pinched hard at the tender flesh under his upper arm. I pulled him unceremoniously back towards me, the pain leaving him no choice but to move as I wanted. 'And Richie,' I said even more quietly, 'if you ever chuck another club at me like that, you'll get it back right between your eyes. And then, if you're capable of standing up, you can carry your own clubs for the rest of the round. OK?'

He stared at me, his eyes glazed. A golden spoilt Californian boy, I doubt if anyone had ever spoken to him like that in his whole life. I let him go and said, 'Right, a three-wood, on the silver birch.'

Like a small boy, Riley did as he was told. He hit a lovely shot into the correct area of the fairway and picked up a birdie. He made a terrible mess of the twelfth hole, though, hitting his drive miles right into the deep rough which lay beyond the pond, but settling down again over the closing holes to return a level par score of 72.

I waited outside the scorer's hut while Riley checked and signed his card. I reckoned that this might well turn out to be my shortest-ever engagement as a professional caddie; I was betting that he'd even refuse to pay me.

When the American reappeared, he managed a smile, somewhat thin, but it was there.

'Shall we try again tomorrow, Chris? I'm off at three.' He fiddled with his glove, looked down at his feet and then at me. 'Look, fella, you were right on all counts and I was an asshole. OK?'

144

'OK,' I said with an answering smile, 'but can I make a suggestion?'

'Sure.'

'Do you play a chip-and-run shot? Because you'll need it here. It's invaluable. It's not like Florida, you know, where you pour millions of gallons of water on the greens. Ours are just not as receptive.'

'So I've seen. But the running shot isn't a natural one for me. I'm not familiar with it.'

I took him by the arm, gently this time, and he had the good grace to grin in acknowledgement of the last time I'd held it. We headed for the practice area. 'I'll try and show you,' I said. 'It's like putting. It's about feel, judgement of distance and the ability to read the line to the pin.'

With some trepidation I showed Riley how I played the basic chip shot. I used a seven-iron just like a putter. I managed to get half a dozen within a couple of feet of the flag and actually holed one.

Then I heard the healthy rumble of Jack Mason's voice. 'Christ, Richie, are you giving that miserable scrote of a caddie a lesson? His short game's good enough already.'

'No,' Riley said quietly, 'he's giving me a lesson.'

'Just the basic chip-and-run,' I put in quickly. 'Jack's the expert, he's got every shot in the book.'

To my great relief, Jack offered to help Riley, and as I headed back towards the clubhouse I heard him say, 'I'll probably live to regret giving you the benefit of these pearls of golfing wisdom but here goes . . .'

Chapter 17

The clock was approaching one and I knew that Toby Greenslade would be well established in one of the many available watering holes. My guess was the sponsor's tent, where the champagne would be flowing freely down the throats of valued clients and key members of the media. Whether Toby qualified as one of the latter was debatable but his jovial presence was invariably welcome at such occasions.

He was not difficult to spot in the throng, whose noisy good humour was fuelled by the attentions of the pretty waitresses, their smiles glued firmly into place. Toby was in his favoured position by the bar, a champagne glass raised and tilted to receive the golden nectar which issued from a magnum held by an attractive, dark-haired girl. He waved when he saw me and ordered another glass.

'This is the lovely Sarah,' he boomed. 'She's been looking after me. Sarah – meet my friend Chris. He's also in the golf business.' I exchanged smiles with her and wondered how many chat-up lines went winging her way each day. She smiled, however, as if she really meant it.

Toby raised his glass and told me to drink up. 'I hear you've been caddying again, young Chris. Doing a bit of moonlighting. I expect Calvin will want a share of your fees. What's Riley like?'

'Great swing, spoiled brat, but he'll learn.'

'If he listens to his caddie,' Toby said sarcastically. I shrugged and he continued in a low tone, 'I hear rumours of trouble in the camp, that all is not sweetness and light between Gresham and the AMC warlords. Is that right?'

'What have you heard?' I asked cautiously. Although Toby was a trusted friend, he was also a journalist with a thirst for a scandal which almost equalled his thirst for champagne. I didn't want to be known as the source of one of his *Daily News* scoops.

'Come on, Chris. You had a long and intimate lunch with Gresham and Fairbairn yesterday. Well done, by the way. Second prize was bloody good going considering some of the bandits who were playing in that pro-am.' Toby paused, finished his champagne with a gulp and smiled his thanks as it was once more replenished. 'I'm not going to drop you in the mire but I heard that Dick Fairbairn has put a rocket behind old Gresham. Told him to dig deeper into his treasure chest and put the course and the clubhouse to rights. Otherwise, he'll take the Classic elsewhere. How'm I doing?'

'Very well, Toby. You sure you weren't under the table?'

'Quite sure. Talking of under the table, did I ever tell you about Hughie Jackson's stag night? A dozen of us . . .'

'Yes, you did.' Quickly I steered him away from the subject. 'I don't know how you gather your information when you never seem to move more than ten yards away from the sponsor's bar. When did you last follow a match out there on the course?'

Toby tapped his nose and grinned. 'No need. All the best bits are on the telly in the press tent. Anyway, my readers don't want to know what club this or that golfer hit into the twelfth green; they want to know who he's bonking and how much he earns. Now let's stick to the point. My impeccable sources tell me that Gresham is far from pleased because he doesn't want to spend any more money on Shere Forest.'

'Of course not. He tried to do just enough to the course to placate Fairbairn, who is far too sharp to be fooled and is even less pleased at the state of the clubhouse. But – and this is strictly off the record, Toby – Fairbairn has offered to bail Gresham out, backing him with AMC money.'

'Which might not be welcome.'

'Why not? Calvin would be pleased, and so would I, because then we could really go to town on the old course and the new course would be guaranteed as well.'

'Quite right, but Gresham isn't the sort who'd want to get involved with a big international corporation. All that red tape, budgets, monthly reports, meetings and yet more meetings. He's a dyed-in-the-wool autocrat. No, he'll go elsewhere for the money. You remember what I told you when we had lunch – that there was an approach from a property company, masterminded by Simon Hanley, the son-in-law. My guess is that he'll plight his troth there.'

'Do you have any concrete evidence?'

'No, but if you look over there,' and Toby indicated the far corner of the sponsor's dining area, 'you'll see two men in dark suits in earnest conversation. They're probably not discussing the merits of Shere Forest's short holes nor why Sam Snead never managed to win the US Open. They're more likely to be carving up the shareholdings in this revered golf club.'

'I can see that one of them is Hanley.'

'Correct, the fat one, and the other is Mervyn Slater,

millionaire property dealer. Make a lovely couple, don't you think? Like a couple of porkers preparing to dunk their snouts in a large trough.'

I focused first on Simon Hanley. His face with its pale blue eyes seemed even pudgier. He was wearing the traditional City garb of pin-striped suit and club tie, whereas his companion had a light grey suit with a waistcoat. Slater had thinning fair hair, a scrubby ginger beard and a pallid face.

'As you say, Toby, an unattractive pair to put it mildly.'

'What on earth the fair Francesca saw in Hanley, I'll never know. She could've had me, for heaven's sake.'

Toby walked down to the end of the bar and came back with a plate of smoked salmon sandwiches. 'Look, Chris, there's a good story here . . .' As I opened my mouth to interrupt, he held up his broad hand for silence. 'Don't worry, I wouldn't dream of implicating you. Shere Forest is a fine old club. OK, it's a toffs' club, old-fashioned, but it has prestige because of the Classic. Along comes a property spiv like Slater, he gets his hooks into it because the owner is too impoverished or too stupid or too mean to spend the money needed to knock it into shape. So Slater gets an absolutely top-class leisure asset at a knock-down price. With the connivance of some of the Gresham family.'

'You make it sound like a golfing *Dallas*,' I said, 'but I think you're being much too harsh. I've never met Slater but I know a bit about him and his company. He's got a good public image – won awards for some of his buildings in London and in Bristol, I seem to remember.'

'Oh yes,' Toby replied, 'and he sponsors things too – some sort of inner-city arts trust among them. He hobnobs with minor royalty and, just to show that he's a man of the people, he's a shareholder in Fulham Football Club. Probably got his eye on it as a site for a hypermarket.'

'Well, they stopped playing football there years ago. You don't seem to have taken to Mr Slater, Toby old man. Why's that?'

'I don't give a toss what his public image is, nor how caring and compassionate his press agent and PR people make him out to be. To me he's a property spiv and an asset stripper. If he ever gets his greedy hands on Shere Forest, he'll sell it on in a few years' time for tens of millions of pounds of profit.'

'But at least I'll have had a hand in designing a great golf course,' I said flippantly. 'If Gresham can't see the possibilities at Shere Forest, perhaps it would be better if he let Slater take the helm.'

'You don't really mean that, Chris,' Toby declared. 'I know Shere Forest has its faults. It seems to be stuck permanently in the fifties, it's racked with social snobbery and needs new blood. But the ordinary members' clubs have an important role in golf and we don't want to see them disappearing into the balance sheets of companies like Davina Holdings.'

'Davina Holdings?'

'Slater's company. Or like AMC, for that matter, even though they are our benefactors at this moment.' He waved benignly at Sarah who strolled over and topped up our glasses. 'Davina was Slater's first wife incidentally – he named the company after her. She died. I vaguely remember something about her. I'll have to look it up.'

'Toby, this business about Slater is pure conjecture, isn't it? You don't have a shred of evidence that it's true. Not that a minor inconvenience like that would ever hold you back.'

'Now then, don't be unkind. It's educated conjecture and

I'll bet the gallant Captain Burnside will know plenty. I would guess that he's in his accustomed place in the club bar now and will drink his way through the day. Over the next hour or so, I'll rough out my report for the News, dramatic and uniquely insightful as always, and then I shall get Burnside going on an even bigger bender than usual. I'll get the information I need.'

'I'll come and join you later,' I said.

'Good idea. Bring along a liver donor, will you?'

Chapter 18

Back in the office, Calvin had left a note saying he had gone up to town to dub some commentary onto a late-night golfing summary for one of the satellite TV channels, and would I please take a look at the draft design for a new course in the South of France? So I spent a couple of hours looking at the layout, pleased that Calvin wanted my involvement with it.

Shortly before five o'clock I walked over to the clubhouse and headed for the bar, a cavernous room with windows overlooking the eighteenth green and its broad fairway. Many of the members had already settled down in the old leather armchairs by the windows. The long, crescent-shaped bar was crowded with the kinds of people who make up the essence of a professional golf tournament: officials, equipment manufacturers, business managers and agents, journalists, radio and TV commentators, and even a few golf enthusiasts, who were there simply to watch the golf.

I found Toby in a corner, his back to the hubbub. Leaning on the wall close by was the lean frame of Nigel Burnside. If the Secretary had been drinking throughout the day, he showed few signs of it. I noticed, however, that his eyelids were drooping slightly and, in answer to one of Toby's questions, he spoke more slowly than usual.

'You see, Toby, I'm absolutely against it all. This is a traditional club. It's run for the members. Not by the members, I grant you that, but then I look after their interests . . .' He broke off to take a long drag at his cigarette and an even longer pull at his whisky.

'You know Chris, don't you, Nigel?' asked Toby.

'Yes, yes,' Burnside muttered and waved at the steward, who brought fresh drinks for the two of them. I decided to have an orange juice.

Burnside continued with an admonitory wag of the finger: 'Now, Toby, this is all off the record and I'm only telling you because I've known you for so long. Gresham is under pressure from all sides, from Fairbairn to tart the whole place up and from Hanley and from young Nick. He's going to sell out to Slater and then this place will change out of all recognition. It'll become a bloody country club,' he said bitterly. 'Full of second-hand car dealers with their second-hand tarts.' Burnside looked around and grinned. 'Whoops, better mind my language in view of our sponsor.'

'I wonder why Simon Hanley and Nick are so keen,' Toby prompted gently.

'How about greed? Hanley is Slater's lawyer and will get the benefit of some fat fees . . .'

'And a bonus no doubt.'

'And a bonus. Also there's the Lloyds problem. Ludlow here, he was in the City, I'm told. He can tell us all about that, I'm sure.'

I nodded. Losses of several billion pounds over the past few years had devastated the fortunes of many members of Lloyds syndicates, who had taken on unlimited liability for any losses incurred.

Burnside blinked a couple of times and continued, 'Both Simon and Nick are members of syndicates that have lost heavily. They need money, and lots of it, to meet their commitments.'

Burnside grasped Toby by the arm. 'None of this is to be repeated, Toby – promise? And you, Chris. I'm counting on your discretion. It's going to be announced in a few days. A tragedy, a bloody tragedy,' he muttered.

He looked across the room, focused on someone and said, 'There's Francesca. I'll bring her over, must introduce you.' With great care, he pushed himself upright and walked reasonably steadily towards her.

Toby shook his head ruefully. 'I'll have to get a lift home. I daren't go near my car. Burnside's capacity is unbelievable; he's a monument to the strength of man's constitution. He should go on show – the Incredible Human Sponge.'

'He found a worthy companion in you, Toby.'

'Thanks a lot. The things I do for the integrity of the fourth estate. Uh-oh, here they come.'

Still straight-backed, Burnside ushered Francesca towards us. For a moment his hand hovered on her shoulder but she shook it off with what seemed a practised motion. Like her mother, Francesca was quite tall and what made her oval face so appealing were the dark eyes she had inherited from her father. I hoped that they were the only characteristics he had passed on.

'Toby, how lovely to see you again.' Francesca said the words not just as a form of greeting but as if she really meant them. Toby smiled broadly and pecked her on the cheek. Such was her warmth that I found myself smiling in anticipation as she said, 'And I've heard about you, Chris, from my father. He can't understand what a stockbroker is doing working as a caddie or a course designer. The old boy is confused, I'm afraid.'

'I'm not in the City at the moment,' I said.

'I don't suppose you miss it, do you?'

'Sometimes I miss the money, but that's all.'

We finished our drinks and I told Toby that if he wanted a lift, it was now or never. He elected for now with some relief and we edged past Burnside and Francesca. As we moved away, I heard the Secretary say, 'It's ages since we've had a chat, Francesca. Come over here and let me catch up with your news.'

I glanced back and saw him trying to manoeuvre her into the corner of the bar recently vacated by Toby but she sidestepped him.

'Burnside's quite an all-rounder, isn't he?' I said. 'A world-class boozer and now he's making a play for Francesca.'

'He's a trier, all right. He's had the mother and now he's after the daughter. That's a very high tariff, Chris.'

Toby hoisted himself into my car and, despite whingeing about the discomfort of the bucket seat, began to snore as soon as we hit the main road. Unceremoniously, I dug him in the ribs. 'What did Burnside tell you?'

'You heard the important bits,' he said sleepily. 'Gresham will throw in his lot with Davina Holdings. He's had enough hassle from everybody and he wants to keep the Classic at Shere Forest. He reckons this is the best way to do it. According to Burnside, the deal has been on the table for some time and they'll formalise it next week.'

'And the dashing Captain is presumably agin it?'

'Of course he is. He knows he'll have to work for a living when the new régime takes over. All that nonsense about the interests of his members . . . he's an idle bugger. Thinks the job's here to keep him in drink and female companions. He's had a very cushy number for a long, long time.'

We sped along the A3 for a few miles and Toby nodded off once more. When we stopped at some traffic lights he spoke again. 'He did say one odd thing, though, old Burnside. He said he could stop the whole charade and that he had a mind to. I wonder what he meant?'

'Wishful thinking,' I said lightly.

On the second day of the tournament I made a determined effort to get into the office early. When Calvin arrived shortly after seven, I was already poring over the drawings of the French course.

'I'm very impressed,' he said. 'I think we can look forward to some long hours, though. Jack Mason tells me that Gresham got a good old-fashioned rollicking from Dick Fairbairn.'

'Yes. The course must be right for next year. And I think that the money will be there for the second course.'

'Friends in high places, have you?' Calvin said sharply.

'Come off it, Calvin. I played the pro-am with Gresham and Fairbairn, as you well know, and Fairbairn as good as offered the money required.'

'Sorry, Chris. Bad night with Jane – she's still suffering. I suppose Gresham will turn AMC down?'

'I don't know for sure but Toby tells me that the money will probably come from another source – and quickly. Next week, with a bit of luck.'

'No worries for us then. We'll have a lot of fun building that course. I'll make some tea.'

Several hours later I switched to my role as a caddie and stood on the practice ground making encouraging noises as

Richie Riley sent his shots spiralling high and handsome into the blue sky, which was lightly speckled with drifting scraps of fluffy cloud. His swing looked in immaculate shape, but so were virtually all the others on view. It was only later, out on the course when the tensions of the round took hold, that one would see whether a swing was reliable and in the groove. Towards the end of his practice, Riley showed me his new repertoire of pitch-and-run shots. He had also acquired a punch shot which travelled at just above head height for sixty or seventy yards, pitched and stopped on the second bounce.

He grinned delightedly at me. 'Jack taught me that one as well.'

Lucky lad, I thought, and we headed for the first tee. Riley seemed happier than on the previous day when he had begun his round in too cocksure a mood, convinced that the course would yield birdies to him and becoming frustrated when it did not. In the second round his more relaxed outlook benefited his golf immensely.

Even when the putts refused to drop, and Riley had an easy style which suggested that he could hole out from virtually anywhere, he was unmoved. After nine holes, however, he was still level par for the round and I began to wonder whether he would qualify for the final two rounds. The dangerous twelfth hole was, to my surprise, a turning point. We debated his tactics on the tee and both agreed that he must take his driver and fly the ball into a position from which he would have a chance to attack the hole and get a birdie. Time was running out and, judging by the other scores on the board, the qualifying axe would fall at one over par, which was Riley's score after twenty-nine holes.

The American produced a shot of scintillating power and accuracy under severe pressure: his ball flew over the left centre of the pond and the right-to-left spin brought it back into the centre of the fairway. What a beauty! He was left with a simple seven-iron to the green and I watched with horror as, with the adrenalin thumping inside him, he crashed his ball through the green, down a slope and onto some hard-packed ground alongside the next tee.

'Oh shit,' he said with commendable restraint. 'I sure put some rocket fuel behind that one.'

When we reached his ball, I knew that there was only one possible shot if Riley were to rescue his par. A small knot of spectators had gathered and were speculating how he would play his recovery shot. Riley smiled at them and said, 'Would anyone like to play this one for me? It ain't my favourite.'

I prayed that he wouldn't call for a sand wedge, but instead, he looked at me and said in a mock-English accent: 'Hand me my mashie niblick, caddie. I do believe it's time for a chip-and-run shot.' There was some appreciative laughter from the watching fans.

I handed him his seven-iron while he took a long look at the various slopes between himself and the ball. He asked me if I agreed with his line, and took three or four practice swings. Finally he said, 'Chris, would you like to go and hold the pin?'

I watched intently as I heard the rap of his club on the ball which breasted the slope at a good pace and took the incline towards the hole. I felt certain it would finish within a few inches of the hole. I was wrong, however. As it began to slow down it broke sharply and, as I hastily removed the flag, the ball fell into the cup.

Riley was grinning like a lunatic and so was I. 'Thank you, Jack Mason. Thank you, Chris Ludlow,' he murmured in my ear.

After that, his struggles and his many missed putts behind him, the Fates relented. Over the closing holes, Riley picked up four birdies to end in a very respectable position in the middle of the field. With a bit of luck and good management we might both have a decent pay day on Sunday, I thought cheerfully as I headed for the car park.

Just as I passed across the front of the clubhouse, I heard the boom of an unmistakable voice. Toby was hurrying towards me; he had actually forced his unwilling and well-padded body into the semblance of a trot. It was an unnerving spectacle. 'Whoah,' I said. 'You'll have a heart attack. An interview about Richie Riley's round can't be that important.'

'Too true, dear boy,' Toby said, wheezing like an old steam engine. 'I wanted to catch you because things have started to move on the takeover story. I was going to sit on the information Burnside gave me but now I can't. If I do, I'll be pre-empted by that slimy toad from the *Chronicle*.'

I knew that the slimy toad was one of Toby's rivals, Mike Johnson. 'What's happened?'

'What's happened is that Hanley has leaked the whole bloody story to Johnson.'

'How do you know?'

'Because I saw them chatting away at the bar and about ten minutes later I saw that so-called journalist slither off at a rate of knots for the nearest telephone. Instead of going to the press centre he used the phone in the Secretary's office, for security reasons I suppose. Anyway, I eased my way into the next-door room where Burnside's maid of all work, Alison, sits. There's a connecting door and I took my life in my hands by opening it a crack . . .'

'What a brave boy you are, Toby.'

'Don't mock. Can you imagine the embarrassment if I'd been caught? I'd have felt like some seedy detective. Anyway, Johnson filed his story about the takeover. No mention of Hanley of course, just the usual "sources at Shere Forest". But I wanted to warn you, because you were privy to some of my chat to Burnside. And despite my assurances to him . . .'

'You'll have to use the story?'

Toby nodded.

'It's hardly an earth-shattering scoop though, Toby, is it?'

'No, but there's an interesting angle to titillate my readers.'

'SNOB CLUB RESCUED BY CITY WHEELER-DEALER?'

'You should be a sub-editor at the *News*, laddie.'

'It'll make things pretty hot for Gresham, and Burnside of course,' I mused. 'And how's Fairbairn going to react to having his overtures rejected?'

'Interesting.' Toby looked at his watch. 'Look – I must be off, Chris. I'll just catch the last edition with the story. It should be an intriguing day tomorrow.'

Not half, I thought.

Chapter 19

Saturday morning brought a welcome return to my old routine. Richie Riley's starting time was a civilised eleven o'clock. He had drawn an ideal playing partner in the shape of Nick Spencer, a friendly and uncomplicated golfer from the Midlands with a wonderful swing which mirrored his personality: it was simple and powerful. It was also accomplished enough to have brought him victory in the US Masters at Augusta a few years back.

I was waiting for my newspapers as they thudded onto the mat soon after seven. I weeded out the main sections of the heavies and turned to the back page of the *Daily News*. Despite the month being June, it was full of football news and I had to turn over to find the golf. There was a short report on the Classic and another headline alongside:

TOFFS' CLUB UP FOR GRABS

The report was short and to the point: 'Shere Forest, traditional home of the AMC Classic Tournament, has been offered a financial lifeline by Mervyn Slater, ace property wheeler-dealer and director of Fulham Football Club. Desperately short of funds, Shere Forest (with an average membership age of 62) cannot offer the sort of facilities a modern sponsor demands. With the event about to go elsewhere, mighty Merv, a good friend of royalty and supporter of causes close to their hearts, has stepped in with a rescue package. The old-boy network which runs the club – bankers, lawyers and stockbrokers to a man – had better cling tight to their leather armchairs when dynamic Merv moves in. There'll be changes, changes galore.'

In view of Toby's article and what was no doubt an even worse piece of 'put the boot in' journalism in the *Chronicle*, I tried to keep well away from any area of Shere Forest where I might be collared by Nigel Burnside. He would want to shift the blame for the leakage to the Press onto someone else, and rightly so since he was not at fault. Toby would get the main burst of flak but I didn't want to be a target as well. I parked my car by the office, changed my shoes there and took a circuitous route to the practice ground.

It was a mild and gentle day which had put a smile on everyone's face. Since it was a Saturday, the spectators were out in force and laden with all the accoutrements they thought they needed for a day at the Classic: caps, scarves, umbrellas, walking sticks, rugs, programmes, binoculars, autograph books, cameras, spare sweaters and windcheaters. Many of the people who had settled in seats in the grandstands seemed to have brought enough food and drink for a weekend rather than one day.

Richie Riley's swing was as slow and powerful as before and I had strong hopes that my 'guv'nor' would really do his stuff and get himself into a position to strike out for a big prize on the final day. Even a finish in tenth position would bring him well over £10,000 and a nice little bonus for his devoted caddie.

On the way to the putting green I ran through the important

routine of checking all the equipment in Riley's bag, with particular concentration on the clubs: two woods, one putter and eleven irons. It was extraordinary how often an extra club, which had perhaps been used on the practice ground, remained in the bag. Fourteen was the limit and any extra ones attracted a penalty. All was well in that department but I noticed, as I rummaged through his bag, that there were no spare gloves.

I have known club golfers keep all sorts of odd and intimate things in their golf bags. One of my friends, who had a colourful sex life above and beyond his outwardly contented suburban marriage, used to keep a spare sheet and a supply of condoms in his bag. A professional golfer would be ill-advised to do the same because his secret would not last long with the average caddie.

When I asked Riley about his spare golf gloves, he sent me off to the changing room to get some from his locker. The clubhouse was the last place I wanted to be but I did his bidding and nearly bumped slap into Gresham and Burnside.

Fortunately I heard them coming, their unmistakable voices raised in argument, and I ducked into the unoccupied dining room to avoid them.

Peter Gresham was holding forth and his words came over loud and clear. 'I suggest, Captain Burnside, that we continue this discussion in private in your office. You've been skating on damned thin ice at this club and this latest breach of confidence may be the last straw. I want an explanation . . .'

Around the corner I heard a door slam and remembered Toby's story of sidling into the neighbouring office to listen in to his rival golf correspondent's conversation. A glance at my watch confirmed that I could spare a few minutes to eavesdrop; Riley would be happy enough on the putting green. With a guilty glance to left and right I opened the door to the adjoining room. As all the administration for the Classic was assumed by the PGA, Alison's services were not required during the Tournament and the room was empty.

I walked quietly across it, glad that I was wearing trainers, the standard footwear for caddies. I crouched down by the communicating door, so that I could not be seen through the window, and pressed my ear to one of the panels. Toby would have enjoyed seeing me hunched by the door, eavesdropping like some sleazy private eye.

The first voice I heard was that of Nigel Burnside. 'Calm down, Peter, old boy. I promise you that I said nothing untoward to either of those journalists.'

'My son-in-law told me that you were hobnobbing with that damned hack from the *News* the night before last. And, lo and behold, he has the story of the takeover for everyone to read.'

'It didn't come from me.'

'God Almighty, Nigel, if it wasn't you then who was it? I don't think you can remember half the things you say when you're drunk, *or* what you do for that matter.'

'That's rich, coming from you,' Burnside said, in a voice so low that I had to strain to hear the words. 'I remember you being too pissed to stand, one night in Germany – too pissed to see. Who got you out of that mess? Who paid off that German family to keep their mouths shut? You'd have been disgraced all right, jailed even. So don't you talk to me about being drunk.'

There was silence for a few moments and then Gresham said, 'I've paid for that mistake a thousand times, Nigel, and don't think you can rely on its protection for ever. That line of credit is about to run out. Soon. I won't be able to protect you when

Slater takes control. Do you think he'll turn a blind eye to your boozing and womanising, and your general inefficiency?'

I was getting cramp and, as I shifted my position, a floorboard creaked. Fortunately, the two men on the other side of the door were too hard at it to hear.

'I wouldn't count your chickens yet, Peter.' Burnside's tone was threatening. 'The members of Shere Forest aren't totally decrepit. I've already had a deputation with enough signatures on a resolution to call an Extraordinary General Meeting to discuss this takeover.'

'They can do nothing; they have no power whatsoever,' Gresham responded heatedly. 'I control the voting shares and Simon and Nick own the few others that are left.'

'We'll see about that on Wednesday at the EGM, won't we, Peter? I suggest you check the position with Simon Hanley. He is the club's solicitor, after all.'

It was time to go. I was due on the tee in ten minutes. I slipped quietly out into the corridor, relieved that no one had seen me creeping about like a burglar in a farce, got a couple of golf gloves out of Riley's locker and sprinted over to the putting green, where Riley was chatting to Francesca Hanley.

As I arrived he said, 'I thought a second caddie had deserted me, Chris, and I was trying to persuade this lovely young lady to take your place.'

'Francesca's certainly a lot better looking,' I said. She gave me a broad smile and a wink.

'I won't pinch your job, Chris. Anyway, I have to join Mummy and Daddy for lunch – it's one of our traditions on the Saturday of the Classic. But I'd like to follow you for a few holes, Mr Riley.'

As Francesca walked away to join the other spectators

alongside the fairway, Riley called after her: 'I'll be watching out for you.'

She waved and we moved off towards the tee. Riley asked, 'Hey, who is that chick, Chris? Is she hot to trot or not? Wow!'

'Calm down, Richie, she's married and "Mummy and Daddy" are the Greshams, who own this place. Anyway, she's much too old for you.'

'Don't you believe it,' he replied. As he teed up his ball, he said, 'This one's for Francesca.'

It was a good one too, a long and booming shot that set him up for his first birdie of the day.

Riley strode off in pursuit of his ball and I tried to analyse the conversation I had just overheard, playing it back in my mind as I trudged in the American's wake. First of all, Burnside, by his own lights, had been honest with Gresham. It wasn't him, but Hanley who had blabbed to the Press about the proposed takeover. No doubt Hanley had his own selfish reasons for doing so.

Without thinking about it, I handed an eight-iron to Riley and saw him fly his ball to within a few feet of the pin. He acknowledged the applause from the spectators, most of whom were there to watch Nick Spencer, and blew a kiss in the direction of Francesca, who was thirty yards away behind the ropes which guarded the fairway.

Nick Spencer, who had an eager eye for available women, spotted the gesture and said, in his flat Midlands accent, 'She's too good for a Yank. You leave her to a true-born Englishman – OK?'

I smiled automatically, my thoughts on the veiled threats made by Burnside. Not so veiled were his remarks about some sort of cover-up operation on Gresham's behalf in Germany.

Disgrace? Jail even? Maybe Toby would know the story behind that. And what did Burnside hope to achieve with the members' meeting next Wednesday? If Gresham controlled most of the shares of Shere Forest, the members would be powerless to prevent the sale to Mervyn Slater. Burnside had implied that he knew something which Gresham did not, but I assumed this was just bravado on his part, a mischievous wish to plant a doubt in Gresham's mind.

Over the next few holes, Riley and Spencer threw birdies at each other and began to climb up the leader board. Francesca left us at the halfway mark in order to keep her lunch date. When Riley at once took three putts from the edge of the green, I hoped that her departure wouldn't bring a decline in his inspired play, but he bounced back with a birdie at the dangerous twelfth and was rewarded with a score of 67. Although the tournament leaders had only just begun their rounds, I reckoned that the Californian would be on their tails on the final day.

In the end he made the top twenty and was scheduled to begin his fourth and final round at just after midday. Even if he only had on outside chance of winning the event, it was a nice feeling to be back at the centre of a professional tournament.

Chapter 20

A long day lay in wait for me on Sunday since I had promised to be at the course at seven o'clock to assist Calvin.

The previous evening had been an abstemious one. I had shared a bottle of wine with Mrs Bradshaw and, while she visited some nearby friends, enjoyed the benefit of a superb beef ragout which she had cooked for me. What a wonderful neighbour. Then it was early to bed and I was up, cheerful, refreshed and feeling virtuous, well before six o'clock the next morning.

The roads were empty and I made it to Shere Forest in record time. I saw the first 'Save the Planet' banner strung along a little railway bridge about a quarter of a mile from the entrance to the club. As I drove on, I could see that all the sponsor's posters had been replaced by placards bearing the same slogan. The walls which flanked the entrance to the club had been daubed with messages in green paint: 'The Green Disciples Love the Earth', 'Green is Love', 'Golf is Greed' amongst them. Clearly, certain people had been up and about even earlier than I had.

I turned through the gates towards the car park and saw that they had even managed to exchange the sombre burgundy and green flag of Shere Forest for one of their own. A 'Save the

Planet' pennant flapped at the top of the white pole in front of the clubhouse. I had to give the Green Disciples full marks for enterprise.

A small group of three men were gathered on the eighteenth green; I recognised Calvin Blair, Martin, the head greenkeeper, and one of the latter's assistants. They were peering at the turf and I saw Calvin gesture angrily. Without any delay I parked my car in a member's space and hurried over to him. The cause of his irritation was obvious: two large holes in the centre of the green.

Blair pointed at two hefty posts by the side of the green. I went over to look at the banner which was fastened between them. It was the familiar 'Save the Planet' logo.

'Those bastards,' Blair said bitterly. 'They've ruined this green and the ninth. Where the hell were the security boys? Have you seen all the rest of their tricks?'

'I'd like to get my hands on them Green Disciples,' Martin muttered. 'Still, it could've been worse.'

'Yes,' agreed Blair, with a sigh. 'We can repair the damage. You and the boys had better get onto it straightaway, Martin. I've already told the PGA and they'll position the pins as best they can. Come on, Chris, we'd better make some notes for the insurance claim.'

'Isn't that Burnside's job? He's the Secretary of the club.'

'Quite right. Let the lazy bugger sort it all out. We've got enough to do. Let's go and get him.'

'You'd love to drag him out of bed, wouldn't you, Calvin?'

'Too bloody true. Drunken swine.'

'I just hope he hasn't got company.'

We walked quietly around the back of the clubhouse, across a lawn and past a copse of trees. Burnside's house, a lovely though dilapidated Tudor cottage with its own small garden, lay a couple of hundred yards away. Calvin told me that it was owned by the club and was one of the Secretary's perks. 'Rent-free cottage, free booze, free food, plenty of crumpet . . . the jammy devil doesn't know he's born.'

'Aha – he seems to be up and about,' I observed. 'There are some lights on.'

'Probably so pissed he forgot to turn them off,' grunted Blair.

We paused at the garden gate, noticing that the front door stood open. Blair hammered the knocker and, for good measure, pressed the doorbell. 'That should get him going,' he said with a smile.

But it didn't, so Blair stepped inside and yelled out Burnside's name. 'That's odd,' he said. 'Perhaps he's already over at the club. We must've missed him.'

I joined Blair inside and looked into a small living room to the right. It was sparsely furnished and impersonal. Calvin meanwhile was halfway up the stairs; he stopped and shouted for Burnside once again.

A strong whiff of stale booze hit my nostrils. It came from the room on the other side of the hallway. Whisky. I pushed the door open and sniffed again. Enough to make your eyes water.

For a moment or two I hung about in the doorway, my eyes fixed on an old desk that was pushed up against the opposite wall. A battered leather chair, which seemed too large for the room, was next to it. I could see why the smell was so overpowering – a litre bottle of Scotch lay on its side on the desk, much of its contents spilled onto the threadbare carpet below. I was glad that Toby wasn't there to see such a waste of good booze. The gallant Captain must have really hung one on.

Well, it had been Saturday night after all.

With every intention of righting the bottle I strolled into the room. My eye was caught by a heavy blackened oak beam which ran across the room with hooks fixed on it at regular intervals. Centuries ago the inhabitants of this cottage had used them to hang up their game birds and rabbits and perhaps the occasional leg of bacon.

Something a great deal more substantial was hanging there now. The body of Nigel Burnside was strung on a cord from the central hook, and a wooden chair lay on its side near his feet.

For several seconds I stood, paralysed with shock, staring at his contorted face. With his head askew and his body hanging helplessly down, the Club Secretary had the look of an early Christian martyr. For one moment I had the fanciful urge to push his arms upwards into the crucifixion pose.

The clattering of Calvin's feet on the stairs brought me back to earth. I shouted, 'He's in here, Calvin, in the study.' It wasn't much of a shout, though, more like a croak.

'Bloody hell, Nigel, didn't you hear us calling, man!' Calvin complained as he came through the door. The words died on his lips. 'Bloody hell,' he repeated in a whisper and then sagged heavily against the wall. After several moments he said hesitantly, 'Suicide?' I shrugged and he continued, 'Poor devil. I wouldn't have put him down for suicide, would you?'

'No. It has all the signs, but I wonder. If someone knocked him off, the killer would take great pains to make it look that way, wouldn't he?' I pointed at the overturned whisky bottle and a scattering of pills on the desk. 'Booze and barbiturates and then the easy way out?'

'Christ, I wouldn't call hanging yourself the easy way out.'

'No. Can you see a phone anywhere?'

'In the hall. Look, Chris, I'd better get outside. I'm not very keen on dead bodies.'

I'm not over fond of them myself, I thought, as I dialled the police.

Chapter 21

It seemed only a few minutes before police cars, an ambulance and a forensics van appeared outside and dozens of people invaded the Tudor cottage and its little garden. Calvin and I were questioned closely by a middle-aged sergeant who made it very clear that he had missed his breakfast.

He took a dim view of me and I had to assure him several times that I had not touched anything vital and that I had neither searched for, nor pocketed, a suicide note.

'What sort of a bloke was this Burnside, then?' asked Sergeant Disley.

'I hardly knew him.'

'You worked for him, didn't you?'

'No. I work for Calvin Blair and we're redesigning some parts of the course.'

Disley grunted. 'Why should he hang himself? Money worries? A bit too old for woman trouble, I suppose. He wasn't queer, was he, by any chance?'

'Not queer, no. Quite keen on the ladies, or so I've been told. I've no idea about his finances. As I say, I hardly knew him. The owner of the club, Peter Gresham, has known him for a long time. He might be able to help you.'

Just as Disley released me, with a reminder that I'd have to make a formal statement, I heard the unmistakable voice of Hermione Gresham. She was standing at the door, flanked by her husband and her daughter.

'I demand to know what's happening here,' she said to Sergeant Disley, and her forceful tones brought another police officer from Burnside's study. He was a square-shouldered man with unusually long sideburns. He announced himself as Inspector Goodall.

'I'm in charge here, madam,' he said briskly, 'and any demanding will be done by me.' Brave man. 'Your name, please.'

I noticed Francesca suppress a smile but Mrs Gresham was not to be outgunned by a mere inspector. 'We are the owners of Shere Forest and I'm told there has been an accident on our property, which is why I insist on knowing what has happened.'

'You're Mr and Mrs Gresham, I take it?'

'Yes.'

'It looks as though Captain Nigel Burnside may have killed himself. At first view, there seem to be no suspicious circumstances but we intend to interview anyone who can throw any light on the incident.'

Fortunately, nobody knew that I had been eavesdropping on the quarrel between Burnside and Peter Gresham and I had no intention of enlightening anyone yet, particularly as I was convinced that their disagreement had, in one way or another, a bearing on Burnside's death. Gresham had been adamant that Burnside could do nothing about the changes that were coming and had hinted strongly that Burnside's undemanding position at Shere Forest would certainly be forfeit. The lazy life which the Captain clearly loved, protected by Gresham and cosseted by the lady members, seemed likely to end. Depression is usually compounded by alcohol (whoever coined the phrase 'drowning one's sorrows' didn't know what they were talking about) and perhaps Burnside had opted to take his own life rather than face a bleak future.

I scrutinised Gresham's face as Inspector Goodall broke the news. It revealed very little. A slight frown, a raising of his right hand to his face and the exclamation 'My God' wasn't exactly over the top when you've just heard that your oldest friend has topped himself.

Hermione Gresham went pale and stood motionless for a moment, her hands clasped tightly in front of her. 'Poor Nigel, my poor Nigel,' she muttered and then her composure fled from her. She threw her arms around her daughter and her body convulsed with great sobs. Gresham patted her ineffectually on the shoulder and Francesca murmured gentle words of comfort into her mother's ear as she eased her away into the sitting room and closed the door.

'I'm sorry, Inspector,' Gresham said, 'but Captain Burnside was one of our oldest friends.'

'No need to be sorry, sir. Do you have any idea why he might've done this?'

Gresham looked at the floor and then at Sergeant Disley and then at me. 'Not really. He had no particular worries. A safe job. This house was his, courtesy of the club.'

Gresham hesitated and Goodall waited for more. 'Well, Inspector, Nigel did get depressed. He was a heavy drinker, always had been. I shouldn't really tell anyone this. Sworn to secrecy, you know, but in the circumstances . . .'

Gresham's finger briefly explored his left nostril and then he resumed, 'When we were in the Army in Germany, he attempted suicide. There was an unfortunate incident. I was his immediate superior and I hushed it up. Water under the bridge now, but he tried to hang himself then.'

You lying bastard, I thought, as Goodall made a note in his book.

I was preparing to leave when the sitting room door opened and Hermione Gresham and her daughter reappeared. The mother's eyes were red and rheumy from her tears but I could see that she had tidied up her make-up and was ready to face the world again.

A glance out of the door revealed that a substantial group of newspapermen and photographers had already gathered at the front gate, augmented by a growing band of spectators, curious to know what all the fuss was about. Two policemen were keeping them at bay.

Inspector Goodall decided that the Gresham family should be escorted away in a police car; I said I'd take my chances via the back door. It was only a short sprint back to the safety of the clubhouse and I reckoned I could outrun even the most determined reporter. I went through the garden gate at the back of the house, put my shoulder hard into the most persistent of the half-dozen members of the Press who were gathered there and ran for it.

However, I could not escape the attentions of that fearless seeker after the truth, Toby Greenslade of the *Daily News*. He was waiting for me in Calvin Blair's office.

'I thought you'd be back at base eventually,' he said. 'Calvin here has been kind enough to give me the basics and now I await your valued insights, Chris.'

'I don't think I have any. It all looks very simple. Open and shut.' I shook my head and tried to give him a warning frown.

'Maybe it does to you,' Toby replied, 'but not to me. Why on earth should Burnside top himself? I can't imagine a coherent reason, can you?'

'There'll be some sad and lonely ladies at Shere Forest,' Calvin said quietly.

'Now's your chance, Toby,' I said. 'Do you think you can fill the gallant Captain's shoes?'

Toby told me that I had a singularly disgusting turn of mind. I said I'd have to cut short our discussion as I was due on the practice ground with Riley in twenty minutes.

'You're with Jack Mason, aren't you?' Calvin said. 'Look out for my daughter. Rebecca always likes to follow Jack, if possible.'

'Is Jane here?' I asked.

'No, afraid not. She couldn't face it, so Jack's wife brought Rebecca over. I'm having an early lunch with her in about ten minutes. So I'll be off. Good luck, Chris.'

A few moments after the door closed behind Blair, the telephone rang and it took me a moment or two to recognise the low-pitched voice of Francesca. 'Chris, are you free for dinner tonight?'

'As far as I know,' I said ungraciously. What a way to speak to a beautiful woman, but I was conscious of Toby standing nearby. I had always suspected that he had the magical gift of being able to hear both ends of a telephone conversation without the need of an extension. Also I wondered if she had an intimate dinner for two in mind or whether her boorish husband would be present.

'Please try to restrain your enthusiasm,' Francesca said tartly. I couldn't blame her. 'Look, I need to get away from Shere Forest and its problems and talk to someone about things other than money and takeovers. Will you indulge a discreet married lady? My husband is out, as usual, with the boring Mr Mervyn Slater. How about it?'

'I'd be delighted,' I said quickly and jotted down the name of a fashionable Kensington restaurant, turning my back so that Toby, who was trying to peer over my shoulder, couldn't see what I was writing.

'Judging by your unpleasantly smug expression, you have an assignation,' Toby said when I'd put down the phone. 'And it's probably someone you shouldn't be with. I shall inquire no further, of course.'

'Of course.'

'Who is it?' I shook my head at him and he continued, 'OK, let's to business. You don't think the poor old Captain's suicide is as straightforward as everyone says, do you?'

'I think it probably was suicide but there's something distinctly murky in Peter Gresham's past that Burnside knew about. I'd like to find out more about it.'

It pleased Toby, as I knew it would, when I decided to tell him how I had followed his lead and eavesdropped on the two men.

'Burnside made great play of some incident when they were in Germany – how he'd saved Gresham from certain disgrace, jail even. And what did Gresham do? He told the police the exact opposite, that he'd pulled Burnside's irons out of the fire. And that Burnside had tried to commit suicide out of remorse.'

'Who did you believe?'

'Burnside,' I said firmly.

'So would I, on balance,' Toby said. 'And it makes me take more seriously Burnside's little hints that he knew something important about this takeover business.'

'Something that Gresham didn't know. And that Burnside was prepared to use to embarrass the Gresham family.'

'Then, in the depths of an alcoholic depression about the whole situation, he goes off and kills himself. No, I can't swallow that. For a start it seems that Burnside had some sort of hold over Gresham. Also he seemed confident that he could bugger up Gresham's plans to sell out. It's exactly the sort of situation that Burnside would revel in. Why should he bow out when he had a golden opportunity to twist Gresham's tail?'

'Did he detest Gresham that much?' I asked.

'Oh, I should think so. And I would imagine that sleeping with Hermione gave old Nigel great pleasure on more than one level.'

'Well, I can't see Gresham getting involved in murder,' I said hesitantly. 'And it did look very much like suicide to me. Maybe Burnside had simply had enough. He was an intelligent man, unfulfilled even; perhaps he decided to call it a day.'

Toby shrugged. 'You've got a theory up your sleeve, I'm sure. You can try it out for size on Francesca over dinner. The theory, I mean,' he said with one of his unpleasant leers.

I looked at Toby sharply and then decided that there was no point in making a denial. I still don't know how he does it, though.

Chapter 22

Richie Riley's swing, almost imperceptibly faster than on the previous day, told me that he was nervous. So was I, come to that, and I spent the hour on the practice ground trying to slow us both down. I even spoke a little slower than usual in my efforts to relax his tempo.

I was glad that we were paired with Jack Mason who, though he would be trying as hard as anyone in the field, would never stoop to gamesmanship. On the contrary, when we walked over to the first tee together, he did his utmost to put Riley at his ease.

We were waiting on the tee for the fairway to clear when Calvin Blair pushed his way through the spectators and joined us. He looked anxious even as he smiled his greeting to Jack. 'I'm sorry, Jack, Chris, but have you seen Rebecca? We were due to have a snack together but she didn't show up.'

'That's not like Rebecca,' said Jack. 'Wasn't she with my missus?'

'She came here with Jenny,' Calvin replied, 'but then they split up.'

'Don't worry, Calvin,' Jack reassured him. 'She'll turn up in the gallery. Chris or I will spot her and tell her to find you in the office or the clubhouse.'

Blair nodded his thanks and stepped back as Jack teed up his ball and hit a soaring drive down the left-hand side of the fairway. My efforts to calm Richie Riley hadn't entirely worked; he hit a very high shot, well short of Jack's, but his mid-iron second shot found the middle of the green. He raised his eyebrows with some relief and grinned at me. He would be fine now, I thought.

And so he was for seven holes, during which he managed a birdie to improve his position. Jack was playing very accurate golf and, with the help of three birdies, had now got to within four shots of the leader. On the eighth hole, Riley hit an appalling shot from the tee, a towering push to the right which headed relentlessly for the middle of a grove of trees. He slammed the clubhead irritably into the turf and I thought that he would drop at least one shot.

However, we heard Riley's ball hit a tree with a resounding *clunk* and then watched it loop sideways and settle in the light rough not far from the fairway.

Jack laughed. 'A bloody woodpecker. You're a lucky guy, Richie.'

Riley offered a muttered thanks to some higher agency and took full advantage of his piece of good luck by putting the ball close to the flag and holing out for another birdie. A par at the ninth hole put him in an excellent position at the halfway stage of the final round.

I took a close look at the damage to the ninth green. Martin and his assistants had performed a creditable repair, and the new turf which had been patched in was only discernible because of its different colour. Some of the professionals later said that the two damaged greens were impossible to putt on, but they were the ones who finished with lousy scores. Another excuse to add to the list. Neither Jack nor Riley seemed aware that any damage had occurred.

Calvin Blair took me aside as we walked to the tenth tee and asked whether we had seen any sign of Rebecca yet. I said no and he shook his head unhappily.

'I've been all over the course and the clubhouse and there isn't a sign of her. It's not like her, Chris. She's a sensible girl.'

'Have you put out a message over the public address system?'

'Yes. Several.'

'She hasn't gone home for some reason?'

'No, I rang Jane to check. She's coming over.'

Richie Riley was looking anxiously in my direction which was no surprise since I had his clubs on my shoulder. 'Look, I've got to go,' I said. 'Rebecca probably got bored and went off to see a film or something, but speak to the police about it anyway.'

'I expect you're right, Chris, but all this Green Disciple business has got me worried. If they've decided to kidnap her . . .'

Calvin's voice trailed away. As he looked anxiously around and fidgeted with the keys and the coins in his pocket, his distress was evident. I understood his concern; the Disciples had, after all, attacked his family a few weeks before. I didn't believe they would make them a target for a second time and I tried to reassure him.

'Calvin, the Disciples have already had a pop at you and your family. I don't believe they'd have another go. Anyway, as you said, Rebecca's very sensible. I know that, too. She'd have screamed blue murder if she felt she was in any danger.'

Although he was unconvinced, Calvin gave me a nod and a

weak smile. He said: 'OK. Don't mention this to Jack. Let him finish his round, he's in with a chance.'

It was very much an outside chance now that the Tournament leaders were out on the course and able to accumulate birdies of their own. Under the immense pressure of the closing holes of an important tournament, neither Jack nor Richie was able to make any more significant progress. Vital putts refused to drop into the hole and Jack Mason finished in tenth place and Richie in a tie for fifteenth. Nevertheless, it was a highly satisfactory performance by the young American and his winnings were as welcome to him as the bonus of several hundred pounds was to me.

Riley had to catch a flight back to the United States that evening and I waited with him while a courtesy car was found for the journey to Heathrow.

'Thanks, Chris,' he said, as the car arrived with an attractive girl at its wheel. 'I learned a lot on this trip. Particularly about my short game, or lack of it.' I tried my modest smile. 'I'm coming over for the Open at St Andrews. Can you carry my bag?'

I hadn't thought about the Open Championship, beyond leaving the week clear in my diary. I wasn't going to miss the Open, even if I had to be there in the unaccustomed role of spectator.

'Richie, you realise that you'll have to qualify, don't you?'

Thousands of hopeful golfers each year tried to win through the various qualifying stages, to realise their fantasies of playing in the most magical of all the golf championships. It was a tough proposition, even for a classy golfer like Richie Riley. At least, as a member of the US Tour, he would have the benefit of being exempted into the final stages of the qualifying tournament

– two rounds which were played on the Sunday and Monday before the Open began.

'No sweat,' the American replied as he got into the car. 'I'll see you at St Andrews on the Tuesday.'

I had been looking around in vain for Calvin Blair and eventually decided to try the office. The place was crowded. Not only were Calvin and Jane in there but Jack and Jenny Mason and the solid presence of Sergeant Disley. By the looks on their faces, I could tell that Rebecca had not yet been found. Jenny Mason, whom I had known for many years, had her arm resting supportively on Jane's shoulder. Calvin's wife looked tormented and afraid. I looked questioningly at Calvin who shook his head despairingly.

Sergeant Disley was the first to speak. 'Mr Blair's opinion is that his daughter has been spirited away by some group called the Green Disciples. Would you have an opinion on that, Mr Ludlow? You know one of their leaders, apparently.'

'I know a lady called Jodie Hesse, who's a spokesperson for them. But I'm sure she wouldn't condone the kidnap of a child.'

'They're a bunch of bloody lunatics,' Blair stated heatedly. 'They've already attacked my wife and Rebecca. They bombed the Department of the Environment. And look at the damage they did to the course this morning.'

'I think you're on the wrong track, Calvin,' I said mildly. 'I still think Rebecca has wandered off on her own. She's probably lost all sense of time.'

'I agree with Chris,' Jenny Mason said. 'She's practically a teenager, she lives in a different world to us adults.' I was glad of Jenny's support because, although I was convinced that Rebecca was an intelligent and capable girl, I was aware that my instinct to protect Jodie Hesse was selfish. I liked her and I also fancied her; I was getting as bad as Max.

Jenny continued, 'I hope you don't mind my asking you, Jane, but how are things between you and Rebecca? Any problems, like arguments or pre-teenage sulks?'

'Well, I can't say things have been easy,' Jane replied. 'Since the attack I've wanted her near me. I suppose I've been clingy and she has fretted a bit . . .'

'That's understandable,' Calvin said firmly.

Jenny nodded in sympathy and Disley interrupted: 'Let's stay with these jolly Green Disciples, shall we?' He turned to me. 'Mr Ludlow, you presumably have an address for this Hesse person?'

'No, I have not,' I said truthfully.

'And you haven't the remotest idea where she lives?' he asked sarcastically.

'No.' I saw Blair glaring at me and added, 'All I know is that she's in London somewhere – I think.'

'That's a great help,' muttered Disley.

'Your brother Max knows her well, doesn't he?' Calvin Blair asked.

'He's got a phone number for her, but he's in Edinburgh somewhere. The University might know where he is. I don't.'

I also had Jodie's phone number in my flat but I was damned if I'd become part of a witch-hunt against her. Nevertheless, I felt guilty. I was certain that she would not involve herself in anything as despicable as the abduction of a young girl and I said so. But I wondered whether Jodie had organised the Green Disciples' fun and games at Shere Forest earlier in the day. Comparatively mild though the protests had been, they bore the marks of a hardened political extremist such as Jodie. I decided to try and talk to her as soon as possible.

Meanwhile, I tried to divert everyone's attention away from Jodie by asking if anyone had checked whether Rebecca, in the absence of her mother, had returned home.

Jane Blair looked at me imploringly. 'The police sent someone over but she's not there. Oh Chris, are you sure you've told us all you can about these Green Disciple people?'

The pleading in her voice made my heart lurch in sympathy and I said, 'I'll do anything in my power to help, but there's no point in picking on someone as the bogeyman. It's too easy. There's probably a very simple explanation.'

Sergeant Disley put his heavy stamp on the discussion. In a world-weary manner he said, 'The problem is that Rebecca is probably in London. Which doesn't narrow it down much because most of the two hundred thousand kids who go missing each year end up in the Smoke.'

Well done, Sergeant Disley, I said to myself. That'll really comfort her desperate parents.

He was proved right, however, and very quickly. A few minutes later the phone rang and, since I was closest to it, I picked it up.

'Is that you, Chris?' It was the clear voice of a child and I knew at once that it was Rebecca. I hoped that it was not to be the prelude to a ransom demand but it was better that I intercepted it than Jane or Calvin. I held the phone tightly to my ear.

After a pause, she said, 'Chris, I've done something stupid. I ran away. It was Mum. She's been so awful since – you know. She's really been on my back. Didn't like me being out of her sight. Didn't want me to go out, even with friends. And when I did escape to someone's house, she'd be on the phone checking I was OK every five minutes. She's been impossible. And then today, she wouldn't go to the golf like Dad wanted her to. She said she was ill and I was so fed up, I—'

I brought her diatribe to a halt. 'Where are you?' Everyone's eyes were on me. 'Where are you, Rebecca?' I saw hope brighten Jane Blair's face and nodded at her.

'I'm at Victoria Station. I'm catching the next train home. I'm really sorry.'

'Speak to your mother,' I suggested gently and handed the phone to Jane.

'Thank God,' said Calvin, and closed his eyes. Jack clasped his friend comfortingly around the shoulders.

Jane Blair was doing nearly all the listening now and, after another minute or two, she put the phone back on its rest.

She looked very composed. Calvin began to speak but she silenced him. 'It's over, Calvin. She's fine. Rebecca ran away on an impulse. She was fed up – with me, I might add. And I don't blame her one little bit.'

'Oh come on, Jane,' Jack began to protest.

'No, I mean it.' Jane rode over his words. 'I've been selfish and neurotic. After that attack, I couldn't cope. I neglected Calvin, which was bad enough, but I also let Rebecca down.'

Jenny Mason walked over to Jane and gave her a hug. 'Don't be silly, darling, everyone understood. You'd been frightened out of your wits.'

'I daresay, but girls of twelve don't understand human frailty and especially not from Mum or Dad. She'd had enough of my moping about, refusing to go anywhere. So she ran away. It was her protest. It's lucky for us that she didn't have much money with her and that she got cold feet.'

'This is what usually happens,' Disley said. He sucked in his breath importantly and added, 'They run away and realise after a few hours that home isn't so bad after all. It means hot food and a comfortable bed.' His tone was so complacent and know-it-all, I'd cheerfully have punched his teeth in.

'That doesn't make it any easier for the poor parents, does it, Sergeant?' said Jenny Mason in a waspish tone. 'Rebecca is only twelve, she's still a baby.'

'The trouble is, she looks like an eighteen-year-old,' said Calvin.

Disley moved towards the door. 'I'll call the search off,' he announced. 'Let's all thank our lucky stars that she saw some sense.'

Calvin Blair slumped in a chair and said on a shuddering breath: 'What a day! Am I glad it's over. Poor old Burnside is found dead. Then there's the little matter of the damage to the course – on the last day of the Classic, for God's sake. And our daughter disappears.'

'But not for long,' Jane added. 'Come on, we've got to meet Rebecca at the station and then the Blair family is going out to celebrate.'

Chapter 23

Just like the Blair family I too was anticipating an enjoyable evening. I entered the grand, if impersonal, surroundings of a Kensington hotel and headed for the restaurant, which had attracted many plaudits from the critics over the previous few months. The kitchen was now in the care of one of those celebrity chefs who seem to haunt the style sections of the posh newspapers. I wondered if I would have the courage to send a dish back, if necessary. Toby Greenslade took a positive delight in bruising inflated culinary egos, but I wasn't in his brass-bound class.

Francesca Hanley was already in the restaurant, sitting at a discreet corner table. She was wearing a black silk jacket over a cream shirt which was open at the throat. Classy. Sexy. I felt a decisive lift of my spirits. I tried to kiss her on the cheek but she turned her head and kissed me on the lips instead. It was a promising start. I still had no clue as to Francesca's motives for inviting me out. Was she as straightforward as she appeared – did she really want to escape the stifling atmosphere of Shere Forest and the Gresham family? Or did she fancy a brief fling? Or a long fling? As I looked into her dark, intelligent eyes and listened to her warm voice, I certainly hoped so; and when I saw the prices on the menu, I decided that if she could keep me in this style, I was hers for as long as she wished.

She emphasised her appointed role as the hostess as we pondered our choice of food. 'No arguments, Chris, about the bill. I asked you out and I'm paying.'

I didn't object. It was only courteous to lie back and enjoy it.

Murmuring 'The wine list, sir,' a slim, Latin-looking waiter tried to hand me a thick leather-bound tome, but Francesca plucked it from his grasp and said firmly, 'That's for me, thank you.'

She ordered a bottle of Roederer champagne and, after the waiter had opened it with a flourish and poured a little into her glass, she sniffed it and told him to fill our glasses.

'Will that be all, madam?' he asked nervously.

'No,' she replied. 'Do you have any of the Léoville-Barton left? Seventy-eight?'

'Yes, madam. At once, madam.'

The waiter scurried off and Francesca asked me how she'd done. I grinned my approval, we clinked glasses and she said, 'We've all had quite a day, haven't we? Poor Nigel. I suppose we ought to drink to the memory of the old lecher.'

'To a ladies' man,' I said politely. 'We should really be toasting him in whisky rather than wine, but I don't suppose he'd mind. Your mother seemed very upset. Is she feeling any better yet?' I'd decided that I should take the chance of finding out as much as I could about the Gresham family. Why hold back when Francesca seemed to be a very forthright woman?

'She's OK now. She has her memories.'

'Memories?'

'Of dear old Nigel. Don't play dumb, Chris, I'm sure you're privy to the fact that he and Mummy had been at it for years. She loved him, I think.'

This was a much faster start than I had anticipated. 'Did your father cotton on?'

'I don't know. I certainly can't remember any discord in that department. He probably blind-eyed it, if he noticed at all. Daddy has a remarkable facility for ignoring what he doesn't want to see.'

The wine waiter was hovering at the table and he showed Francesca the bottle she had ordered. She nodded and he opened it very carefully.

'Your father and Burnside were great chums, weren't they?'

'Yes, from way back. They met at school, but they really became buddies in the Army in Germany.'

The conversation went into neutral while the first course was served and we savoured the superbly cooked dishes. No complaints for chef, so far. I decided to pursue the theme of Germany since Francesca was in a receptive mood. She might know the answers to some intriguing questions.

'Is it true that your father got Burnside out of trouble in Germany?' I asked. 'What was all that about? He mentioned it to that policeman, Goodall.'

Francesca looked puzzled and shook her head.

'Your father called it "an unfortunate incident",' I prompted her. 'He said that Nigel tried to commit suicide.'

'That's news to me,' she replied. 'Of course, the Army would hush up an attempted suicide. As for any unsavoury incidents, it could only be booze and women if Nigel was involved.'

I asked whether her mother had ever referred to any scandal in connection with Burnside. We paused while a waiter removed our empty plates.

'Mummy has never mentioned anything untoward. The

scandal was her affair with Nigel. What have you heard and from where?'

Her tone was sharp and I sidestepped her question. 'Booze and women,' I repeated. 'A deadly combination. I couldn't help but notice that the gallant Captain seemed as keen on you as he once was on your mother. The other day, in the bar, I saw you avoid his clutches with what looked like practised ease.'

'The other day was nothing. Captain Burnside was after me as soon as I'd turned sixteen.' Francesca smiled at the memory and fixed me with her dark eyes. 'The dirty old devil cornered me after a Christmas party at the club. I didn't believe that such an old man – he must have been all of thirty-five then – could be after me. I was naive, of course. I'd noticed his looks and his sly touches. Anyway, Nigel saw his chance, grabbed me and started kissing me – his tongue in my mouth. Yuk, I can still remember the stink of whisky and stale cigarettes.'

'Sounds like a truly romantic encounter.'

'His next move was a hand up my dress.'

'Well, you could fault his technique but not his ambition.'

'I dented his ambition. I kneed him where it hurts and ran for it.'

We both laughed and I said, 'The ladies of Shere Forest never seemed to object to his advances.'

'So I'm told. I guess his advances were more subtle than his attempt on my virtue and possibly his brand of well-oiled charm worked well on bored suburban housewives.'

Several waiters appeared to serve the main course and the wine waiter was punctilious in securing Francesca's approval of the Léoville-Barton.

With a chorus of Thank You Madams they eventually withdrew. The chef was on form: my rack of lamb was superb and perfectly complemented by puréed flageolets. This was the life. After several mouthfuls, I told Francesca about Rebecca Blair's temporary disappearance and her parents' fears that it had been the work of the Green Disciples. Francesca confessed a sneaking admiration for the group.

'They're uncompromising, they really believe in what they're doing. Do you think they'll campaign any more at Shere Forest?'

'It looks like it, after this morning's episode. Though the ironic thing is that I suspect Burnside knew something that might have stopped the new course anyway.'

'Chris, are we talking about the same man? In a few months, you've discovered hidden depths in Burnside that I never suspected and I've known him all my life. I really think you're way off beam. I know quite a bit about it. After all, my husband is the club's solicitor.'

'Henry the Sixth Part Two, act four.'

'What's that?'

'One of Shakespeare's many apt lines. "The first thing we do, let's kill all the lawyers."'

'I couldn't agree more,' she said with gusto. 'Nevertheless, you can bet your last share certificate that Simon has everything buttoned up tight with his chum, Slater. They make a nice pair. I wouldn't have backed boozy old Nigel against them.'

Just as I knew that Burnside had had important information about Peter Gresham's past, so was I convinced that he knew something relevant about the proposed takeover. Francesca didn't appear to be devoted to her husband, so I decided to approach the problem from that angle.

'Why is your husband so keen on the Shere Forest deal?' I asked.

'Because he loves deals. Business, business. Money, money.

That's all that motivates him. And he'll make a packet out of Shere Forest in the short and the long term.'

'Does he need the money?' I asked boldly.

'Yes. Losses at Lloyds, just like my brother Nick. They're both pretty desperate.'

'So you're pleased for them?'

'No, I'm not. They'll ruin Shere Forest. And I don't give a damn about Simon's business any more. It took me a few years to realise that money was just an end in itself for him. Deal followed deal. All those awful people we have to entertain – creeps like Mervyn Slater – all they can talk about is money.' Francesca took a hearty swallow of her wine and went on, 'So you see, if Simon gets his financial comeuppance, it really wouldn't bother me.'

'Surely your father would help him out?'

'My father is as mean as they come. No, the only way he'd help Simon is if I begged him to.'

'And would you?'

'No.' Francesca grinned cheerfully at me.

I learned nothing further about Burnside and his supposed secrets, but reflected that I knew exactly where she stood in the marital ranks. It seemed she would be happy to fall out and march smartly away.

We lingered over coffee for a while and Francesca told me something of her domestic life. With both of her children at boarding school and her husband away in the City throughout the week, her existence mirrored that of the typical suburban housewives whom she had earlier condemned.

She settled the enormous bill and to my disappointment said, 'I've got to drive home now, Chris. No time to visit your flat. In Putney, isn't it?' I nodded. 'Well, why don't you ask me over in the near future? How about next week? I'll ring you.'

I strolled with her to her car. We embraced briefly but enthusiastically and, as her car drew away into the traffic, I anticipated that good times lay ahead with the fetching Francesca Hanley.

Chapter 24

There was very little that Calvin and I could do during the first few days after the Classic Tournament. Shere Forest was in disarray as contractors moved in to dismantle the tents, the hospitality suites, the portable lavatories and all the other paraphernalia which attends a major sporting event.

A forlorn air affected the whole place. It was like the aftermath of a very good wedding. The club flag, at half-mast in memory of the late Secretary, seemed to embody the general mood.

Even Calvin Blair seemed rather wan when he appeared in the office, the day after his daughter's disappearance, later than usual.

'A good celebration?' I asked.

'Top notch, that's why my mouth tastes of old golf gloves.'

'Rebecca's OK?'

'As good as gold and I've got Jane back too.' He groaned gently. 'Now then, my most pressing need is a large mug of tea. I'm suffering from severe dehydration.'

Calvin busied himself with the kettle and the teapot and, just after he had taken the first satisfying swallow, the telephone rang. It was a short and one-sided conversation which required only a few grunts from Calvin.

He said, 'Gresham. He wants a meeting at eleven. Says it's important so you'd better come along, too. Perhaps he wants to offer one of us the job of Secretary.'

If Blair had seemed wan, Gresham's fleshy face looked long enough to trip over. He was sitting in the Secretary's office, his dog stretched out by the side of the desk. Hannibal's tail gave a couple of welcoming thumps on the carpet as we entered, but we ungratefully headed for the chairs furthest away from the animal.

Gresham came straight to the point. 'I've called you in, Blair, to tell you that the new course will go ahead as planned. The money is available. We're going into business with a property company. There'll be an announcement tomorrow.'

'Davina Holdings?' I asked.

Gresham grunted. I noticed that he couldn't bring himself to admit that it was a takeover.

'Mervyn Slater is taking Shere Forest over?' I prompted him.

'In a manner of speaking, yes,' Gresham muttered.

'But what about the members?' I asked. 'What about their EGM on Wednesday? Aren't they going to have their say?'

'They don't have a say in the finances of the club,' stated Gresham emphatically. 'Anyway the EGM has been put off, as a mark of respect to the late Secretary.' After what he felt to be an appropriately solemn pause, he continued briskly: 'Now, this is strictly confidential. I don't want any more leaks to the newspapers.'

Calvin Blair sat up, bristling with irritation. 'There were no leaks from *my* office, Peter. They came from your side of the fence.'

'Yes, yes,' Gresham replied. 'Poor Nigel never could hold a confidence.'

It was my turn to bristle. 'With respect, and especially to the late Secretary, I think the breach of confidence was nearer to home than that.'

While his finger probed deeply into an ear, Gresham looked fiercely at me for a moment and then his shadowed gaze slithered away past my right shoulder.

'I disagree, young man,' he said. 'That sort of carelessness was typical of Burnside. I should know, I'd worked with him for years. I'm not saying that he killed himself just because of that particular gaffe. No doubt there were other reasons. He was unstable, as I well knew.'

So that was the party line. I also noticed that Gresham couldn't bring himself to acknowledge Burnside as a friend; he had already been reduced to a former employee. How would Hermione react to that?

Gresham sat up straighter in his chair. 'Anyway, it's all water under the bridge. We've got a lot to do. We want to start building the new course as soon as possible. Is the design finished?'

Blair told him that the outline design had been completed months before but he had held back on the detailed drawings from which the contractor would work, until he received the final go-ahead.

'Slater wants the contractor to move in within a couple of weeks,' said Gresham.

'That's all right,' Calvin replied. 'I can stake out the line of the fairways and they can begin clearing the ground. In the meantime, the detailed drawings can be done.'

'Slater is anxious to know how long the whole project will

take. When will the new course be in play?'

Calvin sighed and said, 'You mean, how can we cut corners and make sure that he starts getting a return on his investment as soon as possible?'

Calvin gave Gresham a rapid summary of the building process. A lot of time and money would be spent clearing the ground for the teeing areas, the fairways and the greens. The bulldozers and other heavy machinery would move in.

'Everything must go. Trees, heather, bushes. Of course we'll save a lot of trees and replant them. And then we've got to go over the ground with a fine-toothed comb and take out all the roots, rocks and any other debris. No one wants to hit down with a seven-iron and find a small boulder in the way.'

Blair went through the whole process of shaping the contours of the course, the grading of the slopes, the drainage, the laying of the topsoil, the design of the irrigation system and the seeding process. 'And we're going to excavate a couple of lakes. In that way we can conserve water and recycle it. We can also use the earth we excavate on the course.'

'This is all very interesting, Blair.' Gresham didn't mean that and was getting impatient. 'But can you answer my question? How long?'

'It's difficult to be accurate.' Blair shook his head in the manner which plumbers and other tradesmen invariably use. At least he didn't suck his teeth. 'Even if the machinery turns up within a month or so, we've only got a few months before winter sets in. So we won't be ready to seed the course until the spring after next.'

'That's when Slater wants the course open for play,' Gresham said.

'Don't be bloody ridiculous,' Blair replied. 'If this was

Florida we might do it. No problems with winter weather and so on, and the growing season is much longer. But not in Britain, no way. It's just not on.'

Gresham drummed his fingers impatiently on the desk and the faithful Hannibal lifted his head in expectation of a walk, realised there was nothing doing and slumped back on the floor. His master spoke: 'Slater will provide whatever money is needed to finish by the required time. We have to take his wishes seriously.'

'And we have to take the new course seriously,' Blair said. 'I don't want to ruin what could be a great track for the sake of opening it prematurely. What do you think, Chris?'

'Well, if he provides enough machinery and they're on site within a month, with lots of other ifs, we might just have it ready to seed by May of next year, don't you think?' I said tentatively.

'Maybe,' said Blair. 'Of course we could buy turf for the tees and greens, rather than grow from seed. It's bloody expensive, but if he's got money to burn . . .'

'There are quite a few things in our favour,' I added. 'Not an enormous amount of tree clearance, hardly any rock and the soil is sandy.'

'Yes, it's great for growing grass, I agree,' said Blair.

'So you think it can be done?' asked Gresham.

'No,' Calvin said, 'but we'll give it a try. And you'd better tell Slater that he'll have to invest in some security.'

'What do you mean?' Gresham demanded.

Calvin produced a postcard from his pocket. In green ink there was a simple message: 'Don't even try to build the new course.'

'It's those confounded Green Disciples again,' Blair said. 'God knows what they'll do next.'

'Oh, they're just a minor nuisance,' Gresham said dismissively. 'The police will deal with their antics.'

'That'll be the day,' Calvin said. 'Chris, you and Max could lend a hand here. That girl must be made to see sense. Shere Forest isn't high profile – surely she can see that!'

I agreed with Calvin about Shere Forest's place in the environmental scheme of things. But I also guessed that the Green Disciples would not see it his way. However, I promised to try to talk to Jodie Hesse. It suited me rather nicely to have a legitimate reason for seeing her again . . .

Chapter 25

Max turned up on my doorstep that evening. He enthused about his trip to Scotland, mainly in terms of the golf on offer there, particularly at St Andrews. 'I managed to get on the Old Course, courtesy of one of the guys at the University. There's something magical there, I can see why everyone raves about it.'

'Not everyone. When Snead first saw it he asked a local the name of the old abandoned course he'd just seen from his train window.'

'I'll bet that went down well.'

'What did you score?'

'Seventy-four.'

'Off the back tees, I suppose, you bloody bandit.'

Max attempted a modest shrug but spoiled it by grinning widely at me. He was trying to teach me to play chess and, while he set up the chess board, I told him about the takeover of Shere Forest and of Calvin Blair's renewed fears about the Green Disciples. 'I hope to God that they'll lose interest in us,' I concluded.

'Don't hold your breath,' Max said emphatically. 'Now you've got Davina Holdings, a property company, in the driving seat. That's exactly what Jodie was on about. They'll have executive apartments all over Shere Forest before you can blink.'

'That's not the plan. Anyway, I want to talk to Jodie and get her to call the campaign off.'

'You can try but I think you'd be wasting your time. The Green Disciples aren't like normal pressure groups. They're not open to persuasion – they're revolutionaries. The best thing you can do is try to get a line on who's behind the movement. You probably won't succeed because I doubt whether even Jodie knows where the money and the policies come from. But you'll stand a better chance than me.'

'Why do you say that?'

'She thinks I'm frivolous and only interested in one thing.'

'And are you?'

'Sure, and so are you. Why don't you give her a ring?'

Jodie and I arranged to meet the following evening at a fringe theatre in Camberwell. She gave me the address and said: 'We'll have a meal afterwards. The theatre has a good vegetarian restaurant.'

It had to be vegetarian, of course. Although Jodie had a magnetic physical appeal I wondered if she was able to take an interest in anything other than the environment. And why was she so willing to see me? Did she fancy me? Doubtful. Did she view me as a potential convert to her cause? Even more doubtful. Or did she have some Machiavellian scheme in mind which would involve me . . . ?

Max asked me what we were going to see and I admitted that I didn't know. He delved into his briefcase and produced the current edition of *Time Out*. 'Let's see. The six o'clock performance at the Broken Rib Theatre.' He chuckled for several moments and my heart sank. 'You'll enjoy this. It's the musical version of *The Bone People* with an all-female cast.'

I sniggered reluctantly, then with an effort of will, tried to concentrate on the chess. Max was giving me the benefit of some advanced tuition; it was difficult, but it probably beat an evening at a fringe theatre.

The following afternoon I was hard at work checking paperwork for the new course when Toby Greenslade phoned to tell me that he'd been to the Davina Holdings press conference earlier in the day. 'It's all signed, sealed and delivered,' he boomed. 'Slater now owns most of the shares in Shere Forest, and he intends to develop it as an international golf centre.'

'God help the members,' I said.

'Quite. Slater looked like the cat who's just stuck his paw in a very rich vat of cream. Hanley and young Nick Gresham were wreathed in smiles, while old man Gresham looked as though he had the winning line on the football pools but had forgotten to post the coupon.'

'We've been told to move heaven and earth, mainly the latter, to get the new course ready in under two years. At least Slater will provide whatever money is needed.'

'He does seem to have coffers which are full to bursting. Maybe he should thank his first wife for her beneficence.'

'Tell me more.'

'You will recall my misgivings about Slater . . .'

'An unprincipled property spiv?'

'Precisely. I did some research, hacked through the newspaper reports and gossip columns from over a decade ago. Slater married an extremely rich woman, Davina Charlesworth. She inherited millions from a family trust and Slater married her in the mid-seventies. Davina looked lovely in their wedding photographs, but by the end of the seventies she was a heavy user of drugs and booze, in and out of various clinics. There are pictures of her in a headscarf and dark glasses looking like death warmed up – you know the kind of thing. Eventually the poor girl died of a drug overdose in about nineteen eighty and Slater copped several million quid in the will.'

'No children?'

'No.'

'So what?' I said. 'Is there a point to this story or are you just jealous?'

'The point is that there was a lot of criticism of Slater, both during and after the inquest.'

'He was bound to get it in the neck. A beautiful, rich wife who becomes a junkie . . .'

'That was one of the critical areas. Her family and friends claimed that she had never touched drugs before she married Slater. Not even an illicit puff of marijuana. She was straight.'

'And you believe that, do you? So what are you really suggesting, Toby? That Slater had a long-term plan to kill off his wife by drug abuse? It seems fanciful to me.'

'Almost Gothic, dear boy. But that was the implication of the press reports. Even more interesting were the comments of the coroner. He criticised Slater for not making sufficient efforts to save his wife's life.'

'What did he mean?'

'According to Davina's maid, who came in each day to clean and to cook an evening meal, she left her at around seven o'clock on the night of her death. Davina was in a cheerful mood, apparently, but had been drinking for most of the day.'

'You'd be cheerful too if you'd been on the electric soup all day.'

'Less frivolity, Chris,' Toby said, 'and pay attention. Mervyn Slater was out at a business dinner that evening and got home at one in the morning. The pathologist put Davina's death at around that time. She was found sprawled on the carpet in the main lounge, but Slater had noticed nothing untoward.'

'They used separate bedrooms, presumably?'

'Oh yes. But Slater was aware of her habits and yet he didn't check that she was OK. He didn't look in any of the downstairs rooms.'

'He went straight to bed?'

'Yes. It was the coroner's opinion that, if she had been found and prompt action taken, her life could've been saved. And the beak went on to say that anyone living with a drug user should take that elementary precaution of checking that they're OK before retiring for the night.'

'Was there an implication that Slater did a Nelson?'

'Yes. I can just imagine the selfish sod leaving the poor girl to die while he went off to bed.'

'You're not fond of our Mervyn, are you?'

'He was named Shit of the Year in *Private Eye*,' Toby said triumphantly.

'Oh well, that wraps it up. Hand me the black cap,' I said sarcastically. 'Mind you, I can think of better owners for a golf club.'

'An unscrupulous property yob with a decidedly murky past is what you've got,' Toby said judiciously.

'Maybe it's time to join the Green Disciples.'

Within minutes of that conversation, Francesca was on the phone, suggesting that we meet the following evening, take in a movie and then have supper at my place. I was more than happy to fall in with her plans, especially when she mentioned that her husband was abroad on business.

Chapter 26

Camberwell on a cool and cloudy June evening would not normally be high on my list for a night's entertainment. About a quarter of an hour before the performance began, I arrived at the theatre on my bike. It was the quickest way to travel and had the added bonus of showing my Green credentials.

The Broken Rib Cultural Centre was housed in what had once been a congregationalist chapel – a grim concrete edifice which resembled a scaled-down aircraft hangar. The vegetarian café occupied the front of the building; an eclectic collection of wooden tables, benches and chairs, no doubt culled from junk shops and car boot sales, was scattered around the room. Dozens of posters espousing political causes and minority rights were tacked to the walls, the 'Save the Planet' poster of the Green Disciples among them. The two skinny women behind the counter wore identical black smocks and had long black hair. One of them wore round granny glasses.

I glanced at the menu chalked on a blackboard: *Nutty Buckwheat Paté, Cream of Aduki Soup, Red Bean Goulash, Sweet Potato and Aubergine Africaine*. Luckily, I'd eat anything and there was no sign of the dreaded nut cutlet.

Jodie was easy to spot among the other customers. In her bright yellow jeans and mauve sweatshirt she cut a vivid figure among the predominantly black clothing. I hadn't seen so much long hair and so many beads since the seventies; it was like being whizzed back in time to a Pink Floyd concert.

Like Max, Jodie would have looked special in any surroundings: they both had a presence – 'charisma'. They'd make a lovely couple, I thought sentimentally, as I made my way towards her. Or rather, they wouldn't – not if *I* had anything to do with it.

Jodie introduced me to the group she was talking to with a vague, 'This is Chris, an old friend.' We were then summoned into the theatre.

The sparse audience distributed itself among the wooden chairs and narrow benches which faced a small makeshift stage. Before the show started I glanced nervously at my watch and wondered how long the performance would last.

Jodie noticed and whispered, 'Don't worry, the first act is only about forty minutes. We'll give it a try.'

It seemed a lot longer than that, almost as long as a Fidel Castro speech. I think he was mentioned in one of the songs but I wasn't sure because the heavy masks which were worn by the actors distorted their words. As far as I could tell the story was about man's oppression: of women, of blacks, of just about everyone. A surreptitious look around the audience told me that I was one of only three men there. I was glad I had Jodie to protect me.

Raucous cheers and applause greeted the curtain at the halfway mark. I applauded too – with joy that it had stopped.

'What do you think of it so far?' Jodie asked.

'Do you mind if I go home now?' I replied. 'I need to wash my hair tonight.'

Jodie smiled. 'I ought to support my sisters but I think I've

216

seen enough too. The message *is* a little heavy-handed. Let's go and eat.' Heavy-handed? I felt that I'd been bashed over the head with the hardback edition of *The Female Eunuch*.

I followed her to a corner table, my eyes roving over her body. She had a lilting swagger that made me want to grab her there and then. As we sat down, a square-faced woman, her heavy shoulders filling a dark blue donkey jacket, looked at me with evident contempt. I smiled back at her.

'Someone you know?' Jodie asked.

I shook my head. 'How does this place survive?'

'It probably won't much longer. The odd grant finds its way here but funding is difficult, so I'm told.'

'What about your benefactor at the Green Disciples? Perhaps he'd help.'

'I don't think he's interested in women's co-operative theatre groups.'

'What is he interested in?'

'We've had this conversation before, haven't we, Chris? We, the Green Disciples, want to save the planet from the havoc wreaked on it by man. Before it's too late.'

Here we go again. I said diplomatically, 'Yeah, I read *Silent Spring*.'

'That was written more than three decades ago. Can you imagine how much more damage has been done since then?'

'But do you think you can do anything against the big battalions, the international corporations, the governments?'

'It's our duty to try.'

'And anything goes if it helps you achieve your objectives?'

'Not at all. We're against violence.'

'Except in Brazil.'

Jodie looked down at the table and then hard at me. 'So Max

217

told you what happened. I had to defend myself, it was kill or be killed. When a maniac comes at you with a machete . . . Of course I regret it. It was a dreadful thing to happen.'

Jodie led the way to the counter and we collected our first course and a jug of water. My aduki soup was delicious.

There was no point in hanging back with Jodie. I said, 'You may be non-violent but you're not averse to engineering some major disruptions – like the mayhem at Shere Forest. Were you involved?'

'Not actively, no.'

'But you condone it?'

'Of course. Golf is one of the things we're against, on a world-wide scale. Where the needs of the environment and of deprived human beings conflict with big business – and golf is usually about big business – we go into battle.'

'Idealism is so wonderful to behold,' I said nastily. 'And idealists always make the best tyrants.'

'Very good, Chris. One of your own?'

'I can't claim it – Danton can. A perfect example of the whole grisly process. By the way, there aren't any deprived people in the vicinity of Shere Forest.'

'I daresay, but what we do there helps us to focus on the global problem.' Jodie listed a familiar catalogue of objections to golf courses: they take land and water, overuse pesticides and kill off the wildlife. I'd heard it so many times, especially from her. 'And this is all for the benefit of a few fat businessmen who want to play golf,' she concluded.

'Shere Forest isn't like that,' I said patiently. 'Our use of fertiliser and pesticide will be minimal and we'll conserve our water and recycle it. Come on, we're an exception. This isn't Thailand. Can't you call these people off? We don't want any more disruption. The course will be built whatever you do about it.'

'We'll see. You talk a very good environmental game, Chris, but the course is now owned by Mervyn Slater, a property dealer. We'll see how long your good intentions last once he gets his hooks into the prey. He'll want to make money at Shere Forest, lots of it, and screw the cost to the environment.'

I had a gloomy premonition that Jodie might be right but I wanted to get her off the subject of golf and try to find out more about the Green Disciples. I asked her why she had become involved with them.

The second course was now in front of us and she finished her mouthful of food before replying. 'I thought they represented a bit of hope in a sick and uncaring world. They were prepared to fight hard for what they believed in. I suppose it was a stark contrast to my father. He only believed in money, as much of it as he could get his grubby hands on.'

'I gather that you're somewhat anti-business,' I said mildly.

'True, but my father was in a particularly unpleasant business. God knows why my mother married him. She told me that he was once handsome and charming. They met when he was in the British Army. He was one of the occupying forces in Germany.'

'This all sounds a bit Freudian to me. What did he do when he left the Army?'

'Used his contacts to set up in the arms-dealing business. I hated everything he stood for. He sold arms to anyone who'd buy them.' Jodie looked at me with deep despair in her lovely eyes.

'So you became a pacifist . . .'

'Every kind of "ist". And I reverted to my mother's name.'

'Where's your father now?'

219

'Dead. Killed by an explosion in Bosnia last year. Ironic, isn't it, that he probably supplied the instrument of his own death.'

With one of those leaps of intuition that occasionally enlivens the mind I said, 'And I suppose Daddy's ill-gotten gains are now at the disposal of the Green Disciples.'

'Don't be crazy. My mother inherited the money and she gave it away. She's a rich woman in her own right.'

'Wouldn't it be just if the money helped your own good cause?'

'No. It's from a tainted source.'

'So who puts up the money for the Green Disciples? Somebody must. You don't go in for raffles and door-to-door collections.'

Jodie called for a bill, pulled some money out of her pocket and said: 'I've no idea where the funds come from. The Green Disciples have become a successful pressure group because lots of local cells united for the cause. There isn't some Mr Big at the centre, that's not how we work.'

I didn't believe her but there was clearly no future in belabouring the point. We paused at the door and I was more relieved than disappointed when Jodie told me that she had to go on to a meeting. My ambitions to get into bed with her had been tempered by her obsession with the problems of the environment. For all her beauty and intelligence, she was hard work.

Nevertheless, a glimpse inside her house would have been beneficial; it might have revealed some useful information about her and the Green Disciple movement. I also wondered what the meeting was about. I considered following her – but then abandoned the idea as impractical. Just as well, as a few minutes later, a motorbike roared past me; Jodie's bright yellow jeans were unmistakable on the pillion and I also recognised the driver's donkey jacket.

On the ride home I wondered what made Jodie Hesse tick and in the end put her down as a blinkered radical. I admired her dedication and her courage but wished she'd leaven it with more humanity. I also wished that she'd leave Shere Forest alone.

It occurred to me that the Green Disciples' benefactor could well be Jodie Hesse herself.

The following evening spent in Francesca's company was a lot less taxing and much more entertaining. The local cinema's offering of a racy French cops-and-robbers drama was funnier than *The Bone People* – and when we returned to my flat, Francesca left me in no doubt about the further entertainment she had in mind. She was certainly an enthusiast. It was a lot of fun and I looked forward to more.

Chapter 27

At Shere Forest the pressure was already being firmly applied to Calvin Blair to get the new course ready on time. It brought me a bonus since Blair asked me to work there on a full-time basis from now on until the course was finished.

The new owner, Mervyn Slater, made his presence felt in many ways. Plans to refurbish and extend the clubhouse were rushed through and an army of builders appeared on the scene to do his bidding.

We were among the first to feel the force of his ambitions when we were summoned to a meeting, not in the Secretary's office, which had already been ripped apart by the builders, but in the committee room. This was a lovely room, with oak-panelled walls and a magnificent collection of antique golf clubs on the walls. I didn't like to speculate how much they would make at auction, especially if there were some Japanese bidders present.

Slater rose from behind the polished elm table to greet us, and offered us some coffee, which immediately put him well ahead of Peter Gresham in the courtesy stakes. I had only seen him from a distance in the sponsor's dining room at the Classic and now registered his pallor and the dark rings around his eyes. As for that wispy gingery beard . . . How on earth had he managed to capture a beautiful woman like Davina Charlesworth? She'd been extremely rich, what's more. Where, oh where did I go wrong?

As Slater went quickly through the logistics of building the new course, it was clear that he had mastered its basics. He listened intently to Calvin's views on where time could be saved and said, 'The clearing of the course seems to be the first priority, doesn't it? You'll have all the machinery you need on site in ten days.'

He poured more coffee for all of us and continued, 'Whatever you need, Calvin, you shall have it – within reason. You come straight to me.' He handed a card to Blair. 'That's my direct phone line. If I'm not there, my assistant will find me.'

Whatever my misgivings, Slater talked a good match and he certainly went a long way towards getting Calvin on his team when he said, 'I believe in incentives, Calvin. There's a twenty-five grand bonus if you do your stuff and we open on time. I'll send you a letter to that effect.'

The bulldozers arrived in six days, not ten, enough of them to clear the site for a new town.

Calvin and I had worked to all hours to mark out the new fairways, hammering white-painted stakes into the ground at intervals of about fifty feet. Even with the extra help which Calvin brought in, it was bitterly hard work. In addition, we marked the trees on the edges of the fairways, those which were to remain and those which would eventually be uprooted and replanted.

By the time the construction crews arrived, the first six holes on each half of the course had been marked out. The plan was to begin clearing both the first and the tenth holes at the same time.

With several huge machines in action it was like being in the middle of a major land battle. The juggernauts crashed through the heather and scrub and swept all before them. The debris was piled up at intervals and I began to see the size of the disposal problem. The rubbish was burned and with great care: the last thing we wanted was a fire raging out of control in the Berkshire countryside.

Calvin saw me eyeing one of the piles of wood and scrub and said, 'I hope the Green Disciples don't strike now. If they dropped some matches in the wrong place they could do untold harm.'

'Surely they wouldn't do that,' I replied. 'That would be environmentally unsound.'

But strike they did – and the first salvo of their new campaign against Shere Forest was rather more subtle than arson.

About a week after the clearing had begun, Calvin and I were following the bulldozers' trail down the first fairway. Hearing the roar of one of the machines to our left beyond a rise in the ground, Calvin looked puzzled. 'What's going on over there?' he said. 'That's not a fairway.'

We ran up the slope to our left and saw a bulldozer churning its way through the undergrowth. A couple of small trees went down with a tearing snap and a crash. I heard Blair screaming at the driver to stop – in vain because, apart from the noise of the machine, the man was wearing protective ear-muffs.

We ran down the slope on the other side and Calvin waved his arms frantically in front of the bulldozer. 'Be careful,' I shouted uselessly. I wondered whether the driver, high up in his cabin and concentrating on shifting the undergrowth, would see him. He did, thank God, and switched his engine off.

'Christ, boss,' he said, 'I could've killed you. What's the problem?'

'The problem is that this isn't going to be a fucking fairway,' Calvin fumed. 'Who sent you out here?'

'The foreman. Look, there are the stakes. This is the second hole, isn't it?'

He was right. The stakes stretched away into the distance. 'They've been tampered with,' I said quietly. 'Let's go and see what else they've done.' I didn't need Calvin's muttered curses about the Green Disciples to tell me who was responsible.

The stakes which marked several of the new holes had been removed, but only two holes had been repositioned. Not a lot of harm had been done but valuable time was lost while we put matters right. Our hearts sank at having to mark out the holes all over again.

'I quite liked the shape of their second hole,' I remarked to Calvin in a meagre attempt at humour.

His initial glare turned reluctantly into a tight-lipped smile and he said, 'Sorry, Chris, I can't see the funny side. Just in case they try the same trick again, we'd better take some precautions.'

'I doubt they'll pull the same stunt twice.'

'Nevertheless, we'll mark the edges of the fairways with whitewash. A container each, on our backs. I'll get it sorted out tomorrow.'

On the Friday morning Max turned up and viewed our progress with great interest. While he played nine holes, I piled into numerous tasks which all seemed to have the same priority: immediate action. It was a relief when my brother insisted on visiting the local pub for lunch. Calvin and I had got into the habit of grabbing a sandwich and a cup of tea at midday instead of taking a proper break.

The landlord, Edgar, was as welcoming as ever and the excellence of his partner's cooking had not wavered.

We sat in a corner and Max told me that he would be in town for a few days. At first I thought his presence in my spare bedroom might pose a problem, as Francesca had promised to visit me that evening and no doubt she wanted to be as discreet as possible about our liaison. To my relief he said, 'I'll move in tomorrow, if that's all right.'

'What are you up to tonight?'

'I met a nice young lady on the train with a flat in Knightsbridge. I have a pressing invitation to visit.' He grinned at me. 'Talking of crumpet, how are you getting on with the beautiful Jodie?'

'Not as well as you're getting on with Knightsbridge ladies on trains.'

'Oh, this'll be a one-night stand, that's all. Her American husband's due back tomorrow. Anyway, you like Jodie, don't you?'

'Yes, but don't tell Calvin. The Disciples struck again last week.' I explained how they'd rerouted some of the holes.

'Clever, aren't they?' he said. 'But it doesn't sound like Jodie's style to me.'

'Why not?'

'She's a lot more serious than that. There's an element of humour in pulling up a few stakes and redesigning a golf course.'

'Yes, Jodie *is* a bit short in the humour department,' I agreed. 'Idealists often are. I'm crossing my fingers that the

Green Disciples won't become more than a minor irritation. We can cope with that.'

'You're underestimating them, Chris. They can be very heavy. Their creed of non-violence is just a veneer. And I'll show you just how they can operate when they want to. Tomorrow.'

'What's happening?'

'You know the new road south of Swindon that's going to cut through Marlborough Downs?' I did because the controversy over its route had dragged on for over a year. The conservationists were furious that its four lanes had been planned to run right through a noted beauty spot rich in wildlife. In the end, the Secretary of State for Transport had got his way and all objections had been overruled.

Max continued, 'The bulldozers are scheduled to make inroads into a particularly beautiful part of the Downs tomorrow. A big demo is planned, with all the usual groups, including our buddies the Green Disciples.'

'Will Jodie be there?'

'I don't know, but you can bet she's involved. It's going to be really big. And you'll see what that young lady and her chums can do when they mean business. I'll be at your flat at eight o'clock in the morning.'

Chapter 28

In an effort to get Francesca out of my flat well before Max's arrival, I set the alarm for seven o'clock. A languorous early morning cuddle turned into more urgent lovemaking, however, and Francesca made it to her car only a few minutes before eight o'clock.

But Max was late anyway and he arrived wearing some old jeans, a bedraggled Led Zeppelin T-shirt and a sleeveless sweater. He stopped me shaving and made me change into the oldest clothes I could find. 'We're going to a demo,' he said, 'not the Sunningdale foursomes.'

An hour later we parked the car in a field somewhere south of Swindon. It was already crowded with all manner of transport, from large buses to mini-vans and mopeds. A man and a woman were doing a brisk trade in bacon sandwiches and hot coffee from a van near the entrance. We paid our money and sampled both.

Banners and placards of all shapes and sizes proclaimed the allegiances of the demonstrators. Many of them belonged to a group called Swindon Socialists Against Motorway Madness and there were lots of SAM T-shirts to be seen. They seemed to be well organised, with their own stewards identified by armbands. There were family groups among them; young children clinging to their mothers' arms, babies in buggies and a number of dogs. With all the good-natured babble, the chants and the occasional song, there was more of the atmosphere of a carnival than of a serious demonstration among the SAM supporters.

In contrast to them, we saw smaller knots of demonstrators who looked far from good-natured. Much more vociferous with their chanting, they didn't have any children with them and few seemed older than their thirties. They looked as though they were there for serious business.

Max grabbed my arm and pointed out some tough-looking customers who carried anti-hunting placards. 'What the hell are hunt saboteurs here for?'

'Trouble.'

'You bet. Let's watch ourselves, this could turn very nasty.'

From the far end of the field a man with a loudhailer addressed us: 'Welcome to you all and especially the members of SAM. We're about to move off. The site of the demo is less than half a mile away. We are going there to make a peaceful and orderly protest. We will conduct ourselves with dignity, whatever the provocation. OK, let's go.'

'Some bloody chance,' muttered Max as we joined the tail end of a group. So far, it had been remarkably civilised. I'd almost expected the man with the loudhailer to wish us all a nice day.

After only a few minutes' walk we began to hear the chants of the demonstrators who were already in position. When we cleared the brow of a slight hill we suddenly saw the entire tableau stretched out before our eyes. I can still see the whole scene, frozen at that moment in my mind's eye, and still cannot reconcile it with the chaos that was to follow.

Like opposing armies, the two groups faced each other: on

the right the solid body of demonstrators and to the left the ranks of bulldozers and trucks with a few dozen workmen behind them. On each side of the machines were phalanxes of policemen, equally divided between those on horseback and those on foot. Most of the latter carried riot shields and long batons.

A group of policemen around the two leading earthmovers seemed to be grappling with several other people by the front of the vehicles.

'What's going on, Max?' I asked, and my brother produced a pair of miniaturised binoculars from his pocket.

'A couple of women are chained to each bulldozer. The police have got some heavy-duty cutters at work. Whoops, that's numbers one and two freed.'

As the two struggling women were carried away to one of many police vans parked 100 yards to the rear, the yelling and chanting grew louder. The leader of the SAM group shouted through his loudhailer again and told his supporters to walk down and join the back of the demonstration. 'Keep together,' he yelled, 'no violence. Obey the stewards.'

'Some bloody chance,' Max repeated. 'Come on, let's get a bit closer.' We followed the Swindon Socialists down the hill and stayed on the fringes. There seemed to be well over 1000 demonstrators.

The other two women were cut free from the bulldozer tracks. 'Green Disciples,' Max muttered in my ear. 'It's one of their tactics.' As they were dragged off, one woman broke free and ran for it, only to be brought down by a rugby tackle from a large and determined policeman.

The demonstrators surged forward and, despite the efforts of the stewards, the front line began to buckle under the pressure from behind.

'Get the bastards!' came the cry from the tightly packed ranks. Groups of demonstrators broke away from the crowd, the hunt saboteurs among them.

The police anticipated the attack. The officers on foot formed a solid line in front of the bulldozers as the demonstrators ran towards them. For a moment, as they locked shields, the policemen resembled the 'tortoise' formation used by Roman soldiers during a battle.

Max pulled me away so that we were further up the hill and safely out of the mêlée. 'We'll stay out of this,' he said. 'It isn't our fight. You can bet that the people who want a punch-up are Green Disciples and hunt saboteurs.'

We heard the voice of one of the senior policemen boom out: 'Please disperse in an orderly fashion. Please disperse.'

It was a waste of breath. The demonstrators who were leading the charge launched themselves at the police. From our vantage point it looked like an unequal contest: demonstrators with little in the way of weapons except banners, fists and whatever they had in their pockets against well-equipped policemen. Subsequent newspaper accounts of the brawl suggested that those pockets were filled with Stanley knives, knuckledusters, coshes and an assortment of other offensive weapons. Such evidence supported Max's theory that there were plenty of hard-bitten *agents provocateurs* in the crowd, and that a high proportion of them were Green Disciples.

At a given signal, the mounted policemen moved in from the flanks to break up the crowd. The skirmish didn't last long as the weight of the horses and the well-tried tactics of the riot police took their toll. The mounted policemen pursued some skirmishers back towards their original positions. Intent on a measure of revenge, one officer, his baton swinging, galloped after three men who were fleeing in our direction. But one of the protestors, cool and determined, turned and grabbed the rider's leg and hauled him off his horse. As he went down, the other demonstrators laid into him with their boots.

'Come on,' I said, 'let's even the odds up a bit.' We took two of the men out of the fray with shoulder charges. Max rapped the third man hard in the stomach and he lost interest in the fight. The well-trained horse was standing quietly nearby and we gave the policeman a leg-up onto its back.

As we scrambled further up the hill we saw a few demonstrators, some of them bleeding from head wounds, being led off to the police vans.

The senior police officer once again asked everyone to disperse and some of the protestors, especially frightened family groups, began to straggle away.

'I suppose it could've been a lot worse,' I said. 'It'll still make *News at Ten* no doubt.' The press and television people were there in force.

Max nodded and had just said that we might as well leg it back to the car park when we heard the high-pitched sound of all-terrain vehicles approaching in low gear. There were six of them and they ground their way towards the scene.

'Police reinforcements?' I asked Max.

'I doubt it. No markings.'

The trucks stopped about twenty yards short of the line of police horses and, as several policemen walked towards the drivers, all hell broke out.

Men leapt out of the back of each truck, ran a few yards and then hurled a variety of smoke bombs, thunderflashes and other explosives at the police horses.

The creatures reared and plunged in terror, and many of their riders were thrown from their saddles. I saw one policeman being dragged along, his foot trapped in his stirrup.

That was the first wave of the assault and it was followed by the pop of tear-gas canisters. Max grabbed me, shouting, 'Let's get going! This is bloody dangerous.'

By the time we'd run a couple of hundred yards, the police were in disarray and in retreat. The demonstrators had wasted no time in making a run for it, either, in the other direction.

Their work done, the all-terrain vehicles had churned their way to safety, bearing their victorious passengers with them. It had been an efficient and cold-blooded piece of disruption which had the character of Jodie Hesse stamped all over it.

But the ordeal of the police was by no means over. Their efforts to regroup were hindered by eyes streaming from the effects of the tear gas and the jumpy state of the horses. For all their training, the animals were not keen on thunderflashes and smoke bombs. Neither was I.

Most of the demonstrators had taken the opportunity to leave the field of battle, but a few were taunting the police, throwing stones and clods of earth at them. Just as the police seemed to have things under control again we heard the drone of powerful engines overhead. Three helicopters appeared in the sky.

'Christ! Hold on to your hat,' Max said. 'There's more action to come.'

'It looks like something out of *Apocalypse Now*,' I joked nervously.

'Without the Wagner.'

It wasn't napalm and high explosive which rained down on the police but more of the same recently dished out from the all-terrain trucks. The noise from the helicopters was staggering enough as they swooped low over the scene and discharged a second helping of thunderflashes and smoke bombs on the hapless officers.

The aircraft veered away, soared high into the sky, circled and then made another run at the enemy below.

'I wonder what's coming next?' I said to Max. 'More tear gas?'

A deluge of liquid fell on the police ranks and it didn't take long for our noses to tell us what it was. The poor bastards were covered in a blanket of stinking liquid manure.

'Right – that's it. We're out of here,' I said with feeling.

We turned to make the rest of the journey up the hill to the car park, as the leading helicopter made one last pass over the police, who were fruitlessly trying to wipe the evil-smelling substance from their uniforms.

A banner trailed beneath the machine and it read: *'Eat shit, fascist scum – guaranteed organic!'*

'You've got to give them the credit for a sense of humour,' Max said.

'I don't suppose the er, "filth" are laughing. Will they be able to trace the helicopters?'

'Hired, I suppose, probably from the airport in Bristol. Paid for in cash, no names, so it'll be a dead end for the fuzz.'

'Whoever's behind this, they're real pros,' I said.

'Typical of the Green Disciples. They must've spent thousands on this little jaunt. Helicopters and go-anywhere vehicles don't come cheap.'

We toiled up the rest of the hill in the company of a man who had clearly been in the thick of the encounter. His clothes were coated with mud and he was holding a stained and dirty handkerchief to his left cheek.

'Are you OK?' I asked. 'Here, use this.' I offered him my own clean handkerchief.

'No, it's all right, mate,' he said. 'I'll be home soon. Anyway, it's only a bit of a cut. Bastard policeman. I gave him a bloody good kicking anyway.'

'Who were you with?' Max asked. 'SAM or the Green Disciples?'

The man grinned. 'Nah – I'm only here for a bit of fun, like. Couldn't give a toss about the bleedin' motorway. But a bloke give me and me mates a century each to cause a bit of aggro. In cash, like.'

'Who was he?' I asked. He shrugged. 'What did he look like?'

'What's it to you? You the fuzz or what?' he asked aggressively.

'No, the press,' Max lied smoothly. 'And we want to do a good story. So where did this character spring from?' He produced a twenty-pound note, handed it over and the man's tongue was magically loosened.

'Oh, 'e was in the pub, like. We're all out of work, and an 'undred quid's an 'undred quid, innit?'

'How many of you?'

'There's 'alf a dozen of us. But 'e found a lot more lads in the other pubs.'

We had reached the car park and parted company. Max thanked him and told him to have a drink on us.

'The Disciples really went to town, didn't they?' my brother mused. 'Rent-a-mob must have cost them another few grand. Now you can see why I told you not to underestimate them. Green Disciples are big trouble.'

'Do you think Jodie is putting up the money?'

'I'm not sure. Could be – but I get the feeling that whereas she really believes in the environmental cause, whoever planned today's little set-to has much nastier motives.'

'Disruption of society – that kind of caper?'

'Yes. There's some nutter behind it, I think.'

'And he or she is obviously loaded. Money no object.'

'And well organised and sophisticated.'

'I'd like to know more about him – or her,' I said, 'and I bet Jodie could tell me, if she wanted to.'

'I wouldn't be too sure,' Max replied, as we backed the car out and turned towards the exit. 'A bit of pillow talk might have been helpful. On the other hand, she may not even know who he or she is.'

'She's a tough nut to crack in every sense,' I sighed. 'What about your old pals in the Intelligence business, Max? Can't they tell us anything?'

'They might – I'll have a try. In the meantime, I suggest we get well away from our comrades in arms. I suspect that the police will try and stop anyone who remotely looks as if they had anything to do with the morning's entertainment. Let's head east on the minor roads and get well clear.'

Chapter 29

The media feasted on 'The Battle of Marlborough Downs', as one newspaper dubbed it. Both of the national television news programmes showed extensive footage of the incident and, even on the small screen, it looked spectacular. The usual talking heads were asked for their reactions. While those of one political persuasion placed the blame for the confrontation on the police and condemned them for their 'brutality', their opponents pointed to 'a sinister Leftist conspiracy'.

A particularly vehement denunciation of 'the extremists in our society' was made by backbench Conservative MP Julius Sparkes. A familiar figure on the television screen, he usually popped up when law-and-order issues were in the news. He was decidedly one of the flog-'em-and-hang-'em brigade. On this occasion he told the nation that the fracas had been politically inspired and that he was pressing the Home Secretary to introduce more drastic punishments for those guilty of violence at such demonstrations.

A tall and powerful-looking man, Sparkes was a remarkably effective speaker; in a gravelly voice, he spoke his mind in a direct, almost abrupt style. The House of Commons and national television were not his only soapboxes. Sparkes owned a conglomerate which numbered among its assets an advertising agency, a commercial radio station, a string of provincial newspapers and an organisation called TripleVision. In turn TripleVision owned a television franchise, a satellite station and a production company. Sparkes was in the communications business in a big way and understood how it worked. I knew his company well from my days in the City when many of our clients had invested heavily in it.

Tantalised though I was by the mystery that surrounded the Green Disciples, I knew I would have very little time to devote to solving it. The work on the new course was making increasingly heavy demands on my time. I was also honest enough with myself to acknowledge that much of the fascination of the Disciples lay with the puzzling personality of Jodie Hesse.

On the Sunday morning after the demonstration Max and I went for a long run together around Richmond Park. It was good to have company as we blew the cobwebs away from mind and body, and we were looking forward to a few drinks with Mrs Bradshaw, who liked a tipple or two before her Sunday lunch.

On our return, Max suggested I should ring up Jodie. 'Congratulate her on the demo. Go on – flatter her. You never know, she might open up and tell us something.'

Conscious as I was of Jodie's self-contained and wary personality, Max's suggestion seemed overly optimistic. However, Jodie was in when I rang, and I jumped into the conversation with both feet. 'Loved the demo at Marlborough Downs,' I began. 'Would you call it a successful venture?'

There was a moment's silence and I heard Jodie's quiet laugh. She said, 'I think we made our point, don't you?'

'Great coverage from the media. But you won't stop the road going through.'

'Not this one, but we're putting our message across. We're

showing the public that we care.'

'You don't seem to care much about the poor old police. We were there, Jodie, someone could've been badly injured.'

'You're not telling me that you have any sympathy for the police, are you? They're just the agents of capitalism, and they deserve everything they get.'

'They're human beings, I know that. What if one of them had been killed – or one of the demonstrators? There were women there with young children.'

'All the better, Chris. We'd have got even more publicity.'

'You're not serious?'

'This isn't a game,' Jodie said harshly. 'The future of our planet is at stake! I'm prepared to fight for that future along with lots of other people. We don't need more roads, more cars, more pollution. We need *less*. We've got to get back to a simpler economy.'

'I'm not so sure that you're putting that message over,' I said. 'You spent an awful lot of money yesterday and yet the majority opinion classes you as hooligans. Will your backer be pleased with the result?'

'He takes the long view, like me.'

'I just hope his patience and his money don't run out.'

Jodie retorted, 'He's extremely rich and extremely caring. He'll keep on putting our case until it sinks in.'

'I'd like to meet him,' I replied. 'Does he live in England?'

'Very funny, Chris. Now I must go, I've got to catch a plane. Let's meet in a couple of weeks and continue this fascinating conversation.'

Jodie's sarcasm was clear but I pretended to take it at face value and said that I'd like to see her again, soon. The trouble was that I meant it.

'That didn't seem very productive,' Max said.

'No. All I learned was that the Green Disciples are backed by a very rich and powerful man.'

'Wow – that really gets us a long way, doesn't it,' Max said sarcastically.

Calvin took more than a passing interest in the Battle of Marlborough Downs, but I didn't let him know that I'd actually been present. He was more than ever convinced that the Green Disciples would make further attempts to sabotage the new course. Having seen them in action, I agreed, although I tried to calm his anxieties by saying that the Disciples now had more important considerations than Shere Forest. Nevertheless, I backed up his request for improved security. True to his promise to provide whatever was needed, Mervyn Slater made no objections and extra men were drafted in to patrol Shere Forest around the clock.

With the death of Nigel Burnside, new administrators employed by Davina Holdings moved into Shere Forest, and it wasn't long before they made their presence felt. The first cold draught of the new commercial climate took the form of a letter to the members. A copy of it was posted on the main notice board in the clubhouse and it set out in great detail how the many improvements were to be paid for.

On the way to a meeting with Peter Gresham, Calvin and I stopped to read the letter. The first, most predictable change was the proposed increase in members' subscriptions. I did a quick calculation and said to Calvin: 'Subscriptions more than doubled as from April next year. Slater'll have a riot on his hands.'

'So what? He wouldn't give a damn if there was a mass

exodus. In fact, he'd welcome it. New members have to stump up a hefty entrance fee as well as the first year's subscription. That would be great for Slater's cash flow. And we both know he could fill the membership list several times over without any trouble.'

Calvin flicked over to the second page and said: 'Here's the really interesting bit.' I peered over his shoulder at the paragraph headed 'Company Debentures'.

'It is proposed to create a new class of Debenture Holder. Up to a maximum of fifty companies will be invited to purchase a ten-year Debenture for the sum of £750,000. This will entitle each company to nominate ten members a year and to hold a company golf day each year.'

'If Slater sells even fifty of those,' I commented, 'he'll cover his investment in Shere Forest several times over. Very clever.'

'He'll sell them all right,' Calvin replied. 'No bother. Those are aimed at Japanese companies, who'll snap them up. Three-quarters of a million is about what they pay at home just to get into a golf club. It's chicken feed.'

'Did you see the sting in the tail, though? They not only get a company golf day per year but the debenture holders are granted priority tee times at the weekend and on certain other days.'

'The members will go potty. Second-class citizens. I can hear the comments already.'

'And you know how slowly the Japanese play golf. The five-hour round will be the norm.' I had to grin.

'They'll probably have a sushi bar and Sapporo beer on draught,' Calvin said, po-faced.

'Is this the end of civilisation as we know it?' I asked.

'As near as dammit,' Calvin responded sadly.

Throughout June and the early part of July I'd been checking the results of American tournaments for Richie Riley's name. He appeared consistently in the top thirty or so, most notably in the Western Open when he finished in eighth place. I wondered whether he would bother to come over for the Open; it was a daunting and expensive undertaking to travel to Britain to try to qualify.

In the week before the Open began I had a call from Riley who confirmed that he was arriving in Britain in a couple of days for the qualifying event.

'I'm gonna make it, Chris,' he said confidently, 'and I want you there with me. I can't tackle St Andrews without you.'

I promised to be there on the Tuesday of the Open if he qualified. 'No ifs, Chris baby,' he said ebulliently. 'Just be there.'

Chapter 30

Richie Riley was as good as his self-confident word and qualified easily for the Open. I left London at first light on the Tuesday of Open Championship week to meet him at St Andrews.

As I headed north in my old and faithful Porsche the sky brightened and so did my anticipation of the next few days. I had been working long hours at Shere Forest and was looking forward to a change of scene; the Open fitted the bill perfectly. It is the most spectacular of all the major golf championships and takes on a special aura when it is held at the home of golf, St Andrews.

As usual, I had arranged to stay with Toby Greenslade. He and some of his press cronies had hired a house not far from the course. A few days in such company was hard on the constitution, since they kept late hours and full glasses, but it was infinitely preferable to paying outlandish sums of money to rent a broom cupboard.

My first practice round with Riley was not a propitious one because he could not believe the directions in which I told him to aim his shots. The key to a successful round at St Andrews is to navigate your way through the bunkers which lie in wait on nearly every hole. Some of their names are enough to make ordinary golfers tremble: Hell, Coffin and Grave for example.

Severe retribution awaits inaccurate shots.

During that first round Riley saw more sand than Lawrence of Arabia; his wedge must have been red hot. On the dreaded fourteenth hole he hooked his ball into the Beardies, hacked it out, hit it well over the cavernous Hell bunker but landed in the Ginger Beer bunkers at the front of the green. So it went on, but he kept smiling and I hoped that his self-confidence would survive.

He fared much better on the following day when he dared to believe in the seemingly eccentric lines I gave him. We finished the day with a long session on the practice ground and I was impressed by his range of short approach shots. With justifiable pride he demonstrated his pitch-and-run, punch and cut-up shots; all essential strokes for links golf.

Riley was drawn to play his first round in the Open at just after eleven o'clock; nobody likes to start at the beginning or end of the day. I didn't know either of his partners – a qualifier from Japan with an unpronounceable name and a Swede who was in his first year on the European Tour. Even though the fairway, which is shared between the first and the eighteenth holes, is remarkably generous in width, it was a far from relaxing moment for the three players. They were about to hit their first shots in the Open Championship in the lee of the most illustrious clubhouse in golf. But they all acquitted themselves well, and Riley hit a very long drive down the middle of the fairway. The second shot, over the Swilcan Burn, to a hole cut on the front of the green was an unnerving prospect but the players sensibly took no chances. They put their balls beyond the flag and settled for par fours.

With very little wind to protect it, St Andrews had its teeth drawn and Riley was three under par at the turn. Another visit into the Beardies cost him a shot at the fourteenth but he retrieved his mistake with a birdie at the next hole. A rasping drive at the sixteenth sent his ball over the Principal's Nose, a set of three bunkers, but it finished in an insidious pot bunker, called Deacon Sime, about thirty yards further on. That meant another dropped shot but Riley negotiated the famous Road Hole safely and finished with another birdie at the final hole. An opening round of 69 in his first Open was a splendid start.

When I woke up on the following morning to hear the wind whining and opened the curtains to see the clouds racing across the sky, I knew that the young American golfer would have to play the round of his life to record a similar score. I hoped that Riley's ability to manufacture bump-and-run shots along the twisting terrain of the Old Course would stand up to a stiff examination later in the day.

Toby did not conceal his delight when he saw the change in the weather. 'This'll sort the men out from the boys. This is proper Open weather. Let's hope it blows right through to Sunday night.'

'You're a sadist, Toby. It's all right for you, sitting comfortably in the press tent. It'll be no fun out there, either for the golfers or the spectators.'

'The Open isn't meant to be fun. It's supposed to be the ultimate test of a golfer's technique and of his bottle. That's why only those with the very best credentials ever win it. Nonentities have very rarely won the Open, in contrast to the American version, by the way, and that piffling PGA Championship. And they've got the nerve to call it a major!' Toby snorted in his indignation.

'Come on, Toby, the PGA has a marvellous tradition . . .'

'Had,' he interrupted me, 'when it was a matchplay

tournament. Now it's just another strokeplay event, usually played at some hopelessly unsuitable course in the wilds and with hardly any non-American players. Days like this are what championship golf is all about, especially here at St Andrews.'

'I don't suppose Richie Riley would agree with you,' I said, as I refilled his mug with tea.

'I'm sure he wouldn't and I'll bet you a tenner that he doesn't break seventy-eight in this wind.'

It was a shrewd wager but I won it, partly because the wind eased slightly in the afternoon when Riley began his round. It was desperately hard labour, especially for the American who had rarely encountered such conditions. I cajoled him into hitting low, running shots in an effort to counteract the effects of the wind. He stuck courageously to the unfamiliar task and, despite one or two bad holes, he completed his round in seventy-six strokes. At one over par for the two rounds, he was eight shots behind the leaders but qualified comfortably for the rest of the Championship.

In contrast, his two playing partners lost their composure in the fierce conditions and made early exits from the Championship.

Toby Greenslade was rarely able to concede a bet outright and, having grumbled about the very small improvement in the afternoon's playing conditions, he bet me another £10 that Richie Riley would not finish in the top thirty-five in the tournament. Since just over seventy players had qualified for the final two rounds it was a reasonably fair proposition.

When we set off on the following day, we were accompanied by a tall strong American player called Billy Joe Horton, yet another product of the college golf production line.

Richie hardly filled me with confidence about my bet when he dumped his second shot at the opening hole into the Swilcan

Burn. It unsettled him and a very poor shot into Cheape's bunker on the next hole incurred another dropped shot. Fortunately the breeze, although persistent, was not as strong as on the previous day and Riley fought his way back with some spirited play during the middle section of his round. He covered the eight holes from the fifth to the twelfth in four under par and played the difficult fourteenth with great verve to grab another birdie. Although the Road Hole brought a dropped shot, he retrieved it with yet another birdie down the eighteenth to leave himself at two under par for the Championship.

'You've done very well, Richie,' I congratulated him, as we headed for the putting green.

'Yeah, I'm lying around thirty in the field,' he replied, 'but I want a top twenty place and then I qualify for next year automatically. That qualifying event is a sweat. I can do without it.'

My attention was diverted as a man pressed a leaflet into my hands. I glanced briefly at it, expecting an advertisement for yet another device which would transform my golf overnight, but the leaflet was headed: 'The Green Disciples Love the Earth.'

When we reached the practice putting green I scanned the contents and recognised most of the arguments which Jodie used in her condemnation of the game.

I admired the enthusiasm and tireless energy of the Green Disciples in putting their views in front of the golf fans, but reckoned it was a naive tactic. As Richie and I walked back towards the clubhouse I saw that the waste bins were overflowing with abandoned leaflets. I trained an eager eye on the crowds in the hope of seeing a familiar blonde head, but of Jodie Hesse there was no sign.

Chapter 31

My American employer was just in the top half of the field and scheduled to start his final round at 10.50. We agreed to meet on the following morning in time for an hour's practice and then went our different ways, mine to a drink with Toby and a quiet dinner.

We raised our glasses in the champagne tent and Toby produced the Green Disciples' leaflet from his pocket. 'Very brave of them. It's a wonder they didn't get lynched. Talk about preaching to the unconvertible.'

'They regard everyone as suitable for conversion. Even you.'

'Not while they're anti-golf, I'm not. Are they still on your backs at Shere Forest?'

'Not at the moment. All's gone quiet, thank goodness. And I'm going quietly because I've got to be out of my bed early in the morning at six. I want to walk the course. Are you going to come with me?'

Toby's inquiry whether I'd taken complete leave of my senses was predictable. He was more likely to be getting into his bed at such an hour than leaving it.

My reason for taking a look at the course before play began was part habit and part superstition, rather than necessity. I

251

already had all the measurements I needed. I could tell Riley the exact distance to a flag from any point on any hole and it was essential that the information was accurate. He knew to within a few feet how far he could hit a specific club. The adjustments necessary for the strength of the wind, the lie of the ground, the shape of the intended shot, and even the level of his own adrenalin were second nature to him.

I didn't have to check where the holes had been cut on the greens. Each golfer was given a chart with the positions marked and their distances from the perimeters noted. Nevertheless, I felt it was a part of my job to be out there early to scout the course.

The alarm clock buzzed at six the next morning. My unwillingness to move from the comfort of my bed was overtaken, after only a few moments, by a sense of anticipation. There is nothing to equal the final round of the Open Championship: the fervour of the crowds, the vitality and ambition of the players, the intensity of the occasion. And I was lucky enough to have a part, albeit minor, to play.

After a mug of tea I strode down the road towards the famous clubhouse. My caddie's badge took me through the gate and I headed down the side of the Royal and Ancient Club's building towards the first tee. The stands waited, skeletal and silent, in the pallid morning sun.

I didn't expect to see so many people clustered around the famous eighteenth green, the scene of so much golfing drama over the years. There seemed to be another kind of drama going on, with at least a dozen people talking animatedly on and around the green. I recognised the Secretary of the R & A, the head greenkeeper, one or two security men in their green uniforms and a scattering of policemen.

'What's going on?' I asked a Scottish security man who was standing on the fringe of the green.

'We have a crisis on our hands, man. Look.' He pointed at the vast expanse of the two-tiered green. On the top I could see the message burnt into the velvety turf in large letters: 'Green Disciples Love the Earth.'

'How?' I asked simply.

'I didn't come on duty till six, and it was done by then. Those Disciples take no heed of the law. They need hanging.'

So do the security people, I thought, and wondered what the officials could do to rescue the situation. They might be best advised to try and returf all the damaged areas in time for the arrival of the first two competitors at about midday. The quality of the surface wouldn't be more than mediocre, but it was better, surely, than trying to cut a temporary green.

My ruminations were cut short when I noticed a gaggle of newspaper reporters and cameramen. The television and radio people were already conducting their interviews. Toby would never forgive me if he missed the story completely.

Every telephone near the clubhouse was occupied and I decided that it was quickest to run back to the house and pull him out of bed.

Deep in his early morning slumber, Toby was neither a pretty sight nor a grateful one. Irritably he pulled at the duvet as I tried to rouse him.

'Piss off,' he muttered and turned his face to the wall.

'Toby,' I roared, 'the Green Disciples have burned the clubhouse down.'

He sat up straight in bed and said, 'What are you on about?'

'Get your arse into gear.' I threw his clothes onto the bed.

'This is a big story – the Green Disciples have carved up the eighteenth green. Now get a bloody move on or you'll miss it.'

He certainly got a move on and within a couple of minutes we were hurrying back down the road towards the Old Course. Toby did his usual eccentric staggering jog-trot while I told him everything I'd seen.

The throng around the green had expanded greatly as many early-bird spectators joined the reporters and officials. The police had roped the area off and were keeping everyone, except the R & A officials, well clear. It was no wonder; a few dozen pairs of trampling feet would have ruined the green for the foreseeable future.

While Toby pushed through his fellow reporters, I saw that the repair of the green was already underway. Six greenkeepers were on their hands and knees; some were carefully cutting out the burnt areas while the others were trimming lengths of new turf to fill the gaps. It wasn't quite what anyone expected on the closing hole of the foremost championship in golf, but it seemed a reasonable solution – *if* they could pull the trick off successfully. I hated to think of the recriminations if a player faced a putt of a few feet to win the Open and his ball was knocked off line by a poorly repaired chunk of turf.

As the police began to tell everyone to disperse, Toby shoved through the crowd towards me. 'There's to be an announcement by the R & A at eight o'clock,' he panted. 'What a ruddy cock-up. They'll do the repairs but the pros won't like it.'

'What were the police and security boys up to?' I asked. 'Asleep? On the booze? Out with some tarts from Edinburgh?'

'No. Your pals from the Green Disciples ambushed the security guards around the clubhouse. Apparently it was like a military operation. They tied them up and gagged them, and then set to work on the green.'

'Bloody hell! They really go for broke, don't they?'

'This is only a small skirmish compared to that Marlborough Downs business. Anyway, let's have a cup of coffee and then we'll go and hear the announcement.'

As we waded into bacon sandwiches and mugs of hot coffee, Toby said, 'I want to interview your chum, Jodie. An exclusive. Her thoughts on golf and the environment. I'll give her a good spread. What do you think?'

'All you have to do is read that pamphlet again. Or I could give you her views, I've heard them often enough. I doubt she'll play ball.'

'Why not? It's more publicity for the cause. They can never resist that. "The thoughts of Chairman Jodie." Let's give it a try, eh? She's beautiful and rich as well, isn't she, Chris? And obviously as tough as marble. She's just the sort of woman my readers will love to hate.' Toby slapped me cheerfully on the back. 'Come on, let's go and hear what the R & A mandarins have decided.'

It was all predictable stuff. They had decided that the eighteenth green would be repaired to the best of the green staff's abilities; players could move their balls if they felt their line to the hole was especially impaired, and they could use their wedges or any other club on the eighteenth green if they wished. (There was no ban on this practice in any case. To everyone's horror a few years previously, an American had used his wedge to play a shot on one of the huge double greens that were a feature of the Old Course. Because he had had an Italian name, Toby had lambasted him in the *Daily News* as 'the Mafia Man of Golf'.) Finally, the Secretary said how much he deplored the actions of a misguided group of extremists. 'And so say all of us,' Toby grunted, 'but think of the publicity they've got by this – all over the world.'

By the time I'd walked back to the house with Toby, had a shower and downed another mug of tea, it was time to meet Richie Riley. Toby reminded me that we still had a £10 bet.

We had been drawn to play with an unobtrusive and highly efficient Spanish professional called Luis Miguel, who seemed to score well by stealth. You blinked and suddenly he was two under par. Riley was showing very little in the way of nerves. He told me that he was here to enjoy the occasion, and for the first eight holes we both had plenty of fun as he improved his position by three shots.

On a reasonably benign day, too benign for Toby's tastes, Riley was one of many who were scoring well. It was the relatively innocuous ninth hole which interrupted his progress. I imagine that he had visions of driving his ball very close to the green, but it came to rest just under the back lip of a bunker about fifty yards short, a bizarre and cruel outcome to a good shot.

Riley looked at the ball from several angles, tried this stance and that, and decided that his only recourse was to play the ball backwards out of the bunker. His third shot was mediocre and he missed his putt to drop a shot. He compounded his misery by taking three putts at the tenth and so I did what a good caddie has to do occasionally; I took him aside, told him that he was playing well and he had eight holes left in which to make the best he could of the tournament. 'Come on, Richie, you need a par at the short hole and then there's a real chance of a birdie at the twelfth.'

The American reacted bravely to the circumstances. He duly pulled a shot back at the twelfth with a deft pitch to a few feet, and plotted his way carefully down the next hole which is pitted with dangerous bunkers: Coffin, Cat's Trap and the Lion's Mouth among others. His second birdie of the tournament at the long fourteenth hole set his adrenalin pumping and he picked up two more shots against par over the closing holes. He nearly had another but his birdie putt at the Road Hole hit the back of the hole and stayed out.

We all inspected the damaged eighteenth green suspiciously. The greenkeepers had done a more than adequate job of the repairs, but you could still see the outline of the Green Disciples' message. Riley had no traumas over his putts because he laid his approach, from a distance of around twenty feet, dead alongside the hole.

He was rightly excited by his performance and, after checking his card carefully in the scorer's caravan, dashed into the clubhouse to telephone his parents. When all the players had finished, we learned that his courageous play had put him into a tie for eighteenth place. Richie went home with a substantial prize and I benefited to the tune of nearly £1000; even more important, I won my bet with Toby.

'I'll see you next year, Chris,' were Richie's parting words as he pumped my hand enthusiastically. 'I loved every minute of it. Just like Gene Sarazen, I'd make it to the Open even if I had to swim across.'

After the prizes were given out and the speeches made, I took one last look at the famous course and trudged back to the house. I'd decided to drive home to London that evening. I owed it to Calvin Blair to be at Shere Forest bright and early the following morning.

Chapter 32

My desire to arrive early was thwarted. The excitements of the previous day and a protracted journey south on motorways clogged with weekend travellers took its toll. When the alarm clock sounded, I turned it off and went straight back to sleep. A late start meant that I reached the outskirts of Shere Forest just after nine o'clock.

The first hint that something was amiss was a small queue of cars waiting to get into the drive which led to the club. It was being monitored by two policemen. I decided to walk down to find out the cause of the delay. It was only then that I registered the acrid smell of burning. I peered through the line of trees and saw a pall of smoke hovering above the clubhouse.

The leading car, its occupant muttering indignantly, was turned away. Down the drive I could see an array of fire engines and police cars.

'Can I get in?' I asked one of the policemen.

'Not unless you've a good reason.'

'I work here. I'm trying to build a golf course.'

'Blair Associates?'

'Yes.'

'I've got bad news then. Your offices are burnt out and so is most of your equipment. You'd better drive through, but park well away from the clubhouse.'

I parked as instructed and picked my way past the haphazardly parked fire engines and over the hoses which snaked out from their bellies. I soon found Calvin. He was standing, shoulders drooping and hands in his pockets, about fifty yards from where our office used to be.

There wasn't much of it left, just some blackened pieces of wood and twisted pieces of metal. Four of the bulldozers were wrecked, their cabins blown apart and their huge tyres burnt out. Covered in foam laid down by the firemen, they seemed to have fallen in on themselves and to have subsided in a sudden fit of despair. Alongside our burnt-out office was the skeleton of a large van.

As I walked towards Calvin I felt guilty at being late, which was absurd, particularly in the context of the fire. He shook his head slowly and said, 'It's all under control now, but it's been a bit of a shock.'

With an unpleasant sensation in my stomach, I asked, 'Deliberate?'

'Oh yes. The Green Disciples left their calling card – a note posted through the clubhouse door, telling us to call off the new course, to leave nature in peace or something. The police have got it.'

'So what happened?'

Blair gestured helplessly at the chaos around us. 'They torched the office and blew up the bulldozers. This time, they've gone too far.'

I looked at Blair and waited. He pointed at the wrecked van. 'Young Terry's dead. He was asleep in his camper van. The poor lad wanted to get a very early start so that he could finish the clearing of the third hole this morning. I told him he could park it there. He never stood a chance.'

I didn't know much about Terry Ball, beyond his cheerful and hard-working personality and I saved myself from an inadequate silence by asking where the security men had been hiding. It seemed to be a recurring theme at the moment.

'There was only one man on. They were cutting down since everything seemed quiet. He was probably asleep in the clubhouse.'

'They've certainly got it in for golf, haven't they?' I said soberly. 'You heard what they did at St Andrews, I suppose?'

'Of course. I was glued to the action. Wouldn't miss it for the world. What they did up there was child's play compared to this. Your friend Jodie Hesse has got a lot to answer for.'

'Just a minute, Calvin. You don't know that she had anything to do with it. She wouldn't condone this kind of thing.'

'Says you,' he replied. His tone was dull, bitter. 'The police will have a different view and so have I. They scared my family half to death, they bombed the Department of the Environment, they tried to sabotage two golf tournaments and now this. And Jodie Hesse is one of their spokesmen.'

'So that makes her guilty of manslaughter, does it?'

'In my book, yes. She speaks for them, so she must condone their actions. You only defend her because you fancy her,' he added disgustedly.

Maybe Calvin was right. Jodie *was* ruthless in her pursuit of a better environment for the people of the world, but I was convinced that despite her vow to the contrary she didn't support the kind of extremism that would result in the death of bystanders. If she did, it was no step at all to the terrors inflicted by the IRA, the PLO or any other murderous organisation.

The arrival of Peter Gresham saved us from a serious

argument, one which might even have terminated my short career as a golf course designer. Much to my surprise, Hannibal was on a lead in deference to the dangerous conditions. At least the smoke-affected atmosphere blotted out the retriever's own distinctive stench.

Gresham said, 'I've spoken to Slater. He'll be over in an hour or so. You'll have a new office by tomorrow night. New machinery within days. You've plenty to get on with in the meantime, I'm sure. Use the clubhouse facilities.' He paused and scratched his ear. 'I'm very sorry, Calvin, very sorry. Especially over young Ball. He seemed a good man.' Gresham grunted a couple of times, turned and headed for the clubhouse.

'I suppose he's right,' Calvin said wearily. 'The show must go on.'

'What about the drawings for the course?'

'I've got copies. The contractor has some and I've more at home. Come on, let's go and find ourselves a corner in the clubhouse.'

While Blair went off to talk to the course contractor's foreman, I put a call through to Jodie Hesse's number and left a message on her answering machine. I was not hopeful that she would reply but, a few minutes later, I heard her high, flat voice on my line.

'I heard the news, Chris,' she said, 'and I can guess what you're going to say . . .'

'Yes – a convenient death to bring you some extra publicity. If you can only put your message across by murdering innocent people, you should—'

'Stop, Chris. That was an accident. But I admit that some of the Green Disciples are out of control. They're not my people. I'll fight till I drop for the environment but I won't kill for it, whatever I've said and done in the past. You must believe me. I had nothing to do with the fire at Shere Forest.'

'What I believe doesn't matter. It's the police you have to convince. They'll be around to ask you some very searching questions. And they won't be as gullible as me.'

'You're not gullible. But I intend to state my position tonight on television. There's a special programme about the environment and I'm involved. It's at seven o'clock. BBC. Watch it.'

'OK.'

'And then come round to my house afterwards for supper. We'll talk. I want you to believe in me. I've got a couple of things to do, so not too early. Say half nine.'

Calvin Blair walked through the door as Jodie gave me an address in Camberwell. 'It's near the Broken Rib Theatre,' she said. I hoped that the woman with the donkey jacket and big shoulders wasn't going to be a fellow guest.

Within the next half-hour I had calls from both Max and Toby. They said they were calling to check that I was still alive, but Max wanted to confirm that he could still use my spare room and Toby was pressing for his interview with Jodie. As Calvin had said, the show must go on.

'Watch the BBC tonight,' I said to Toby. 'An Environmental special . . .' I heard him groan. 'You should learn exactly where she stands and then I'll try and get you face to face.'

Calvin looked up questioningly. 'I suppose you're on about your friend Jodie, are you? What a pity I can't watch her.' I didn't believe him but nodded politely and he continued, 'I've got to dub some comments on a tape of the Open.'

'Well, put in a good word for Richie Riley, won't you?'

* * *

Later that morning we were asked to join Mervyn Slater in the committee room. He was pacing up and down, with Peter Gresham sitting silently at the table. There was no offer of coffee on this occasion.

Slater went straight to the point. 'As you can imagine, Calvin, I've had my bellyful of these Green Disciple loonies. We can bounce back from the fire this morning, thank God, as all the insurance is in place and so on. Peter's told you that we'll be in action again within days, hasn't he?'

We both nodded and Slater continued, 'But this bloody Hesse woman is a real pain in the bum.' He walked over to the table, opened a file and waved some papers at us. 'This lot arrived on my lawyer's desk this morning. She's only filed an action in the European Court to stop us proceeding with the new course.'

'On what grounds?' I asked.

'On the grounds that we are "irretrievably altering an ancient tract of land to the detriment of its wildlife and its ecological balance" – whatever that means. Also that "ancient common land rights have been ignored".' He threw the papers back on the table.

'In other words,' I said, 'Mr Gresham had no rights to the land and therefore neither does Davina Holdings.'

'It's bullshit, of course,' snarled Slater. 'My lawyers have already applied to have the action set aside. But – and this is the point, Calvin – I want you to press on as fast as possible.'

'The case could take months, even years, to get to court,' Gresham said comfortably.

'By which time the course will be more or less built,' continued Slater. 'So, really push on and if anything gets in your way, don't worry.'

'What do you mean?' Calvin asked, suddenly suspicious.

Slater winked and said, 'Nature reserve areas, Dartford Warblers, whatever. Just ignore them, plough on regardless.'

'But we've made undertakings with the local wildlife people and the conservationists,' I protested. 'Charley James is on the committee – we can't go back on our word.'

'This is business, Chris,' Slater stated, his cheeks turning pink above his beard. 'There's lots of money at stake and I'm not going to let some bloody Kraut anarchist get in the way. I'll deal with her and anyone else who rocks the boat in my own way.'

'Someone should sort out those bloody Green Disciples,' agreed Calvin heatedly.

Slater's face visibly relaxed and he smiled at Calvin and me. 'That's the stuff. This project means a lot to me. I've acquired a great club from Peter and I want to make it even better. And I can see that you're keen to earn your bonus, eh, Calvin?'

Slater walked us to the door and reminded us that he was always available if we needed any help.

Chapter 33

At seven o'clock that evening, Max and I were settled in front of my television with a bottle of wine between us.

The programme had been hastily cobbled together and took the form of a studio discussion, chaired by an unsmiling television journalist called Jeremy Kelly, who clearly mistook abrasiveness for intellectual integrity.

Jodie sat to his left, svelte in a black shirt with a round neck and long sleeves, while Charley James, perky and smiling, sat on his other side. In the cause of balance there was a spokesman on the environment from each of the two main political parties.

The politicians were given a few minutes to state their respective party's commitment to the environment, and then Charley James put over her conservationist message with practised charm.

It was obvious that the real meat in this programme's sandwich was going to be Jodie. Jeremy Kelly asked his first question:

'Jodie Hesse, you are the spokesperson for the Green Disciples. Do you think that their methods, which embrace disruption and anarchy and the death of innocent people, are appropriate?'

'I think your question is put in a biased way,' Jodie replied, 'but I'll answer it. All radical movements attract extremists and the Green Disciples are no exception to the rule. You're referring to the accident at Shere Forest. It's a cause of great regret, as is the death of any human being. Like the people who've been poisoned by insecticides or those who die of thirst in Southern Africa only a few miles from golf courses which use millions of gallons of water a week.'

'But you intend to put your message across whatever it costs in social disruption?'

'We've got to ensure that people listen because time is running out. The earth's resources are finite and we can't go on plundering them. This manic pursuit of economic growth must be replaced by a conservationist approach. Descartes' dream of a marvellous science that would bring a mastery of nature has become a nightmare . . .'

'So, if I can bring you back to earth,' Kelly said, 'you're against big business, against modern agriculture, against most things?'

'I'm against the waste of resources. Society is best organised in a series of smaller self-sufficient communities. Why pollute the atmosphere and use up some more of the earth's precious resources by driving in a Japanese car to a hypermarket to buy American beer, French apples and New Zealand lamb? Wouldn't it be better to walk to the local market and buy or barter fresh local products?'

'It's an idyllic picture you paint,' Kelly replied, 'but it hardly matches up with the methods employed by the Green Disciples, which embrace extremes of violence. Do you stand with them or not?'

Jodie pushed her hand wearily through her hair as the camera closed on her face. 'My ideals, my dreams are still intact. I'll try to realise them. "The force that through the green fuse drives the flower, drives my green age." That's taken out of context but isn't a bad metaphor for what I believe. But you asked about the Green Disciples. I'm not sure about their motives any more. Maybe they've become a little tarnished, maybe they've lost sight of their original objectives.'

'Are you saying that you no longer believe in their ideals?' Kelly asked.

'No, but perhaps they no longer believe in mine,' Jodie said. Max looked over to me with a raised eyebrow as the programme veered off into a discussion of the morality of active and passive resistance. The two politicians interrupted each other as they tried to put over their respective party's views and Charley James made a lucid and good-humoured plea for more conservation. Finally, Jodie reaffirmed her commitment to the environmental cause but, significantly, did not mention the Green Disciples by name. With a brief summary from Jeremy Kelly the programme ended and Max said, 'Christ, she did a neat job of distancing herself from the Green Disciples, didn't she?'

'It was you who told me that their motives were much more sinister than mere concern about the environment. Jodie has obviously worked it out, too.'

'And wants to plough her own furrow?'

'Very appropriate, Max. Maybe she really is a true idealist. She's nuts, of course, because we're living smack bang in the middle of the industrial age and it can only get worse.'

'In its twilight, Chris, I'd say.'

About an hour later I prepared to set out for Jodie's house on my bike. 'I'll tell you more about Jodie's road to Damascus later,' I said cheerfully to Max.

'Tomorrow, you mean. Do your best for England, you jammy bastard.' He's a coarse man sometimes, my brother.

I looked in my wallet for Jodie's address. It wasn't there – I must have left it at Shere Forest.

'Hell, I've left her address behind. I'd better phone her.'

'Did you write it down?'

'Yes and it's on the tip of my brain. It's near that awful theatre in Camberwell.'

'If it's in your head, you can retrieve it.' Max enjoyed mental games. 'Where's the A to Z? I'll throw some street names at you.'

'It's OK,' I said. 'I've got it. Twenty-five Berwick Road.'

During the ride east towards Camberwell I wondered just how much I was looking forward to seeing Jodie. She had a peculiar slant on life, the universe and everything, but her physical charms were undeniable. If some of my motives for seeing her again were ambiguous even to me, I was clear on one thing; I badly wanted to haul her into bed and stay there for a while.

Just after 9.30 I arrived at her front door and rang the bell. It was a narrow, three-storeyed house in a uniform row of buildings. Brightly coloured doors and window boxes here and there showed that a certain amount of gentrification was underway.

There was no reply to my ringing, although I could see the glow of lights behind the curtains as I looked up at the first floor. Perhaps Jodie was juggling with saucepans in the kitchen. It was not really an image that fitted her and I quickly flicked to a more acceptable one. She was in the shower, lithe and suntanned . . .

Don't get ahead of yourself, Ludlow, I said to myself. I hammered on the door and it swung open slightly. Jodie had left it on the latch. Perhaps she was in the shower after all, waiting for me to join her.

I fumbled for the hall light and called out Jodie's name. There was no answer and I headed for the stairs. Music floated down from above and I assumed that was why she couldn't hear me. I couldn't smell anything cooking. Oh well, champagne and smoked salmon would do.

'Jodie, where are you?' I called as I reached the top of the stairs. A sitting room at the front of the house and a bedroom at the back were empty.

One more flight of stairs lay ahead of me and I was beginning to wonder if Jodie had slipped out to buy wine or a take-away meal at one of the local shops.

The top floor was one big room, which had been made out of what was formerly a loft. With its wood panelling and skylights it was spacious and immediately appealing. The long wooden table, a dresser filled with china plates and another table covered in bottles of various kinds indicated that it was the dining room; a kitchen area took up one corner. The lighting was dim, as if for an intimate dinner party.

Jodie was sitting at one end of the table, her hands spread out on its top. Her head was lolling forward and I thought that she had fallen asleep. The words 'Wake up, Jodie,' congealed on my lips as I moved towards her.

In the dim light I could see a black stain which had spread outwards from her neck. I lifted her head gently. The wide grimace of the cut spread in a jagged line from under her left ear to beneath her chin. A second cut ran from the other side but didn't quite marry up with the first.

I lowered her head and fought the urge to vomit. I took some deep breaths and looked for the dimmer switch, even though the last thing I wanted was to focus any more light on what had been done to that beautiful girl.

With my hand covered by a handkerchief, I turned the lights up and forced myself to approach the table again. It was set for two people. I looked at Jodie, and saw how the blood had drenched her T-shirt and trousers. How pathetic the 'Save the Planet' logo looked now. I couldn't bring myself to touch her brutalised face but reached over to stroke her hand in farewell.

I suddenly realised the extent of the savagery inflicted on Jodie. A broad steel nail had been hammered through the centre of each hand and into the table beneath. It was then that I wept. I collapsed into a chair and bawled.

After a while, I began to get control of myself. I could just about comprehend the extremes of emotion, the temporary madness, that might lead to murder, but I had no inkling of how someone could torture and kill another human being in such a perverse way. With my head between my hands, I offered up a prayer that one day I'd find the sadistic bastard who had done for Jodie. Five minutes alone with him, that would be enough.

The only sensible course of action now was to call the police. But if I did that, any meagre chance I had of finding the killer would disappear. I was damned if I was going to walk away from it all like that. I'd do some freelancing; I knew as much about Jodie's background as anyone and I had Max to help me, with his contacts in the murky reaches of the Intelligence industry. The first thing to do was to have a good look around the house. There ought to be something that would give me a line to Jodie's killer. And then God help him.

Wiping my eyes free of tears, I took one last look at Jodie. The glitter of something at the base of her chair caught my eye and I stooped down. It was a button, brass or maybe gold, and it bore the emblem of the Shere Forest Golf Club. That was a start. I put it in my pocket, dimmed the lights again and trod carefully down the stairs. A look into the first-floor rooms revealed nothing untoward and I headed slowly down the final flight to the ground floor.

The hall light gave enough illumination for me to see into the last two rooms; at the back there was a small sitting room with a television set and a video player. Finally I pushed my way gingerly into the front room. It was set up as an office, not a tidy one. I stumbled over some papers on the floor. I risked putting on a light and saw that the equivalent of a small cyclone had paid a visit. The drawers of the desk had been thrown open, their contents strewn on the floor; books from the shelves were scattered about; and files from a small cabinet were upended here and there. A personal computer was humming in the corner, its index showing on the screen. The abbreviations made very little sense to me. Golf was listed but I wasn't going to stick around to call up the file.

There was a sudden buzz and a whirr from the corner of the room which had me jumping up and sweating with fright. It was a fax machine and I watched as a short message came through to confirm a meeting in Paris in a few days' time.

A previous message lay above it. Short, to the point and unsigned, it read: 'See you after the show.' I tore the messages off the roll and shoved them hastily into my pocket. I had no idea whether they were clues or not, but they were certainly worth taking.

It was time to go. I switched off the light and peered out at the street through a crack in the curtain. There didn't seem to be much going on. I thanked my guardian angel that I hadn't gone to the house in my Porsche, which might have been noticed by a neighbour. Easing my way out of the door, I detached my bike from its lamp-post and pedalled like hell for the anonymity of the main roads.

My mind was mercifully blank for several minutes as I concentrated on pedalling fiercely to get well away from the area. It was only later that I started to wonder at the senseless waste of a life and ask myself who and why . . .

The one thing I couldn't bear was leaving poor Jodie sitting there in her own blood. An anonymous phone call to the police was the only solution. I stopped by some telephones opposite Chelsea Bridge and dialled 999. After a few delays and queries about the nature of the inquiry, I got through to Camberwell police station. In a phoney London accent I said, 'Twenty-five Berwick Road. Woman dead.' As the policeman began to ask me for my name, I put the phone down.

Cycling hard towards Putney, I desperately tried to think who, apart from Max, knew that I had a date with Jodie. I was hopeful that she herself would not have told anyone of my intended visit. The habit of security seemed to be ingrained in her. I went back and forth over the events of the day and decided that I hadn't spoken of it to anyone, not even Toby. If I was wrong and the police tracked my visit down they would give me an exceedingly bad time.

But someone else *had* got to Jodie. I remembered that she'd told me she had things to do before I arrived. That was vague enough to mean that she was expecting a visitor ahead of me. The murderer could well be someone she knew.

The presence of a Shere Forest blazer button was too good to be true. It belonged in the pages of a 1930s country house murder mystery and seemed to be an amateurish attempt to plant some misleading evidence. But what about the fax?

Chapter 34

My hand was trembling violently as I put the key into the front door of my flat. The music from my sitting room told me that Max was still up. No wonder – my watch confirmed that it wasn't yet eleven o'clock.

Stretched out in a chair, a magazine in his hands, Max grinned up at me. 'Blimey, Chris, that was quick.' Then he looked hard at me, rose from the chair and said, 'What the hell's the matter? You're as white as paper.'

'It's Jodie. She's dead.' I spoke as calmly as I could. 'Murdered.' I sat down heavily on a sofa. Max stood motionless for a moment and then moved rapidly towards the kitchen. I heard the clink of glass and he reappeared with two tumblers and a bottle of brandy.

'Drink,' he said.

That first shot disappeared in one steady gulp and Max wasn't far behind me. He seemed almost as shocked as I was and it was some time before either of us spoke. Then Max suggested I told him everything I had seen. 'However trivial. Everything – from the moment you arrived at her front door.'

With numerous questions from my brother, I stumbled through the whole heartbreaking sequence.

'Are you sure nobody saw you?' Max asked. 'A neighbour, for instance?'

'No one. It's a quiet residential street. They were all in front of the telly, I expect.'

'Good. Just in case anyone asks, you were here in the flat all evening. You'll probably get a call from the police, so it's best to be prepared.'

'What did we do?'

'Watched Jodie on the box, had a few drinks and a meal. Chatted, as brothers do.'

'That reminds me, Max, I haven't eaten. It seems indecent but I'm starving.'

He offered to cook me an omelette. Silent, we stood in the kitchen. Max whisked a few eggs while I wondered why someone would murder a woman like Jodie in such a sadistic way.

'If someone just wanted her out of the way for some reason, why not make it quick and clean?' I asked Max. 'The murder looked sort of personal, like an act of revenge.'

I heard my brother's voice as though from a distance. 'Who had a reason to kill her? Who wanted her dead? Could it have been a casual killing, even?' He slid my omelette onto a warm plate. 'Some nutter who knew she lived alone and took his chance. Was there any sign of rape?'

'No, I don't think so. She was fully clothed.'

'Anyway, Jodie could look after herself. I wouldn't have fancied my chances in unarmed combat with her.'

'She's been a great embarrassment to Shere Forest,' I pointed out, 'especially with this action against them in the European Court. Mervyn Slater has lots of money riding on the club's back. If it's a success, he'll make huge profits. And then there's Peter Gresham and his son and the odious Simon Hanley, his son-in-law.'

'I can't see what Gresham would have to gain, Chris. He sold out to Slater and he's already got his money. He's simply not the type, anyway. What about Hanley?'

'I'm sure he's on some kind of profit-sharing deal with Slater. He'd want to protect that and apparently he's already taken a hammering at Lloyds. The question is whether he's capable of murder. I don't know.'

'He might be capable of it but there are very few people around who are capable of a murder like this one. There's a very significant difference.' Max poured us both another brandy. 'How important is Shere Forest to Slater's company? Is he as mega-rich as everyone makes out?'

'You never know with property-based businesses. A couple of bad deals and they can go very rapidly down the tubes. The other point about Slater is that he's got a murky past. Toby suspects him of having disposed of his first wife to get his hands on her money.'

'OK, so he's got form. He's definitely on the list of suspects.'

'I don't think we should totally exclude Nick Gresham and Simon Hanley. Maybe one of them lost a blazer button while he was in Jodie's dining room,' I said.

'Possibly, but I think it's more likely to be a plant. Someone wants to throw suspicion on Shere Forest. I think that the fax may be much more pertinent, Chris.'

We looked at the sheet of paper and, apart from the time of its dispatch, there was a call-back number on the sheet. 'It's Central London somewhere,' I said. 'How do we find out where it came from?'

'Isn't there a directory of fax machines?'

'I don't think so. Anyway, they'd be listed in alphabetical order by subscriber. That wouldn't help.'

'We'll take the direct route,' Max decided. 'Tomorrow we'll fax that number and ask them to call back. We'll say we've received a scrambled message and could they confirm what it says.'

'That's fine, Max, but if it's come from the killer, he won't bother to answer, will he?'

'No, but that'll tell us something in itself and we can then turn the fax over to the police. They've got the machinery to trace the source, haven't they? Anyway, it probably came via a public fax.'

I cut myself a lump of cheese and noticed with surprise how little brandy was left in the bottle. I said, 'Max, could this have been a *crime passionnel*? The brutality of the killing indicates something very personal.'

'A lover, perhaps even a rival from another extremist movement? It's possible.'

I remembered the tough-looking woman in the donkey jacket who had roared off with Jodie on the pillion of her motorbike and told Max about her.

He laughed. '"ANARCHIST DIES IN LESBIAN LOVE-NEST MURDER." You've been mixing too much with Toby and his like. Come on, let's give it a rest. I'm off to bed. We'll see everything from a different perspective in the morning.'

After the evening's horrors, I expected nightmares, especially on top of several glasses of brandy. Instead I had the dreamless sleep of a truly exhausted man. When I padded into the kitchen in the morning, Max was already up.

'Nothing on the news yet,' he said, 'but the police are

bound to let it out later. I'll phone you at the office as soon as they do. You can act suitably shocked and so on. And Chris, what about that piece of paper with Jodie's address on it? Seek and destroy, as they say, just in case.'

Max asked me where the nearest fax machine was and I directed him to a nearby newsagent. 'Why don't you ask Toby to do it?' I added. 'He's got a machine at his elbow.'

'How much do I tell him?'

'Only as much as you need to,' I said, 'but we'll meet him tonight and reveal all. A journalist, even Toby, could be very helpful to us.'

The first thing I did in the office was to look for Jodie's address, jotted down on a message pad the previous day. I knew I'd left it on the top of my temporary desk and experienced a nasty surge of panic when I couldn't find it. I hunted through the drawers and then the wastepaper bin, without success, and a look on the floor revealed nothing. In desperation, I glanced at the bin alongside Calvin's desk and there it was. The message had been thrown in there. But I couldn't remember doing it. No matter, I went to the nearest lavatory and flushed the evidence away.

Calvin was later into the office than usual and mentioned that he'd gone to bed in the small hours. 'I was dubbing that tournament from Biarritz so I missed your friend telling us all about the environment. How was it?'

'OK. She was good, very lucid.' I found it hard to behave as if Jodie were still alive and hoped that my voice didn't sound too odd.

The ring of my telephone saved me. It was Max. 'Chris, I've just heard the bad news. Jodie Hesse is dead. OK? Act natural. See you later. I've been in touch with Toby.'

For the sake of authenticity, since Calvin could hear my side of the exchanges, I asked a few questions. It wasn't a problem to assume a state of shock and sorrow because Max's words brought the reality of Jodie's death home to me. I sat down and stared at the desk for a moment and said, 'Calvin, I've just had some very bad news. That was Max. Jodie Hesse has been found dead.'

'Dead? How?'

'I don't know. He didn't tell me.' I could say no more because the phone rang once again to bring the gruff voice of Toby Greenslade.

'My boy. Max has been in touch. Dreadful thing. I watched her last night. Beautiful and twice as bright as that bumptious fool, Jeremy Kelly. What a waste. The official word is that it's being treated by the police as a suspicious death.'

'That means murder, does it?' I asked for Calvin's benefit. He looked at me keenly.

'Yes,' said Toby quietly. 'Max has asked me to do something for him and I'm to meet you both later.'

Blair walked across to my desk and put his hand on my shoulder. 'I'm sorry, Chris, you were obviously fond of her. Do you want to take the day off? Might it help?'

I refused on the grounds that I'd be better off working and ought to be around when the reporters arrived, as they were bound to do.

It wasn't long before the vanguard of hacks and photographers had made their way to the club. Slater's security guards came in handy in denying them entry to the clubhouse but anyone who went outside was guaranteed an interview. Several of the members obliged and I shuddered to think how their comments would be recycled for the titillation of readers on the following day.

Peter Gresham, Hannibal by his side, complained his way into our office. In such cramped surroundings, the retriever's smell verged on overpowering and I edged my way to the window, opening it as widely as I could.

'Damned reporters,' Gresham said irritably. 'Slater's Press Officer, or whatever he's called, is on his way over to deal with them. Do you know, one of the blighters had the damned cheek to phone me and say that the Green Disciples had accused us, here at Shere Forest, of assassinating this Hesse woman! Have you ever heard such nonsense?'

'How did they justify that?' asked Calvin.

'The fact that she was the brains behind their opposition to the new course and that she was taking action in the European Court to stop us.'

'It's an obvious assumption to make,' I said. 'After all, Jodie's death means that the embarrassing legal action will no longer take place. I imagine that the police will ask us all some pretty searching questions.'

Gresham glowered at me. 'They can ask all they want. I'm glad to say that the Gresham family were all present and correct last night.'

'That's very convenient for you all,' I said nastily. 'But what about Mr Slater – was he with you too?'

'As a matter of fact, no,' Gresham replied. 'It was a family affair, a birthday celebration. Not that I can see what business it is of yours.'

'Chris didn't mean anything,' said Calvin placatorily. 'We're all rather shocked by this. Chris knew Jodie Hesse and her death won't do us any good. You know how the press love to dig up all the dirt they can.'

'Well, they'll get nothing from me,' Gresham muttered as he stamped out of the office.

Calvin and I sought refuge amidst the turmoil of the machinery and the men who were building the new course. It was a relief to lose myself to other pressing problems, though Jodie's face kept imposing itself on my mind's eye.

Chapter 35

With Calvin's blessing, I left the office early. My flat was empty – a note from Max informed me that he'd be back at around five o'clock and that Toby would be joining us later. Disappointed that I had no one to talk to, I decided to invite Mrs Bradshaw in for a cup of tea but she'd gone out. I thought about going for a run but opted instead for a session on the weight-training machinery.

Just as I was coming to the end I heard the front door open and close. I padded quietly to the bedroom door and peered out. It was OK – it was only Max. I was getting paranoid, I thought. Who else would it be?'

'Glad to see you're keeping fit,' Max grinned. 'Have a quick shower. I've made a bit of progress, I think.'

By the time I was ready, Toby had also arrived. He looked at me and said: 'God, you look disgustingly healthy. What are you in training for?'

'Life,' I said pompously as Toby flopped onto a sofa and groaned.

'What's this all about?' he said. 'Max has had me faxing people and chatting up a lovely-sounding girl on the phone. And Jodie Hesse is dead and you, Chris, know something about it. So, let's have it. Come on – I could do with a bloody good story.'

283

'I found Jodie with her throat cut,' I stated bluntly. 'In her house, last night. Nobody knows that except you and Max.'

'And that's the way it's got to stay,' Max said emphatically.

'Of course, of course, dear boy,' Toby said with a look of horror on his face. 'God Almighty, what are you going to do? Did you tell the police?'

'No,' I said. Then: 'I've removed some evidence for a start and that's why you were on the fax machine. What did you find out?'

Max answered. 'The source of that fax to Jodie was a company called TripleVision. Toby did his stuff and got me inside the building by chatting up the lady with the lovely voice. The fax had been sent from her machine.'

'It was rather odd,' said Toby. 'She works for Harvey Waters who produces the golf on satellite for TripleVision. Known him for years, so it was easy.'

'And is she a friend of Jodie's?' I asked impatiently.

'No, she'd never heard of her. And I believed her. Liz is a very pleasant, honest girl – incapable of lying. I'd think.'

'So where does that take us?' I asked.

'Not very far,' Max replied, 'because there are several hundred people in the TripleVision offices and they have over fifty fax machines. And Liz didn't notice anyone unusual sending anything out on that particular machine. But then, she wouldn't have because the message was timed at around five-thirty and she leaves the office at five.'

'So, any one of three of four hundred people could've sent the message,' Toby concluded.

Max nodded and I said, 'The fax could well be a red herring. It might simply have come from a friend, don't you think? Jodie was likely to have known people in organisations like

TripleVision. They're into television production, newspapers, public relations. It was her kind of world.'

'Or it could have been an enemy,' Max said. 'Same basic assumptions as yours, but TripleVision no doubt has people of all political persuasions from deep red to dark blue. Someone might have been setting her up for the kill.'

'Julius Sparkes owns that company,' Toby reminded us, 'and he wouldn't take kindly to having any pinkos nestling in his bosom. As for some deranged killer, that would certainly destroy his credibility. He sets himself up as Mr Law and Order, as you all know.'

'It's amusing to think how many subversives must be lurking in his organisation,' Max said.

'Maybe we can flush some of them out,' I suggested. 'Toby can write a piece in the *News* suggesting that the anti-golf movement is rife among certain sectors of the media and especially television. How ironic it is that a company like TripleVision, which covers a great deal of golf, is known to have several Green Disciple sympathisers on its staff. Et cetera. You know the form, Toby.'

He grunted. 'I might get away with it, I suppose, but only because Sparkes owns some newspapers and is therefore regarded as the opposition. The trouble is that our proprietor, like most of 'em in the newspaper business, is well to the right of Captain Bligh. He's not a hanger and flogger, just a straight hanger.'

'Then the article should appeal to him for several reasons, shouldn't it?' I said.

'I'll make some inquiries about the company,' offered Max. 'There are still a few mates of mine left in various corners of Whitehall. If there are any particularly dangerous people ensconced at TripleVision the Intelligence boys will know of them. That doesn't mean they'll necessarily tell me much, but it's worth a try.'

'Of course – old Calvin works a bit for TripleVision. Expert comment on various events. He's quite good at it, too,' stated Toby.

'That's a coincidence,' I said. 'He was working last night, wasn't he? On the Biarritz Open.'

The other two looked quizzically at me as the germ of a very unpleasant idea bloomed in my mind. Calvin Blair had a strong motive and, possibly, an opportunity to kill Jodie. Might he have arranged to meet her on some pretext? Had he confirmed the meeting by sending a fax from the TripleVision offices? He had been there on legitimate business and nobody would have questioned his use of a machine in one of the offices where the golf coverage was produced.

'What's up, Chris?' asked Max.

'Nothing much. I'll ask Calvin if he saw anything unusual in their office last night. And I'll also check out the alibi for Peter Gresham and his family. That should be easy enough.'

So it proved. A phone call to Francesca did the trick. She told me that everyone had gathered at Peter and Hermione Gresham's house for dinner on Monday evening. 'It was Nick's birthday, the son and heir, so we all had to be there.'

'Including your husband?'

'Fortunately not, darling, he's in Edinburgh for a few days. So why don't you pop over at lunchtime tomorrow for a quick bite, if you see what I mean.'

It would have been rude to refuse. In the meantime I began to wonder how I could check if her husband had really been in the

Scottish capital on the night of Jodie's murder.

Calvin Blair wasn't so easy to deal with and I didn't relish trying to question him about where he'd been and what he'd been doing.

My opportunity came when he decided to walk down to look at one of the new holes. There had been heavy rain overnight and Calvin was anxious to see whether it had affected the work. As he strode enthusiastically through the heather towards the distant thrumming of the heavy machinery, I glanced at his good-natured face and found it hard to believe that he could be capable of any kind of violence.

But I had to satisfy myself about my suspicions. Here goes my job again, I thought. 'Calvin,' I said tentatively, 'you were at TripleVision on Monday night, weren't you?' He grunted and I carried on: 'Did you notice anyone odd using any of the fax machines in the golf department?'

'They're all bloody odd there, Chris. Drive you mad. But the answer is that I was in a studio, dubbing my comments onto the pictures.'

'What time did you get there?'

'Oh, about a quarter past five.' He glanced at me. 'What's this about? You're coming on like Inspector Plod. What are you driving at?'

'Someone sent a fax to Jodie Hesse, at five-thirty-five on the same evening she was murdered. It confirmed a meeting with her later on. I'd love to know who sent it.'

'Why?'

'Because it might have been sent by her killer.'

Calvin stopped in the shelter of some trees. 'If you're acting out some fantasy as the great detective, Chris, I'd forget it and leave it all to the police. They're qualified to do the work, you're not.'

It was a dismissive, almost contemptuous remark and I wasn't going to let him off the hook. 'Look, Calvin,' I said fiercely, 'Jodie had everything: brains and beauty. She was an idealist and they're bloody rare in this world. Somebody killed her and I'm going to ask as many questions as I bloody well like until I find out who it was. You can thank your stars that nobody did to your family what was done to Jodie.'

Blair stepped back in the face of such vehemence and I continued more quietly but just as emphatically. 'You can help me if you want to. You are one of the people who had a strong motive for wanting Jodie out of the way.' Blair began to protest but I talked him down. 'The Green Disciples attacked your family, they disrupted your work, and Jodie was trying to put a stop to it altogether at Shere Forest – at your dream course, the one that would show the world that Calvin Blair was a golf architect to be reckoned with. You also had her address. I wrote it down in the office and found it in *your* wastepaper bin!' I realised that I'd begun to shout again. I drew in a trembling breath and gave Blair a chance to reply.

He spoke calmly. 'I *didn't* know her address. I *didn't* go near a fax nor did I go anywhere near Jodie Hesse. I understand your feelings, Chris. When I saw Jane and Rebecca trussed up like turkeys, dead, I thought . . .' He turned away, such was his emotion. 'I know you liked her, admired her. There were times when I wished her dead, I admit it, and the rest of those bloody Green Disciples. But as for trying to carry out that wish . . . I just couldn't.'

'So give me some help,' I pleaded. 'Tell me what you did on Monday.'

Calvin sighed. 'OK. I did the dubbing and was out of the studio before eight o'clock and home just after nine. Now, Chris, that's all I'm going to say on the subject and I suggest that you concentrate on your work here and leave everything else to the police.'

He was right. I was embarrassed at even thinking that he could have committed a murder. Not many words passed between us during the rest of the morning.

Chapter 36

On the following day Toby's article in the *Daily News* expressed regret at the increasing militancy which was afflicting many sports, even golf. He concluded:

'Golf is an easy sport to mock because it is the pursuit mainly of the much-abused middle classes. Those who attack the game for its élitist image are well entrenched in the media, especially so amongst our colleagues in television. To set foot in a TV company these days inevitably means stumbling over all kinds of single-issue fanatics. That even goes for the organisation owned by that doughty defender of law and order, Julius Sparkes. My sources tell me that the Green Disciples is but one of several extremist groups that have their supporters within Sparkes's TripleVision company.'

Just as I was wondering how the *News*'s libel lawyers had passed it, Toby rang to say that Sparkes's solicitors had threatened a libel action unless a full apology was made. Toby's lords and masters opted for a fulsome expression of regret, and this appeared in the following day's edition.

Meanwhile, the Green Disciples were also active. During that week, several newspaper and magazine articles which pleaded the cause of the Green Movement appeared. Great play was made of the events at Shere Forest. In one of them, an unnamed spokesman for the Green Disciples stated that all the evidence surrounding Jodie Hesse's death pointed to a conspiracy on the part of the owners of Shere Forest.

Perhaps the man was right, although the police didn't seem to think so. The statements they took from the Shere Forest people were perfunctory. In my own case the interview, to my intense relief, lasted only a few minutes and no one ever checked the story of my evening with Max. I wondered whether orders had come from people in high places to apply the soft pedal to the investigation. Jodie was an extremist and a troublemaker. Perhaps the unspoken attitude to her death was 'good riddance'. The piece of disinformation about the Green Disciples' links with TripleVision which Toby planted in the *Daily News* stirred nobody up except a few lawyers. Max had gone off to Norway for several days and therefore nothing emanated from his Whitehall friends.

Jodie's story receded from the front pages of the newspapers but she was more in my thoughts than ever, even though the workload at Shere Forest became more severe. Mervyn Slater, free at last from any interference in his plans, really forced the pace. As autumn began to be chased by winter, the expansion and refurbishment of the clubhouse entered its final phase and the new course also began to take shape. We were ahead of schedule and it looked as if Slater's wish to open the course for play two springs hence might even be realised.

Calvin Blair was cautious, however, and rarely failed to emphasise the perils of a British winter: frozen ground, torrential rain, heavy snow. Any of those would disrupt the programme and make it difficult to meet the deadline. We all knew that the course had to be seeded in the coming spring; it was the crux of the matter.

Slater also pressed on with his plans to make Shere Forest a profitable enterprise. The members had protested loud and long about the severe hike in the prices of food and drink in the restyled bars and the restaurant, but it was nothing compared to the unrest which afflicted them as the day of the Annual General Meeting approached. This was the occasion on which the increased subscriptions and the plans for special company debentures would be confirmed. As everyone knew, Slater's company owned the club and the members were powerless to vote the new measures out. But a good number were determined to have their say.

Peter Gresham, as Chairman of the Shere Forest Company, had to chair the meeting which was to fall on the last Wednesday of the month. A few days before, he wandered into our office and said to Calvin, 'This damned meeting on Wednesday – I'd be obliged if you'd attend, Blair, and answer any questions about the course. There are bound to be some. You're best qualified.'

Calvin made a show of examining his diary. 'I can't do it, Peter. I'm speaking at a dinner – the Southern Golf Alliance. I can't let them down, as you'd understand.'

Gresham tapped an adjacent desk with his forefinger, which then strayed up to his nose and down again. 'What about you, young fella? Could you cope with any questions my members might come up with? They're a pretty docile lot, normally.'

'He knows as much about the new course as I do,' said Calvin.

I agreed to attend the meeting.

An AGM at a golf club is like a three-putt green – to be avoided whenever possible. It serves very little purpose. Members can express their views in a truly democratic fashion and it is a golden opportunity for the club bores to pontificate on any aspect of the club's activities, the more obscure the better. But it is an illusion to imagine that their views matter. As in most supposedly democratic situations the major decisions have already been taken. The dedicated minority who exercise the power have sorted everything out behind closed doors.

This was even more of a self-evident truth at Shere Forest where the members no longer had any voting rights.

At six o'clock we all gathered in the elegant dining room, with its high ceiling and its old wooden lockers still in place. Portraits of some of the former captains were on the walls. Although the room had been extended, its original atmosphere had survived. Slater was not a complete philistine.

Such was the demand for seats that members overflowed into one of the adjoining bars. I took my place on the end of the front row opposite the table where the Shere Forest board of directors would face their members. I looked around at the throng. Predominantly male, middle-aged and prosperous, most of them wore club ties of various kinds, their hues as vigorous as the ruddy cheeks of their owners. The dark suits of the professional men mingled with the baggy tweed jackets of the retired members. Most of them were clutching drinks in their hands.

Amid the noisy babble, I made out the occasional burst of complaint.

'They'll let anyone in now, you know, it's just a question of money.'

'It's not the golf club I joined.'

'Corporate members, indeed – spivs who don't know one end of a golf club from the other.'

'We'll have to rename this place "the Brinks Mat Country Club".'

The directors filed in slowly and took their places. There were two men in dark suits on either side of Peter Gresham. His son, Nick, looked rather nervous at one end of the table; Simon Hanley looked smug and overweight at the other. I wondered if any of them had been involved in Jodie's murder. According to Francesca, the two Greshams had alibis. But what about Simon Hanley?

My speculations were interrupted by Peter Gresham declaring the meeting open. In brisk tones, he summarised the management's plans for the club and emphasised the attraction of more members to the club, especially corporate ones who were prepared to pay a premium for the privilege.

In the circumstances there was remarkably little disruption during Gresham's statement. I had expected some barracking but the Chairman clearly retained a valuable residue of respect amongst the members. Slater had been astute enough to realise this and use it.

One of the suits then got to his feet and went through the finances of the club in tedious detail. Several of the members could be seen tiptoeing to the bar for more supplies of alcohol and then it was the turn of another director to report on the current state of the work on the new course. He introduced me and asked the members to direct any questions of a technical nature my way. Fortunately, no one took him up on his offer.

Peter Gresham warily asked the members if they had any further points to raise. A thin, balding man with a heavy moustache was first on his feet and Gresham introduced him as Sir George Hart.

In clipped tones, Hart began. 'Despite all the dissatisfaction among the members over the increased subscriptions, I want to point out how lucky we are in comparison with American golfers, European golfers and especially Japanese golfers ...'

There was some booing and hissing from the body of the room but Hart continued: 'Most of them pay a great deal more than us for much less agreeable golf courses. I would value my membership of Shere Forest as cheap at ten times the price.'

He sat down amid a modest grumble of dissension. A member to my left said, 'It's all right for old George Hart. His second wife brought a few million with her. He'll never have to worry about money.'

Several members next had their say, with varying degrees of dissatisfaction, about the unprecedented increase in the price of beer, the reduced amount of butter on the teacakes, the poor state of one of the practice nets and the imminent penury that the hike in the annual subscription would bring.

By this stage Gresham was clearly impatient. He wanted to close the meeting while he was winning, no doubt aware that he'd got off lightly. Criticism and complaint had been aired but mostly in a resigned, even good-humoured, way. A gap in the questions gave the Chairman his chance. As he opened his mouth to bring matters to a close, however, a tall man with heavily framed spectacles on his face and a pint jug of beer in his hand, interrupted him.

'Through the Chair,' he said, in a rapid voice with a hint of a Welsh accent, 'are the members aware that Shere Forest is being fattened up for sale? Are the members aware that Davina Holdings, which owns our club, is in serious financial trouble?'

Simon Hanley jumped to his feet and, despite the shouts of 'Sit down!' and 'Let the man have his say!' he shouted: 'I hope you can substantiate such slanderous allegations.'

'The interim results from Davina are due in less than two weeks,' the Welshman said. 'They'll show just how far they're up the Swanee. Any members who've got shares would do well to sell them.' There were some good-natured shouts about insider trading and the man continued: 'Mervyn Slater has one excellent asset, however – Shere Forest. He bought it dirt cheap. By the time he's jacked up the subscriptions, sold fifty corporate debentures at three-quarters of a million quid each and added a second championship course, he'll have something of great value to sell.'

The Welshman took a copious drink from his glass and stated firmly: 'And sell it he will – with planning permissions for a hotel and a conference centre and some holiday villas. It'll be a fat and juicy asset and you can guess who'll jump in and buy it, can't you?' He paused and someone shouted in an appalling parody of the Welsh accent, 'Spit it out, boyo.'

'It'll be one of the corporations which are going to snap up the debentures, of course. Our friends from the Land of the Rising Sun, the Japanese.'

Shouts and protests, questions and derisive comments then filled the room, as Peter Gresham banged irritably on the table and called for order. 'The member over there still has the floor,' he shouted.

'So you can look forward to six-hour rounds, caddie carts everywhere and taking lunch on the floor with your shoes off.'

'Bring on the geisha girls,' someone yelled.

'Mervyn Slater will be the one who'll be able to afford geisha girls,' the Welshman concluded. 'He'll walk away with a profit of fifty million quid, I expect.'

The noise in the room reached its height as the man sat down and Gresham had to stand up and yell for quiet. 'Gentlemen,' he said, 'we've just heard what I can only call an entertaining fantasy. I can assure you that Mervyn Slater will act in the best interests of our great club. I wouldn't have allowed him to acquire it otherwise. You all know how proud I am of our traditions here and it hurt me to have to bring in new owners. But it was the only way ahead for us, the only way to safeguard those fine traditions. I'm confident that I made the right choice in aligning ourselves with a lively and forward-thinking organisation such as Davina Holdings.'

There was some muted applause and I reflected that I had never heard Gresham speak at such length before and so lucidly. Either he really believed what he'd said about Slater, or he was a much better actor than I believed possible.

Most people assumed that the meeting was now over and began to make for the bar. But an old man in the centre of the front row stood up and raised his hand for silence. His tweed suit looked rather too big for his shrunken figure and I noticed that he wore a tattered and faded Hawks Club tie. He was tall and grey-faced, with a prominent nose and a resemblance to Somerset Maugham.

Someone alongside me groaned and I asked him the identity of the old man. 'Sir John Milne-Lyon,' he whispered. 'He's our oldest member.'

Despite his great age, Sir John had a rich full ring to his voice. 'Mr Chairman, gentlemen,' he said, 'I'm interested in all these plans for our club but I wonder whether they accord with the conditions laid down in the original Deed of Trust.'

I saw one of the dark-suited directors leaning over to talk rapidly to Simon Hanley as the elderly member continued. 'Young Peter's father, Jimmy Gresham, was a far-sighted man as well as a fine golfer. You all know about his record in the Sunningdale Foursomes and I was privileged to be his partner on many of those occasions just as I was his opponent in the final of the Worplesdon Foursomes . . .'

Peter Gresham stood up and said: 'I'm sorry to interrupt you, Sir John, but the meeting has gone on for a very long time. Could I ask you to make your point as quickly as possible?'

'Yes, yes, of course, my boy,' said Sir John. 'The point is that your father drew up a Deed of Trust to protect this club. Any sale of shares to an outside party had to be approved by the club's membership. I remember that your father showed me the Deed. Let me see, it must have been before the war, I can't quite . . .'

Peter Gresham interrupted him to say, 'Thank you, Sir John, but I really think you must be mistaken. My father passed nothing like that on to me.'

'What would Gresham know about it?' my neighbour said to nobody in particular. 'He was in short pants when his father died.'

Gresham said, 'The Shere Forest solicitor is here with us.' He gestured at Simon Hanley. 'Simon, do you have any knowledge of a Deed of Trust?'

'No, Mr Chairman. I can assure the members that all the official documents relating to Shere Forest and its ownership were carefully checked. Everything was carried out in a strictly correct legal manner.'

'Smarmy bastard,' muttered my neighbour and I had to agree with him.

With evident relief, Gresham declared the meeting closed, and a stream of members headed for the comfort of the bar. It seemed to me that most of them had ignored the significance of the possible existence of a Deed of Trust. Would they really defer to the judgement of a creep like Simon Hanley in such a matter?

I caught up with Sir John Milne-Lyon as he left the dining room and asked him if he could spare a moment. I sat him down and he said, 'How long have you been a member here, my boy?' When I explained that I was helping Calvin Blair build the new course he said, 'I used to know Alister MacKenzie – a great designer. You make sure you get hold of his little book, *Golf Architecture*, I think it's called. There's never been a better summary of how to build a proper golf course.'

I thanked him and asked him about the Deed of Trust. 'Can you remember what it said about the sale of the club?'

'Oh yes, my boy. Whatever young Peter likes to think, the Deed exists. I may be old but I haven't lost all my marbles yet. What do you play off, by the way?'

'Two, at the moment.'

'That's very good. I only got down to two for a short time, when I lived next door to the course at Troon. I used to practise every morning.'

'Tell me a little more about the Deed,' I said gently.

'Yes, the Deed. I saw it, you know. I think Jimmy had it drawn up in thirty-seven or thirty-eight. Let's see, Mary and I lost the Worplesdon final in thirty-seven. It was around then.'

'Can you remember what it said?'

'The main thing was to protect the members. That was Jimmy's big concern. He owned the club but he said that it should never be sold without the approval of the members. Very far-sighted was old Jimmy. Now, he could chip a ball. The maestro, I used to call him. What do you use for your chip-and-runs, my boy?'

'I stick to a seven-iron for the bread-and-butter shots.'

'That's the way. Like a woman, be faithful and they won't let you down, eh?'

'There's some truth in that, sir,' I said. 'Sir John, can you remember what formula Mr Gresham used to protect the Shere Forest members?'

'Formula? Oh, I see. Yes, a majority of the members had to agree. Two-thirds, I think. The bar's a bit clearer now, my boy. Why don't you get us a drink? Mine's a whisky.'

When I returned with a large one for Sir John and a beer for myself I asked him one more question. 'Have you any idea where that Deed of Trust might be now?'

'If young Peter doesn't know where it is, and he claims that he's never seen it, we must assume that it's long gone, mustn't we? Of course, it wouldn't suit him, his son-in-law or the new owner if it turned up, would it?'

Sir John smiled at me, tossed back his whisky and wished me goodbye. 'We'll play a few holes one day,' he said.

The old man walked carefully towards the exit. He certainly hadn't lost his marbles. Whereas I'd had my doubts about the existence of a Deed of Trust when he'd first mentioned it, my conversation with Sir John had convinced me that his memory wasn't faulty. He'd immediately understood the implications of such a document. So had Simon Hanley.

Chapter 37

The following day I bought all the newspapers which had good City pages and went through them thoroughly. There was no mention of Davina Holdings and its share price told me very little; at 248 pence it was close to its highest level for the year, although it had moved down a few points the previous day.

I wondered how much the Welshman knew and how good his information was. More important, how sure was he that Slater was planning to sell Shere Forest to a Japanese corporation? It had been Jodie's contention from the start that Slater would eventually use the golf courses to elbow aside any planning and environmental constraints. Both she and Max had talked of the new course as a Trojan Horse to admit a much greater degree of building development. Maybe they were right after all.

Right on cue, the phone rang and Max greeted me. He was somewhere in Finland but planned to be back in England during the following week. 'I'll miss this place,' he said enthusiastically. 'The women are fan-tas-tic.'

'Good,' I said drily. 'What about your friends in Whitehall – any news?'

'Not yet, they're a bit tight-lipped at the moment. But I'll work on it when I get back.'

303

My mind returned to Davina Holdings. The best source of information could well be my old boss in the City, Andrew Buccleuth. Someone in his stockbroking firm would have tabs on the property sector. A call to his office got me as far as his secretary, Veronica, who watched over his working day like Cerberus in human form. After diligent cross-examination she allowed me to talk to her master, who was as affable as his secretary was chilly.

'Veronica's still on form,' I said ironically.

'Yes, she takes her role as guardian very seriously. She's getting married in a couple of weeks.'

I gasped theatrically. Veronica was around fifty years of age and had spent her life looking after her widowed mother, as well as Andrew. 'Who's the lucky man?' I asked. 'Is he moving in with her and Mum?'

'Mum's now in a home for aged gentlefolk and Veronica met Cyril at one of those singles dinner things.'

I didn't pursue the thread of Veronica's courtship any further but asked Andrew about Davina Holdings. He promised to call me back in an hour or two when he'd spoken to his property analyst.

Andrew was as good as his word. Just before lunch, Veronica, steely-voiced as ever, spoke down the line: 'I have Mr Buccleuth for you, Mr Ludlow.'

'I believe congratulations are in order, Veronica,' I said teasingly.

'Thank you,' she said in a slightly mellower tone before reverting to her usual formality. 'I'm putting you through.'

'Are you sitting comfortably?' said Andrew. 'Davina Holdings is said to be in a mess. Some of it will be revealed in the half-year results at the end of the month. If you've got any shares there, sell them now, that's my unbiased advice.'

'What's the problem?'

'The same one that's scuppered most of the property boys. Slater has quite a number of over-ambitious schemes which, because of the recession, he's been unable to sell or to rent out. There's a big development in Chelmsford, for instance, another one in Cardiff and a huge block in Hammersmith. It's got to the stage where he can hardly service the interest payments.'

'What will happen?'

'He's trying to reschedule the payments with his bankers, and find someone to bail him out.'

So the Welshman had been right.

'What about Shere Forest?' I inquired.

'That's currently his most valuable asset and my analyst here thinks he may have a buyer lined up.'

'A Japanese outfit?'

'How did you guess, Chris? Apparently he's getting a sum not unadjacent to eighty big ones. It won't necessarily save the sinking ship but it may well encourage the banks to carry on supporting him.'

'And no doubt a substantial commission on the sale will find its way to an off-shore company solely controlled by Mervyn Slater.'

'I don't know about that.' Andrew's voice sounded tentative. 'But you could be right. I've never dabbled much in property shares. Much too risky. I'm just amazed that Peter Gresham got involved with someone like Slater. Chalk and cheese, I would've thought.'

'Gresham needed the money. Or, I should say his son and son-in-law, Hanley, needed the money.'

'What a shame,' Andrew said. 'Have you ever had a game with Gresham, by the way?'

'A few holes. He can still play a bit.'

'I'll say. You know that he played in the Walker Cup and he won the President's Putter?'

'Yes, he's a fine player,' I agreed.

'Not a patch on his father,' Andrew stated firmly. 'Now Jimmy won the President's at his first attempt, when he was still at Oxford. And he finished third in the Open in thirty-eight, Reg Whitcombe's year at Sandwich, when the wind was so strong that the exhibition tent blew away. Old Jimmy Gresham was some player, I'll tell you.'

'And he was killed during the war?'

'In Burma. Peter told me that he was tortured to death by the Japanese. They're not his favourite people. This whole business with Davina Holdings is ironic, to say the least.'

I thanked Andrew Buccleuth for his help and he warned me not to divulge any of the information about Davina Holdings.

Although a crisis in the affairs of his company seemed to be behind Slater's proposed sale of Shere Forest, I wondered whether he'd had the plan in mind from the start. It was also interesting to speculate how much Nick Gresham and Simon Hanley had known. If they'd all been in on the plot, it was no wonder that the Green Disciples, and especially Jodie, had been seen as a serious threat. The odds were shortening that one of them was behind her murder. *Or maybe all of them.*

I tried my theory on Max when he returned from his Finnish trip and he agreed that it had some merit. 'Except for the method of the murder itself,' he said. 'I can't imagine any of those three men, from what you've told me about them, killing Jodie in such a brutal way.'

'Maybe they contracted it out to some hit man who gets his thrills that way.'

'That's a possibility. In which case, it's lucky he wasn't still in the house when you got there, Chris.'

We spent the weekend playing golf and toying with theories about Jodie's death. They became more and more arcane and Max promised to concentrate on prising some information out of his various contacts in the Intelligence services. It seemed to be the most promising path to tread – aside from kidnapping Slater or Hanley and trying to knock the truth out of them, that is.

On the following Tuesday I received a phone call from Toby Greenslade, who was keener than I to discuss developments at Shere Forest. A crony of his from the club had 'dropped a few hints'.

'What's this about a Japanese takeover?' he asked sharply.

'I can only give you my name, rank and serial number,' I said facetiously.

'Look, you young pup, I heard you were at the AGM and some member came up with incontrovertible evidence that Slater is selling out to the Japs.'

'He came up with a rumour, Toby, that's all.'

'Do you believe it?'

'No comment. Why don't you ring up Slater or Peter Gresham – or that creep, Hanley?'

'I've tried them. They won't tell me anything. By the way, Chris, are you still seeing Hanley's wife, the lovely Francesca?'

'Even more no comment.'

'Well, I'm going to run a little story in tomorrow's *News*, even though my friends will tell me sod all.' With a brusque farewell, he replaced his phone.

That evening Max disclosed that he had at last gathered a few scraps of information from his contacts. Interesting though they were, they didn't get us very far.

'They know Slater for two reasons,' Max said. 'First, the death of his first wife was never satisfactorily explained. The file is closed on that incident and he was never charged with anything. But he's questionable and they keep an eye on him. There's another reason for that – he's been involved in several dodgy property deals and they know that he's salted away quite a lot of money overseas.'

'That doesn't surprise me. Mind you, any man who supports Fulham Football Club must be put down as questionable,' I said. 'What about the others?'

'Nothing on Nick Gresham, although he's been seen with some curious Middle Eastern gentlemen in a casino in the West End. They think that's just a coincidence, however. Those guys were arms dealers and he's not involved in any business with scum like that.'

'No,' I agreed, 'but Hanley could be.'

'Wrong, Chris. He's in cahoots with Slater, as is very obvious. He's got his own secret bank account in Liechtenstein, by the way – I'll bet his wife would be interested in that. She'd also be interested in the crumpet he visits regularly in a mews house off Holland Park Avenue.'

'OK. So what about the old man – nothing on him, surely?'

'No. What you see is what you get. Of course, his firm has doled out plenty of cash in brown envelopes in their time to councillors and borough surveyors, but that's the nature of the building business.'

'Is there anything about a skeleton in the cupboard? Way back in Germany, perhaps?'

'Well, well. What do you know about that, Chris?'

'Only what I overheard some months ago. There was a row between him and Nigel Burnside. The Captain said he'd saved Gresham from some very serious problems when they were in the Army together.'

'Yes. It's all a bit like Slater's little spot of bother over his first wife's death. In Gresham's case, too, nothing was proven. In the German incident, a young child was killed, by a car that mounted the pavement. It was a British Army staff car and the driver was obviously drunk.'

'And it was Gresham at the wheel and the whole thing was hushed up?'

'You've got it. The German family said it was the child's own fault, she ran into the road. But they moved a few months later to a much nicer house in another town.'

'What a wicked world we live in,' I said mournfully.

'It's the only one we've got,' said Max cheerfully.

Chapter 38

Little had been seen of Peter Gresham since the AGM the previous week but he made an early entry to our office on the Wednesday morning. With Hannibal snuffling at his heels, he strode in and brandished a copy of the *Daily News* at us.

'Have you seen this damned article by that man, Greenslade?' he asked.

Although I had seen it and had already discussed it with Calvin, we both played dumb.

'He's a friend of yours, Ludlow. You didn't pass on any of the nonsense that was spouted at the AGM, did you?'

'No, I did not,' I said firmly. 'There were about two hundred of your members there. Why don't you ask them?'

Gresham looked pointedly at me for a moment. As he realised the injustice of his remark, his dark eyes swivelled away. He scratched one of his ears and grunted, 'Yes, quite right. Unfair of me, damned unfair.'

I asked to see the article. Headed 'JAPS SET TO INVADE NOBS' CLUB' the first paragraph read:

'Shere Forest, the exclusive golf club on the borders of royal Berkshire and stockbroker Surrey, will soon be flying the flag of the Rising Sun. Mervyn Slater, new owner and property whizz kid, is set to make a bundle on his recent investment by selling it on to a Japanese Corporation. It is estimated that Fulham Football Club fan Merv will walk away with a profit of over 8 billion yen. That's 50 million quid to you and me. That'll buy an awful lot of footballs.'

'Is it true?' I asked. 'Is that what Slater intends to do?'

'It's not what Slater *intends* to do, it's a matter of what he's *allowed* to do.' Gresham spoke so forcefully that Hannibal jumped up from his recumbent position on the floor and barked. His doggie smell pulsated strongly through the room. 'I can assure you that there will be no sale of my club to a bunch of damned Japanese. Murdering devils. I won't allow it.'

Gresham turned on his heel as if on a parade ground and stamped his way out of the door.

Calvin aimed a mock salute at his back. 'What's all that about? Is he off his chump or what? It's not his club any more, is it? Slater can do what he bloody well likes.'

'I'm not so sure,' I said cautiously. 'Gresham may have one more card up his sleeve.'

'It'll have to be a good 'un.'

'The Joker, perhaps.'

At midday, in order to get the knots out of my back after a morning spent poring over drawings of the new course, I headed for the practice putting green. I was trying out yet another new method, concentrating on making my right hand push the club through towards the hole. If it worked for Jack Nicklaus, why wasn't it working for me?

On the verge of returning to the drawing board, both literally and figuratively, I was hailed by Sir John Milne-Lyon.

'I saw you from the bar, my boy. Good to see you practising.'

'I need all the help I can get, Sir John.'

'Well, your stroke looks pretty smooth, and that's most of the battle. But could you just do me a little favour and have a look at my putting? I'm all over the place at the moment.'

It was nice to think that a man in his nineties was still trying to improve his game. I watched him hit a few putts and suggested that he stood more upright over the ball and rocked his shoulders to initiate the back-swing. It worked, as most putting tips do for a while.

After he'd holed several five-foot putts, the old man ushered me into the clubhouse and bought me a drink. Peter Gresham was sitting in a far corner of the bar with two of the members. I nodded towards them and said, 'Mr Gresham seems to be in a fair old state this morning. The takeover of the club and so on. Did you read about it?'

'Yes, my boy, I read several papers each morning. Keeps me in touch and my mind active.'

'What do you think about it all?'

'Young Peter's got a thing about the Japanese. Silly. I know they killed his father but, nonetheless, you've got to forgive and forget. I spent two years in France during the Great War. Lots of my friends were killed and one of my brothers. But I don't hate the Jerries, life's too short for that nonsense. Don't trust the buggers, mind you,' he said reflectively.

'He'd say the same thing about the Japanese,' I replied. 'But if he found that Deed of Trust, there wouldn't be a problem.'

'I've tried to help him out there,' Sir John said. 'I gave it a lot of thought and then suddenly remembered that the club's bankers before the war were Coutts in the Strand. Seems the obvious place to look, doesn't it?'

'And has he?'

'I hope so, but you'd better ask him yourself.'

There was no chance to do so because Gresham had headed for the dining room with his two friends. I joined Calvin for a quick pub lunch and we pressed on with our mountains of work during the afternoon. Between times, I received a call from Toby who asked if I'd enjoyed his article.

'Loved the headline, Toby. But Peter Gresham is not pleased with you.'

'My job as a journalist isn't to please people,' Toby replied grandly.

'Obviously, and especially not those who are fond of our mother tongue.' I overrode his protests and continued: 'Toby, listen to me. There's a much bigger story here than a proposed takeover by the Japs.'

'What is it?'

'I don't know yet. Honestly. But I think it'll all come to the boil in the next few days.'

I was wrong. It was sooner than that.

Late that afternoon, as thoughts of going home began to surface, the phone rang once again. I had been speculating about the meal that Mrs Bradshaw would have left for me. Wednesday was the day on which she cleaned my flat, and she invariably cooked me supper. It was an appealing prospect: a good meal and European Cup football on the box. Manchester United versus some Turkish side or other. A hatful of goals for United, no doubt.

It was Francesca Hanley, and I had to hold the receiver away from my ear as she shouted down the line: 'Chris, thank God you're there. Come over quickly. It's Simon, he's going berserk. Please come!'

I heard a crash from the other end and the line went dead. Quickly, I grabbed my jacket, rapped out an explanation to Calvin and raced for the door. He shouted after me, 'Shall I call the police?'

'Not yet. Stay by the phone!' As I legged it out of the office towards the Porsche I hoped that Simon hadn't found out that I'd been sleeping with Francesca. That would put me well and truly on the defensive. You can't bonk a man's wife and beat him up as well.

The Hanley household was only a couple of miles away but it seemed much further. I swept into the drive, skidded to a stop and scrambled out of the car. The front door of the house was open and, as I ran towards it, I could already hear Hanley shouting abuse. Presumably at his wife, but possibly at the world in general. There were bangs and thuds from the back of the house and I went cautiously in that direction, treading softly and staying close to one wall of the large hallway. I heard a sharp crack, a scream from Francesca, and I didn't have to strain to hear Hanley's next words: 'That stupid bastard, he's about to ruin everything. Well, I'm going over there to stop him.'

It didn't take too long to work out who his target was. A moment later, Hanley came floundering through the kitchen doorway into the hall. He had a shotgun in his right hand. I hoped that the safety catch was on.

Hanley was bright crimson in the face and sweat sprinkled his forehead. Francesca clutched at his arm. I could see deep red marks on both her cheeks and she was bleeding from the corner of her mouth. He shook her off violently and she shouted, 'Don't be stupid, there's nothing you can do now.'

For a moment or two I thought Hanley was going to put the gun down but the sight of me seemed to stoke the fire of his anger. 'I can kill your bloody fool of a father,' he roared. 'Now let go of me, and you – get the hell out of my way!'

He levelled the barrel of the shotgun at me. Two barrels, I noted dispassionately. He could hardly miss at the distance of a few yards. One barrel would be enough. For what seemed a very long time I was rooted to the spot. I didn't believe that he'd kill me. I didn't believe he'd kill anyone, face to face, with a gun. But I didn't fancy an each-way bet either, especially when he screamed once again, 'Get out of the way.'

The barrels wavered in the air and then there was a flash and the crushing sound of a shotgun in a confined space. The splinter of wood and crash of breaking glass followed immediately. I looked up from the floor where I'd thrown myself and realised that Hanley had missed me deliberately.

'That's to show you I mean it,' he shouted hoarsely at me. He looked as frightened as I felt. Francesca was cowering in a corner, her hands over her ears. I picked myself up as Hanley moved towards me and it was Francesca who saved the day. I saw her dart towards a small table, grab a pot plant and throw it at Hanley. It was more of a lob, really, but it did the trick. He saw her move out of the corner of his eye and put up his arm as a shield against the unlikely missile.

That was my chance. I threw myself across the few yards that separated us, jabbed him in the eyes with one hand and grabbed for the gun with the other. I smelled aftershave as I got in close but the tussle didn't last long. Hanley let go of the gun and staggered back against a grandfather clock. According to Francesca later, I kicked him in the ankle and then hit him as hard as I could in the stomach and ribs.

Hanley had collapsed onto the floor and lay there groaning loudly. Francesca broke the gun open and removed the two cartridges. She knelt by her husband. 'Come on, Simon,' she said, 'it's all over. Let's get you into the sitting room.'

The telephone was on the wall near the front door. I phoned Calvin and told him to wait for me.

Chapter 39

Simon Hanley was doubled up on a sofa, coughing and retching. I wanted to haul him to his feet by his hair and knock some truth out of him, but the sight of Francesca with tears running down her battered face reminded me that we'd had enough violence for one day. Above all, Hanley was humiliated, his passion spent; he'd probably tell me all I needed to know.

'What's this all about, Simon?' I asked gently.

He didn't move from his position on the sofa. I heard his muffled voice say, 'The stupid old bastard, he'll spoil everything.'

Francesca, busy now with a handkerchief in an effort to mop up her tears, said sharply, 'Tell him, Simon. It's all finished now. Just tell him the truth.'

'He called me in the office,' Hanley mumbled. 'Told me the deal with the Japs was off. I laughed at him. Said it was out of his hands, that Slater was in the driving seat now.'

'And Gresham told you that he'd unearthed a copy of the Deed of Trust and that he could prevent a further sale?'

The hunched figure moved slightly as if in assent and then Hanley sat up a little. 'He told me that he'd called a meeting with Slater at the club, to sort things out once and for all. That he wouldn't disturb the *status quo*, but that he wouldn't allow the club to be sold to a Japanese company either. I knew there'd be trouble as soon as the Japs came into it.'

'What did you expect?' Francesca snapped. 'His father was tortured to death by them. You know bloody well that he won't do business with them.'

Hanley laughed bitterly and then held his ribs as he grimaced in pain. 'The old fool. Slater had no interest in Shere Forest as a golf club. It's just another commodity, an asset which he bought cheap to sell on dear. He had the Japanese deal fixed up months ago.'

'And he needs to move quickly, I hear?'

'You bet. He needs all the cash he can get to prop up his company.'

'And what was your cut going to be?' Francesca asked.

'Five per cent of the gross if you must know.'

'You utter shit,' she said simply.

'I was in a hole. It was my chance to make some real money again. Christ, I've had to pay out nearly a million in losses at Lloyds.'

'Don't expect any sympathy from me. You're greedy, Simon, greedy and corrupt, and you always have been.' Francesca paused and then said nastily, 'I suppose you couldn't wait to spend some of the money on your tarts.' Hanley made no reply and she asked: 'What about Nick? He was in on this, too, wasn't he?'

'Slater paid off his gambling debts. He had a bonus to come, half a million when the deal went through.'

'God, you all make me feel ill,' said Francesca. 'Money, money, money, that's all you think about.' She stood up and walked away, as if trying to avoid his contagion.

'It's all right for you, Francesca,' Hanley snivelled. 'You've always had money and plenty of it.'

To get the questions back on track I asked Hanley what he'd intended to do to Peter Gresham.

'Threaten him,' he replied. 'Get the Deed off him and destroy it, just like . . .' Hanley stopped and was silent.

'Just like the copy that Nigel Burnside knew about,' I finished for him.

'I don't know what you're talking about,' he blustered. I walked towards him, grabbed him by his shirt-front and began to lift him. I raised my fist and Francesca turned away and looked out through the window.

'I know what happened,' I said. 'You might as well come clean. Now, in front of your wife.'

'OK, OK.' I let him go and he slumped back into the chair. 'Burnside was a complete piss-artist, he couldn't keep any kind of a secret. God knows what Hermione ever saw in him. There's no accounting for taste.'

'Too true,' Francesca said sharply.

'Anyway, back at the time of the Classic, he knew about the impending sale of the club to Slater. I thought he was being even more cocky than usual, sarcastic even about Shere Forest. So I got him on one side. He was bursting with his little scheme. He'd found the Deed somewhere in the club's records and planned to produce it at the EGM which had been called for the following Wednesday.'

'Which would've effectively stopped the sale.'

'Dead in its tracks. The members saved by their indomitable Secretary. There's no doubt that they'd have voted the proposal out.'

'And the first part of your bonus would never have materialised?'

'Correct. And of course Burnside told the Press about the sale to make doubly sure that he'd be seen as the white knight riding to the club's rescue.'

I knew that this was untrue and I said, 'It wasn't Burnside who blabbed to the Press, it was you. You dropped your guts to Johnson of the *Chronicle*. I'm betting that you wanted to flush Burnside out, make him demonstrate how clever or lucky he'd been in getting hold of the Deed.'

'It wasn't like that,' Hanley said, 'but who cares?'

'I still don't understand why Burnside should have told you where the Deed was.'

He looked at me with an air of shifty triumph. 'I put some pressure on him. You might even call it blackmail, I suppose. You see, he'd been in big trouble when he was in the Army in Germany. A child was killed in a car accident and Burnside was responsible. Old man Gresham got him off the hook. So I gave him the choice. Hand over the Deed to me and I'd keep quiet or I'd ruin his reputation, such as it was, for good.'

Now I knew that Hanley was lying because Gresham, not Burnside, had transgressed in Germany. A sudden flash of understanding lit up my brain. I thought I knew what had really happened but I led Hanley on a little further. 'So, Burnside knew that his grandiose scheme wasn't going to work. He also knew that you might reveal the truth about that unsavoury incident in Germany at any time.'

'I gave him my word,' protested Hanley.

'No wonder he killed himself,' said Francesca.

'Anyway,' I interrupted, 'the result was that, in the depths of alcoholic despair, he hanged himself. And you destroyed the Deed, is that it?'

'That's it,' Hanley agreed.

'You bloody liar,' I said quietly.

I saw Francesca's body jerk in surprise. 'You didn't blackmail Burnside, you couldn't have done. You got him horribly drunk at his cottage and found out where the Deed was. Then you gave him a nice cocktail of tranquillizers and Scotch and strung him up. You murdered him.'

Hanley had gone chalk-white. He stuttered out his denials but I knew I was right. I stood in front of him and he rose unsteadily to his feet. 'Did you kill Jodie Hesse as well?' I asked him. 'She was in the way of the deal, too, wasn't she? Was it you? Or Slater?'

I grabbed him by the shirt and shoved my face close to his. I could smell aftershave again, mingled with sweat. 'You weren't at Nick's party. Jodie was killed that night. Where were you, you murdering bastard?' I was yelling in his face and I felt someone bashing me on the arm.

'Let him go, Chris.' It was Francesca. I relaxed my grip and retreated a pace or two.

'Fran, Fran,' he gabbled, 'I've got a receipt in my wallet, in my coat in the kitchen. I was in Edinburgh for the night.'

Hanley was telling the truth. There was not only a credit card receipt but also the hotel receipt to match it. 'Two hundred and forty pounds. Two people. Another of your tarts, I take it,' Francesca said drily. 'You can go and join her. Tonight, Simon. I want you out of here.'

'I think I'd better go and talk to Gresham,' I said, 'and Slater, if he's turned up.' As we reached the front door, Francesca stumbled against me. She clung on tight and I held her for a moment.

'I'm OK,' she said quickly. 'Just getting used to the idea of being married to a murderer.'

'I'm probably wrong.'

'You're probably right. I could follow the logic of it. I could never understand why my father kept Burnside in a job. He was useless and he wasn't even polite to the old man. In fact, he was positively nasty. It rings true that he had some sort of hold over him.'

'Let's call it gratitude on your father's part, and loyalty on both their parts.' I nodded towards the open door of the lounge. 'Is it wise to be alone with him?'

'He won't trouble me any more. What little stuffing he had has leaked out now. I'll see you very soon.'

'Yes, Francesca, but . . .'

'Don't worry. I won't be after you on the rebound. Go and sort out my father, Chris. You're the best man to do it.'

More carefully than on the outward journey, I drove back to the club. Calvin Blair was waiting anxiously in the office and fired a volley of questions at me. With a promise to tell him everything later, I urged him to help me find Gresham.

'I must tell him what Hanley and Slater have been up to,' I said.

As we passed the car park, Calvin gestured at a Rolls Royce with the number plate MS1. 'Slater's here already.'

'Well, we'll interrupt the meeting, if we have to.'

We walked swiftly into the bar which was crowded with golfers. A large society had just finished their day and were setting out to demolish the bar's supplies of booze; anything contained in a bottle or a barrel was clearly on their hit list. The noise was such that the barman could hardly hear my question about the whereabouts of Peter Gresham. Craning across the bar counter he eventually shouted back, 'A meeting with Mr

Slater? In the committee room, I expect.'

The room was on the far side of the clubhouse on the upper floor. We clattered up some broad wooden stairs and along a corridor which was lined with the photographs of past captains of the club. Without waiting for an answer to my knock, I threw open the door of the committee room.

Mervyn Slater was alone in the room at one end of the long wooden table. Slumped in the substantial wood and leather chair which was only ever occupied, on formal occasions, by the Captain of the club, he seemed to have fallen asleep.

We both paused in the doorway, surprised that Peter Gresham was not there. As I said, 'I'm sorry to butt in . . .' I was hit by a sickening sense of *déjà vu*. I noticed the curious angle of Slater's head. I walked a few more steps into the room and saw the gaping wound in his neck. Blood had spurted haphazardly over his dark suit, onto the carpet and across the table. The weapon wasn't hard to find. It was a ceremonial Samurai sword which lay precisely in the centre of the table, its blade pointing at Slater's corpse. Beyond the sword handle lay a large brown envelope. It was neatly positioned, its centre aligned with the handle.

Calvin muttered, 'Oh my God,' and I told him to stay where he was. He didn't protest.

I moved closer and noted the distinct and sickening echoes of Jodie's death. Could it be the same murderer? But with a different weapon?

I turned to speak to Calvin and a feeling of unease crawled over me when I saw he was no longer in the room. Quickly I moved to the door and found him squatting in the corridor, his head on his knees. I was also trying to stifle an urgent need to be sick, but I put my hand on Calvin's shoulder and said, 'Take it easy. I've got to find Gresham. He's probably in the office.' The Secretary's office adjoined the committee room. I dreaded what I might find in there. 'When you feel up to it, we'll have a look in that envelope.'

Calvin stood up unsteadily, wiped his face with a handkerchief and said, 'Shouldn't we leave everything as it is? Call the police and leave it all for them?'

'We'll do that in a minute but I'm interested in that envelope.' I walked back through the door of the committee room and carefully slid the envelope across the table towards me. Then I called out Peter Gresham's name as I walked towards the office. 'Peter,' I shouted lustily. 'Peter, are you there?'

My hand was on the door knob when I heard the roar of a shotgun for the second time that day. Once again I dived on the floor and sat there for a moment or two.

Sure now of what I would find on the other side of the door, I said to Calvin, 'Go to the bar and use their phone. Call the police. I'll take a look in there.'

Clutching the precious brown envelope, I turned the handle, opened the door very slowly and peered inside. Gresham was on the floor, a chair tumbled by him. I recognised him by his tweed suit and because the faithful Hannibal was tugging playfully at one of his master's sleeves. There wasn't much left of Peter Gresham's head; the blast had blown the front half backwards against the wall and upwards to the ceiling.

I only ventured into the room for a few moments; I'd had enough of death and destruction for one day. I tugged at Hannibal's collar but he wouldn't move from Gresham's side, so I left them together.

Calvin was nowhere to be seen and I assumed that he was calling the police. With my face averted, I sat at the opposite end of the table from Slater's dead body and tipped out the contents of the unsealed envelope.

There were sealed letters addressed to Gresham's wife, Hermione, and his two children. I put them on one side and unfolded a legal document which had been printed on thick creamy paper. At the bottom there was the wax seal of the Shere Forest Golf Club and the signature of James Gresham. It was dated 1938, so Sir John Milne-Lyon's memory had been pretty accurate.

I scanned the Deed of Trust quickly. In plain language it stated that, in the matter of a sale of the Shere Forest golf club to an outside party, James Gresham or his heirs and successors volunteered to be bound by the decision of the members. A majority of two-thirds would be required before such a sale could take place. Sir John had been right and, when he had found a copy of the Deed, Nigel Burnside had realised what power he had in his hands. Unfortunately for the Secretary, Simon Hanley had discovered the danger to his plans and had taken his own drastic action.

Peter Gresham had written his suicide note-cum-confession on Shere Forest notepaper. His handwriting sprawled across the page but was legible enough. As I began to read, I heard footsteps in the corridor and jumped guiltily to my feet. It was Calvin. He said the police were on their way.

'You didn't tell anyone about this, did you?' I asked.

'No, I told the barman to send the police up here. They didn't hear a thing, it's like a madhouse down there.'

'Good. Come and look at this.' I spread Gresham's letter out on the table and we both read it.

'To my friends at Shere Forest,' it was headed and then it continued:

First of all, I want to thank Sir John Milne-Lyon for alerting me to the existence of the enclosed Deed of Trust. I had no knowledge of it but should have realised that my father would have had the best interests of Shere Forest close to his heart.

For a time, financial considerations and pressure from my immediate family made me cast those best interests aside. My regrets to you all for failing to carry out my duties on your behalf.

I could not allow Davina Holdings to sell Shere Forest from under us. Above all, not to Japanese interests. As some of you will know, my father, along with hundreds of thousands of other brave soldiers, was murdered by the Japanese in direct contravention of the codes of warfare. I could not allow my father's beloved Shere Forest to pass into the hands of such a people.

The discovery of the Deed of Trust has made it easier for me to act. I have taken revenge on a cheat and a charlatan and hope I've acted honourably in taking my own life.

I am convinced that my dead friend, Nigel Burnside, also took his own life, possibly in remorse at what might happen to Shere Forest.

I ask you all to honour the traditions of this great club.

I replaced the letters and the two other documents in the brown envelope and pushed it back into the middle of the table.

'Let's wait outside,' Calvin said nervously and I joined him in the corridor. 'That body gives me the creeps.'

'You wouldn't want to see Gresham in that case,' I said. 'What did you think of the letter?'

'All crystal clear, isn't it? He knocked Slater off and then did for himself. But I don't get his remarks about Burnside. We know it was suicide, and the inquest confirmed it, so what's he trying to say?'

'I think, Calvin, that Gresham was far from convinced that Burnside committed suicide. I reckon he guessed that his old chum was murdered to make sure that the Deed remained a secret. It's a bit of special pleading to protect someone in Gresham's family.'

'Who? Not Nick surely?' I heard the thump of footsteps and the echo of voices coming in our direction. Calvin's face suddenly lit up in surprise and contempt. 'It's that bastard Hanley, isn't it?'

'I think so. Gresham has laid down a bit more smoke for Francesca's sake. I suggest that we leave it like that.'

A squad of police arrived and took over. Though they dealt with Calvin and me sympathetically it was several hours before we were allowed to go home.

Two shotgun blasts, a punch-up, two deaths and far too much time spent in the company of the police added up to a long day in anybody's book. I wasn't sorry to throw myself into bed as soon as I got home. I had hoped for dreamless sleep to heal some of the scars of a violent day. Instead, my uneasy mind projected bizarre images on my unconscious. Invading those images was the tortured form of Jodie Hesse; it was as if she were begging me to unmask her murderer.

Chapter 40

There had been no need for Peter Gresham to kill Mervyn Slater; it was an act of revenge, pure and simple, as Gresham had admitted in his suicide note. Slater's fragile property empire crashed in ruins soon after his death and when the Official Receiver learned of the existence of the Deed of Trust, which technically invalidated the sale of Shere Forest to Davina Holdings, he was very happy to rid himself of the problem. He agreed to sell all the shares back to the members for a nominal sum.

Cajoled by Hermione Gresham, the members put their hands in their pockets and provided the money to complete the building of the new course. There was a messianic look to Hermione and she assumed her husband's role as Chairman of the club and also took on the work of the Secretary. She did the work of the two men in her life with ease and frequently made the point that the expansion of Shere Forest would be completed, on time, as a memorial to Peter.

Hermione was much better to work for than her husband, and her enthusiasm made everyone at Shere Forest rally to her call. Aided by yet another mild winter, it seemed that the eighteen holes would all be ready for seeding in the spring.

All the environmental plans, which had been deliberately

shoved to one side in Slater's determination to meet his deadline, were reimposed, much to Charley James's delight. She became a regular visitor once again. Calvin agreed to slight modifications of two of the holes on the new course in order to offer more space and protection to the Dartford Warblers.

It was an enormous relief to everyone that the Green Disciples now left Shere Forest in peace. Perhaps they had decided that after all the bloodshed, any more harassment would be disastrous for them in PR terms. Maybe they didn't fancy crossing swords with Hermione Gresham – and who could blame them? Although they were active on various fronts and their public profile remained as distinctive as ever, they subsequently concentrated their efforts on mainland Europe.

My affair with Francesca fizzled out gradually. Nothing was seen of Simon Hanley at Shere Forest again and his misdemeanours were never brought out into the open. But I knew, as did Francesca, that he was a murderer and a con-man. As far as I was aware he continued to work for his firm of solicitors. The law, like the City, looks after its own.

All in all, the lid seemed to have been firmly nailed down on all the mayhem which had afflicted Shere Forest. From the start, Burnside's death had been accepted as a suicide and the deaths of Slater and Peter Gresham were seen as the bizarre tragedies they surely were. For some days there was the usual frenzy of coverage in the tabloid Press and then they moved onto some other sensation.

No progress was made in tracking down the murderer of Jodie Hesse. It seemed almost as though word had gone out from Scotland Yard, or from one of the Intelligence bodies, that no one was to try too hard to solve the crime.

Even Max made no headway with his various contacts in

Whitehall. As the winter dragged on I gave up asking him about Jodie, which saved him from having to tell me that I should forget all about her and find myself a nice bit of crumpet.

Max was right to warn me not to dwell on the tragedy of Jodie Hesse. But I couldn't forget my promise to myself to find her murderer, and no day passed without my thinking about her.

Chapter 41

The seeding of the new course was achieved on schedule to general rejoicing. Although the official opening of the refurbished clubhouse was not due to take place until the eve of the British Classic, Hermione Gresham declared that she would host her own pro-am tournament on the first Monday in May to mark the progress made on the project. It was to be her way of thanking everyone who had been involved.

The pro-am was billed as a light-hearted competition but the prize for the leading professional was substantial and he would also become the holder of the Peter Gresham Salver. Hermione had not forgotten her old lover either – the leading amateur was to receive the Nigel Burnside Medal.

A good professional field had been assembled, including Jack Mason. During the week before the event, Calvin Blair had been spending an hour a day on the practice ground and I knew that he was also determined to make a good showing.

Max and I hoped that he would succeed, as we had been drawn to play with him, the fourth member of our group being Toby Greenslade. Whatever the standard of the golf it would certainly be a good-humoured and enjoyable event – particularly as we intended to linger at the refreshment tents which Hermione had placed at frequent intervals around the course.

With a keen sense of anticipation, therefore, I set off for Max's flat on a still and sunny Monday morning – it was a lovely day for golf.

Max was still working for the Swiss Institute which had sponsored the environmental report. Having settled on London as his base for the next year or two, he had bought himself a flat not far from mine. Since I had volunteered to do the driving, Max had offered to supply the breakfast.

As I waited in a traffic jam I glanced at the headlines in my newspaper – and received a shock. They were entirely taken up by the death of Julius Sparkes. 'MP AND MEDIA MOGUL JULIUS MURDERED', screamed the banner headline, followed by, 'GUNMAN'S BULLETS ASSASSINATE SPARKES – IRA SUSPECTED.'

'Kidneys, bacon, mushrooms, eggs, black pudding,' Max said succinctly as he opened his door to me. 'All ready. It'll put ten yards on your drive.'

We both piled into the food heaped on our plates and between a mouthful, I said, 'Have you read about Sparkes?' Max nodded. 'Is it the IRA, do you think?'

'Could be,' he replied, buttering another thick slice of bread. 'He's made some pretty inflammatory remarks about them over the years, hasn't he? He was probably on someone's hit list.'

'Whoever did it was a cool customer, according to the papers. He put a bullet into Sparkes's body and then made sure with one in the head. All done from a distance of at least half a mile.'

'These hit squads aren't mugs. Everyone knows that,' Max said.

'But no one's claimed responsibility yet, have they?'

'Not yet, they'll probably do it later today. They'll get the headlines on the TV news tonight and in the papers tomorrow.'

'Since we're on the subject,' I said, 'you and your security chums never found anything or anyone suspicious at TripleVision, did you? That lead to Jodie Hesse petered out, obviously.'

'Yeah,' Max replied. 'It was never a lead, really. Just some casual contact she had, that's all.' He stood up. 'We'll have a fresh pot of coffee, and then away. How's your game, Chris? Putting well, as usual, I hope.'

As it happened, I was far from happy with my putting. It had recently become wayward and the game within a game had become a puzzle to me.

'Why don't you try a new putter?' Max suggested from the other side of the room. 'That usually helps. Have a rummage in my cupboard in the hall. There are several in there.'

Max was right to say that a new club, a different balance and feel, sometimes helped.

I threw open the double doors of the hall cupboard and saw a collection of suitcases piled high in one corner and various items of clothing hanging from a pole. Tennis and squash rackets, a couple of hockey sticks and various discarded golf clubs, including several putters, lay in another corner. I tugged at a couple of putters and dislodged a flat brown plastic case. I wondered if Max had something special in the way of putters in there.

After laying the other two clubs on the hall floor, I hauled the box into the open and flicked the catches off. Pressed into the foam rubber of the interior were several pieces of tubular black metal, a collapsible tripod, a telescope that I recognised as a gun sight and the other bits and pieces that made up a lethal-looking rifle.

Startled, I looked round as Max said, 'It's a Barrett Light Fifty. American.'

'What the hell are you doing with it?'

'It goes back tonight. I borrowed it to do a job. Come into the kitchen, have your coffee and I'll tell you about it.'

'It's a pity that you had to know anything about this, Chris,' Max began, 'and I needn't tell you that this is strictly between us. Plus a guy I know from way back.'

'From when you were in Ireland?'

'Yeah, we worked together. Fortunately I've got as much on him as he's got on me. He stayed on with one of the security bodies. He's a professional spook. He'll probably end up in charge of something important.

'Anyway, to get to the point, I was suspicious about the fax that was sent from TripleVision to Jodie and later I went back to try and find out a bit more about it. You remember Liz, the pleasant girl who worked in the golf department?' I nodded and Max continued, 'Well, I made sure she became a friend.'

'Max, you didn't . . .'

'No, I didn't. I can make friends with the opposite sex, you know,' he said sharply. I laughed at him and he continued. 'I still thought that Jodie must have had a close contact at TripleVision and I got Liz to ask around. After all, Jodie had become pretty high profile, as they put it in public relations circles. But nothing came of it. According to Liz, nobody admitted to knowing her. In the circumstances, I don't suppose they would.

'I asked my friend at security what he knew about weirdos

and lefties at TripleVision but he had nothing much either. He said that the only real weirdo was Sparkes himself and he came up with some diverting facts. First of all, they'd had him under surveillance for years, because he hasn't always been on the far Right of the political spectrum. In fact, when he was at Oxford, he was a devotee of an extreme form of Communism. In his twenties he travelled widely in Russia and in China, so the spooks had their eyes on him.'

'Youthful idealism,' I replied. 'Nothing wrong with that and it often brings disillusionment and a complete reversal of political ideas.'

'The God that failed,' Max murmured. 'Yes, you're right in some cases.'

'But not in that of Sparkes?'

'No, because his Right-wing stance was merely that. His real sympathies remained on the other flank. As he got richer and richer he was able to support a whole variety of extremist causes. I told you way back when we first discussed the Green Disciples that their aims were primarily to disrupt society and eventually to destroy it.'

'I remember that,' I said.

'Well, according to my spooky chum, Sparkes provided the money that enabled the Green Disciples to do their stuff in such style. And they *were* bloody successful . . .'

'As we saw down in Wiltshire.'

'Exactly. Brilliantly organised, highly motivated, a sophisticated group with pots of money.'

My mind had raced ahead and I said quietly to Max, 'You're about to tell me that Sparkes and Jodie were lovers, aren't you?'

'I'm afraid so. Then I began to wonder about Sparkes. The highly successful businessman, posing as a Right-wing extremist but actually just the opposite. A ruthless espouser of the most disruptive elements on the far Left of European politics. It struck me that he might've been disenchanted with Jodie. And then I remembered something that Liz told me, only a small thing. Sparkes's suite of offices was on the same floor as the golf department where she worked. It seemed a reasonable assumption that Sparkes or his secretary sent that message to Jodie. The fax machine in question was the closest one to his office.'

'That seems a careless thing to do,' I objected.

'I agree. Maybe he didn't think it through. Or maybe he told the bastard he paid to knock Jodie off to collect the fax message on his way out of her house,' Max replied.

'I see. And Sparkes must've had kittens when he forgot. But why didn't he use the fax in his own office?'

'There isn't one. He wouldn't have any machinery in his office, except telephones.'

'This is all pretty flimsy, Max,' I objected. 'It hardly seems enough evidence to condemn Sparkes as the man behind Jodie's murder.'

Max left the room and reappeared a few moments later with a cassette tape in his hand. 'Listen to this,' he said. 'It came courtesy of my contact in security. But prepare yourself, the first person you'll hear is Jodie.'

The buzz of a telephone was heard and then the unmistakable voice of Jodie Hesse. It was an unnerving moment. A man spoke and Max whispered that it was Sparkes.

'Jodie, we have to talk. I'm not too happy at the way things are going.'

'What do you mean? The programme has never been so successful, we've never been so prominent.'

'That isn't the reason why I've poured millions into it. You've begun to believe your own publicity and you've forgotten what our real aims are.'

'You're probably right, Julius. I've been thinking things over in the last few weeks. My aims are different to yours. I believe in the message. Save the planet, that's what I want to do.'

There was silence on the tape for a few moments and then Sparkes said, 'Take it easy, Jodie. We'll talk it through. After your broadcast – OK?'

'OK,' said Jodie.

'So we know that Sparkes is disenchanted . . .' I began.

But Max held his hand up to silence me and said, 'Here comes the conclusive bit.'

The tape hissed and we heard the buzz of another telephone. A voice with a broad north-east accent said hello and Sparkes said sharply, 'Is that you, Tom?'

'Yeah.'

'You remember the problem we discussed? I want you to deal with it. She'll be home at about nine o'clock. I'll pay the usual fee. Agreed?'

'Agreed.'

There was silence in the kitchen for some time and then I said to Max, 'Wouldn't Sparkes realise that his phones were tapped?'

'Probably. But if it came to it he'd claim they were normal business chats. There's nothing about violence, nothing untoward at all. It's only because we know what happened later that we hear the implications.'

'And your contacts understood the implications, that Sparkes was behind Jodie's murder?'

'Sure,' Max replied.

341

'Why didn't they pass the evidence over to the police?'

'For a start it's not hard evidence. Anyway, they don't work like that. The police are the last people they'd help. These security boys aren't in the information exchange business. They're very jealous of their sources, and they *don't* share their secrets.'

'So Sparkes had Jodie killed because he couldn't control her any more. She'd ceased to be a true believer in his grand plan.'

'Partly that,' Max said. 'And perhaps he was jealous of her. She'd become very successful. It's ironic that she'd actually become a convert to the Green Disciples' cause. That didn't suit Sparkes at all. He'd recruited her as a hard-edged social revolutionary and she'd become a wide-eyed environmental idealist. She was a potential danger because she knew far too much about him and his organisation.'

'And her murder was a bonus for the Green Disciples,' I mused. 'They were able to throw suspicion on the people connected with Shere Forest. Very clever.'

A glance at my watch told me that we ought to be on our way in a few minutes. I had a few more questions for my brother, however. 'So you decided to kill him yourself?'

'With the connivance of my security friend, yes. He was glad to see me go freelance and knock the bastard off. Sparkes was just a load of trouble. They were glad to be rid of him.'

'And they'll cover your tracks?'

'I don't leave tracks,' Max said grimly. 'But some obscure Irish faction will take responsibility for his execution. They'll release it to the Press Association today.'

'How did you do it?'

Max grimaced at me. 'Sparkes had pretty good security but he'd become a bit careless, especially at weekends. He's got a bloody great country house in Rutland. I found out that it was a habit of his on a Sunday night to sit and drink a few glasses of champagne, either on the lawn or in the conservatory.'

'Didn't he have men patrolling the grounds?' I asked.

'Yeah, but not the perimeter. As I say, he'd got careless. I climbed up in a tree, not far from the perimeter wall. I had a clear shot at him and with that Barrett rifle you can't miss.'

'I thought the pros used Kalashnikovs.'

'A lot do. I prefer the Barrett. It's very accurate and very powerful. Anyway, I got him first time.'

'And then made sure?'

'I put the second bullet through his head. Then over the wall and away on a motorbike.'

'Were you wearing your white Stetson?'

'Very funny, Chris. But I did it for Jodie. She was special.'

'She certainly was.'

Max stood up briskly, snapped shut the case which contained the Barrett and threw it into the cupboard. 'Come on,' he said, 'let's go and play some golf.'

'Right. You never know, on the way round we might see a Dartford Warbler.'

More Thrilling Crime Fiction from Headline:

MARTHA GRIMES

THE HORSE YOU CAME IN ON

Richard Jury is supposed to be on holiday when the telephone call comes. And in any case, what has sudden death on American soil to do with an English police superintendent? But when the victim turns out to be British by birth, and to have a distant connection with Jury's old acquaintance, Lady Cray, he reluctantly acknowledges that his marker is being called in. Enlisting the aid of reluctant peer Melrose Plant, and accompanied by the irrepressibly lugubrious Sergeant Wiggins, Jury crosses the Atlantic to see what he can find out.

Baltimore turns out to have many attractions – not least that it is the home of avant garde novelist Ellen Taylor, last encountered at The Old Silent inn. Ellen is painfully engaged upon finishing her new book, but takes time out to introduce the trio to the delights of the city – football, Edgar Allen Poe, Bromo-Seltzer and a bar called The Horse You Came In On.

A case of plagiarism, a blind and deaf street-dweller, an engaging child who bears a strong resemblance to Scarlett O'Hara – these are just some of the elements in a complex puzzle whose solution looks set to defy the combined talents of the visiting team and put an end to a very promising writing career...

Also by Martha Grimes in Headline
THE DIRTY DUCK   JERUSALEM INN   THE DEER LEAP
THE FIVE BELLS AND BLADEBONE   HELP THE POOR STRUGGLER
THE OLD FOX DECEIV'D   THE ANODYNE NECKLACE
THE OLD SILENT   THE MAN WITH A LOAD OF MISCHIEF
THE OLD CONTEMPTIBLES   I AM THE ONLY RUNNING FOOTMAN

FICTION/CRIME   0 7472 4221 6

A selection of bestsellers
from Headline

APPOINTED TO DIE	Kate Charles	£4.99 ☐
SIX FOOT UNDER	Katherine John	£4.99 ☐
TAKEOUT DOUBLE	Susan Moody	£4.99 ☐
POISON FOR THE PRINCE	Elizabeth Eyre	£4.99 ☐
THE HORSE YOU CAME IN ON	Martha Grimes	£5.99 ☐
DEADLY ADMIRER	Christine Green	£4.99 ☐
A SUDDEN FEARFUL DEATH	Anne Perry	£5.99 ☐
THE ASSASSIN IN THE GREENWOOD	P C Doherty	£4.99 ☐
KATWALK	Karen Kijewski	£4.50 ☐
THE ENVY OF THE STRANGER	Caroline Graham	£4.99 ☐
WHERE OLD BONES LIE	Ann Granger	£4.99 ☐
BONE IDLE	Staynes & Storey	£4.99 ☐
MISSING PERSON	Frances Ferguson	£4.99 ☐

All Headline books are available at your local bookshop or newsagent, or can be ordered direct from the publisher. Just tick the titles you want and fill in the form below. Prices and availability subject to change without notice.

Headline Book Publishing, Cash Sales Department, Bookpoint, 39 Milton Park, Abingdon, OXON, OX14 4TD, UK. If you have a credit card you may order by telephone – 0235 400400.

Please enclose a cheque or postal order made payable to Bookpoint Ltd to the value of the cover price and allow the following for postage and packing:
UK & BFPO: £1.00 for the first book, 50p for the second book and 30p for each additional book ordered up to a maximum charge of £3.00.
OVERSEAS & EIRE: £2.00 for the first book, £1.00 for the second book and 50p for each additional book.

Name ....

Address ....

....

....

If you would prefer to pay by credit card, please complete:
Please debit my Visa/Access/Diner's Card/American Express (delete as applicable) card no:

Signature .... Expiry Date ....